EVERYTHING'S BETTER WITH MONKEYS

"Without adventure, civilization is in full decay."
Alfred North Whitehead

"Who dares, wins."
Motto of the British Special Air Service regiment

"To infinity...and beyond!"
Buzz Lightyear

Paper Phoenix titles C.J. Henderson

A BRIGHT AND SHINING WORLD:
THE SCIENCE FICTION OF C.J. HENDERSON

eSpec Books titles Including the Work of C.J. Henderson

BREACH THE HULL
SO IT BEGINS
BY OTHER MEANS
BEST LAID PLANS
DOGS OF WAR
THE BEST OF DEFENDING THE FUTURE

THE SOCIETY FOR THE PRESERVATION OF CJ HENDERSON

EVERYTHING'S BETTER WITH MONKEYS

TALES OF THE E.A.S. ROOSEVELT
And the Greatest Crew in the Universe

DTF REISSUED

C.J. Henderson

eBooks
Pennsville, NJ

PUBLISHED BY
Spec Books
PO Box 242
Pennsville, NJ 08070
www.especbooks.com

Copyright ©2013, 2024 C.J. Henderson
Story Introductions ©2013, 2024 Jack Dolphin

ISBN: 978-1-956463-21-7
ISBN (ebook): 978-1-956463-20-0

Shore Leave originally published in *Breach the Hull* edited by Mike McPhail, Marrietta Publishing, 2007
Space Pirate Cookies originally published in *Space Pirates* edited by David Lee Summers, Flying Pen Press, 2009
Everything's Better with Monkeys originally published in *So It Begin* edited by Mike McPhail, Dark Quest Books, 2009
A Meal Fit for God originally published in *By Other Means* edited by Mike McPhail, Dark Quest Books, 2011
Oh Why, Can't I? originally published in *Space Horrors* edited by David Lee Summers, Flying Pen Press, 2010
Space Battle of the Bands originally published in *Space Battles* edited by Bryan Thomas Schmidt, Flying Pen Press, 2012
Lawn Care originally published in *Galactic Creatures* edited by Elektra Hammond, Sparkito Press, 2012
Are We Now Smitten? originally published in *Best Laid Plans* edited by Mike McPhail, Dark Quest Books 2013

All rights reserved. No part of the contents of this book may be reproduced or transmitted in any form or by any means without the written permission of the publisher.

All persons, places, and events in this book are fictitious and any resemblance to actual persons, places, or events is purely coincidental.

Interior Design: Mike and Danielle McPhail
Cover Art and Design: Mike McPhail, McP Digital Graphics
Copy Editing: Danielle McPhail

CONTENTS

DEDICATION _____ vii

INTRODUCTION _____ ix

Prologue: SO IT BEGINS _____ 1

SHORE LEAVE _____ 7

SPACE PIRATE COOKIES _____ 29

EVERYTHING'S BETTER WITH MONKEYS _____ 51

A MEAL FIT FOR GOD _____ 71

OH WHY, CAN'T I? _____ 93

SPACE BATTLE OF THE BANDS _____ 109

LAWN CARE _____ 123

ARE WE NOW SMITTEN? _____ 137

ABSOLUTELY NOTHING _____ 159

SO LONG... _____ 187

ABOUT THE AUTHOR _____ 189

DEDICATION

THERE COULD HAVE BEEN NO TALES OF THE ROOSEVELT, NOT A ONE, IF not for one certain individual.

When I was asked to submit a tale to *Breach the Hull,* the first book in the "Defending the Future" series, I was, well, shall we say... hesitant.

Do understand, while I have nothing against the military, I'm not known for doing military stories. And I'd never done anything even approaching a sci fi military story.

But, for a number of varied reasons I threw myself into the task. I sweat for almost a month, every free writing moment dedicated to trying to think of something, anything that would fit the bill.

Finally, remembering an old interview with Gene Kelly, where he informed the audience that he had played sailors in so many of his movies because the pants were so easy to dance in, I got an idea I finally felt was original. And thus, "Shore Leave," the first story in this collection, was born.

As must be obvious, more stories followed. A book filled. No one is more amazed about that than I am.

The one person who seems to not be surprised about any of this at all, however, is the fellow who tapped me way back when for that first story. The guy who, when I said I had no ideas, assured me I would get one. The editor who did not push or hint or nudge, but who simply sat back and waited for lightning to strike.

And who to this day refuses to take any of the credit (or the blame) for any of what follows. Who keeps saying he had nothing to do with it, that it was all me, and all sorts of other rubbish.

Thus, this collection is dedicated to:

MIKE McPHAIL

The kind of mate who comes along once in your lifetime, just to let you know the gods think you deserve to know what real friendship is all about.

Not one word that follows would exist without him.

INTRODUCTION

THE STORY BEGINS, LIKE SO MANY DO, WITH A PHONE CALL.

This call was to a new editor, one who was organizing his very first book project; an anthology of military science fiction stories. Among his contributors were several big-named authors in the genre, and then there was C.J. Henderson. He wasn't known for his SF writings, let alone MilSF, but he had been invited by the powers-that-be. In the editor's mind, Mr. Henderson (later to be known as C.J.), was a modern-day pulp-fiction writer, who wrote Kolchak: The Night Stalker and the Occult Detective.

Mr. Henderson had a proposal for a story, but wanted the editor's opinion before investing the effort in to write it. He proposed your basic Starship, Starfleet-style, character-driven adventure, but this one included a musical number, sort of like a Dean Martin, Jerry Lewis military buddy-movie.

The editor —who was looking for hardcore Starship Trooper-esque* stories written by real-world military veterans— paused for just a moment, and said, "Right, sounds good, go for it."

In the fullness of time, the story arrived. The Editor hard copied it, got in his car and drove to a parking lot (supposedly to get away from the distractions of the office), and over a box of McNuggets and a Coke he read the story; and when he was done, he smiled. It was the kind of smile one gets when you see an old friend on the street.

Everything's Better With Monkeys

There were none of the typical tropes of blood, gore, death, and destruction, but instead it had heart and camaraderie at its core. It had warm, likable characters set against the backdrop of a great Starship, roaming a universe of endless possibilities and adventure; and yes, the good guys won in the end.

The story proved so uplifting that the editor decided to place it in the last slot, citing the need to end the book —in stark contrast to the other stories— on a happy note; and there they have been ever since (more or less) throughout the course of the Defending the Future series.

It has been proclaimed by Mr. Henderson, that with the release of the book, *Everything Is Better With Monkeys*,** the Rocky and Noodles adventures are now concluded; although this seem most unlikely. Anyone who has attended one of Mr. Henderson's readings knows that inevitably he will reach a point where he'll tear up, and have to push past the lump in his throat in order to finish the passage. For it is most evident that he loves these characters as much as his fans do.

Mike McPhail 2013
Series Editor,
Defending The Future

---

*Many years later in the movie "Starship Troopers 3: Marauders," the Sky Marshall sang, in what we could only call *a music video*, "Its A Good Day To Die".

**The book you have just bought and are now reading.

Prologue
SO IT BEGINS

"WHAT?"

The young man had not actually meant to vocalize—it had merely been the strangeness of the moment. Sitting with friends at a table in the officers' lounge, opening a messagvac, he had been halted by his slight amazement at the archaic means of communication—mildly intrigued as to what would prompt someone to do such a thing.

Hand-written. Hand-delivered. Curious—

I mean...

It had been brought to him by the waitress along with two pitchers of Moonside Fizz, one of those new lunar malts, a house bowl of cigarettes, five slices of pizza and a tumble of the mushroom/hot pepper curly fries—

Why would anyone...

Ultimately, the entirety of his distraction took him but a fraction over a full second. Distracted by chatter, senses dulled slightly from beer and one or two of its heartier companions, his nerves in a twist—

And why the hell not, I mean, with all the waiting, wondering who was going to be posted where—everyone's nerves buzzed, adrenaline pumping, the smell of sweat in the air—

Bother with such a...

As the young man tried to listen to both the conversations buzzing to either side of him at the same time, he finally got past his wondering and opened the pack—actually tearing real paper, only the tiniest part of his mind

Everything's Better With Monkeys

still puzzling at the curiousness of such a thing being sent to him—and then finally, he pulled forth the intriguing article's contents and brushed his eyes over them—

I mean...

And, as he finally began to read, the new graduate actually paled, blood rushing from his head, his body speeding it to his heart to force it to start pumping once more. He sat, purposely frozen for the most wondrous moment he would ever know, suspended outside normal time. As his friends wrangled on, shouting and cursing and drumming their fingers, chain-smoking, calling for liquor, calling for food, calling out to the universe for anything that ultimately equated to distraction, he wrapped his mind around an idea so large he had not actually, seriously, ever *really* entertained it for more than an instant.

She's mine...

Eyes blinking; heart starting once more; all his most wildly imagined possible timelines shattered, suddenly replaced by the one which had just been delivered unto him, an overwhelming new future radiating outward from probability to fill that single instant in the infinite bold spiral—

"She's *mine!*"

The words were shouted with head-turning glee. The cry—more than just a shout, less than a scream, more like a whoop—was a statement of notice, a demanding of attention. Indeed, it was Enthusiasm herself, come to smile among the hills of Earth, like the ancient gods bringing themselves down to Greece to bless some tragic fool.

"Take no prisoners, show no mercy," the young man blurted, self-indulgent joy of the most obnoxious kind gifting his throat with resonance, "bow down you ordinary lads and lasses, I say to you, avert your eyes..."

All about the officer's lounge, attention was refocused, and everywhere around the latest center-of-attention, twos and twos were put together as the brimming-over young officer threw himself upward, twisting in the air as he flew his few feet off the ground, announcing;

"For you are indeed now in the utter and overwhelming presence of *greatness!*"

As he thudded down atop the nearest table, hands on hips, at various of the other tables all about the room those present were suddenly blessed with the necessary amount of understanding. As one, they nodded—they understood.

They got it.

SO IT BEGINS - C.J. Henderson

Some of them smiled, some of them laughed. And, of course, there were those sore few who could do nothing but grind their teeth, refusing to believe what they knew to be true until it was rubbed in their faces.

"Ladies and gentlemen, and any other naval personnel I may have left out in that all-too-brief list of categories...,"

One table in particular thought they knew what the news was, and the notion pleased them all, the notion that their friend and classmate, Alexander Benjamin Valance had received his assignment. An assignment that, judging from his reaction, had to be one quite choice.

"If I could retain your attention for but a moment longer, so that I might share a bit of news..."

Everyone had been waiting since graduation for their share of this particular news. All of them, they had their grades. They had their ranks. The only thing missing in their young lives was that for which those most recently released from the Earth Alliance Military Acadamy had gathered all across campus—their postings. Those assembled in the officer's lounge at that moment were the outside favorites to be given their own ships.

"Ahem..."

There were four new topline cruisers in port, all of them fresh from the Asteroid Works, all of them sleek and deadly and begging for someone as worthy of an active posting as their Alex. Alex Valance was a fighter and a thinker. He maintained; he held on. You could always count on him to stay the course, to hold the line. And best of all for those closest to him, he was that often most hated kind of fellow, the rascal for whom everything always turned out all right.

If anyone could handle one of those new destroyers, take it out to the rim and back again, it was, as he was so often called, their "pal Al." He was—and everyone knew it—a man who understood how to get a job done. He was also straight and honorable and damn lucky; maybe not exactly an all-around great guy, but definitely a good one—and a man who deserved his chance to lead.

"Let it be known," he cried as he raised his arms from his sides, thrusting them out as he shouted, "that this is your first, *official* greeting..."

The Trident, The LaRaja, The Thunderer, The Ulysses, any of them were well worth the years of study, sweat and service it had taken Alex to get to this point.

"From the new captain of..."

Any of them...

"The Earth Alliance Starship..."

Everything's Better With Monkeys

No matter which one it was, they would ship with him if they could, be happy for the rest if they could not, and be proud they "knew him when."

"*Roosevelt!*"

And at that historic moment, newly appointed Alexander Valance became the most envied man in the entire Navy, and several other branches of the service as well, for, unless he was drunk or insane, or anything else besides honest and correct, he had just received his orders to take command of the greatest fighting ship ever conceived.

"The *Roosevelt*?"

The room said the words, repeated them first as a question, then as one of the many typical means to unconsciously register surprise—

"Oh my God!"

That first shout was cascaded by a hundred more. Then, screams and oaths and cheers in fifteen languages thundered throughout the lounge. The din was such that the ranking officer on post declared the next round of drinks on the house. And well they should be for those present were witness to a moment about which they would be able to tell their grandchildren. And a true thing it was. For the man who captained such a ship as had Valance was certain to be remembered.

The *Roosevelt* was the first of the long-awaited Dreadnought class, a single ship stretching for a mile and a half, inconceivable tons of metal and plastics, crystal and biomechanical feeds brought together from Earth, the Moon and the asteroids that, when ultimately combined into an end product, became something unheard of—something utterly unthinkable. And thus... so the prevailing wisdom of the day went...

Unbeatable, as well.

She was, in the end, a sum far greater than her parts. She was known as "the cowboy ship," for it had been that cocky gang of rocketeers known as the Moonpie Cowboys who had built her. They were the wildmen of the mightiest nation in the system's Advanced R&D Team, and it was their spirit that infested her. And programmed her mind.

The *Roosevelt* was the first of her class, the eldest child of interplanetary war wagons—the all or nothing-at-all of the Federal Enforcement Troops—big because she had to be. The first ship with functional energy shields, she needed room for massive engines to power such revolutionary devices. And for her thousands of attack aircraft, hundreds of them merely hanging off her sides. And for her extensive guns, her big guns—the pounders and the whisperers—and all those hundreds of thousands of missiles and bombs.

SO IT BEGINS - C.J. Henderson

She was the solar system's first spacecraft carrier, a prairie outpost, a relentlessly strong, mobile fort in space. She was meant to house 10,000 sailors and marines. She was meant to keep the peace.

She's mine

And she had been given to a captain straight from the Academy. In the weeks to come there would be those who said it was bold thinking, putting a fresh captain in a fresh ship, a tactician who would not come to such a new thing with the prejudices of the old—some past-their-prime functionary—fighting the last war, as it were. There were also those that wondered at what previously unsuspected connections the Valance family might have.

Then, there were those who had correctly assessed the situation. They were the ones who believed that Valance was in the grips of forces he could not yet begin to understand. Like any captain, this one had been picked with due and careful consideration. But, unlike those chosen to further this or that corporate or political or family ambition, Valance had been chosen because he was, when all was said and done, simply the best man for the job.

In a stunningly, some might say preposterously bold moment, those in charge of such things had decided that the first vessel to go beyond the edge of the solar system, that humanity's flagship, as it were, should be piloted by someone not beholden to anyone. Or, more correctly, by someone beholden to all. Someone who thought words like "duty" and "honor" and "home" still had meaning. Someone like Alexander Benjamin Valance whom, those in charge felt, had the best chance of going into the far beyond and representing the race fairly and honestly, doing what he would end up doing with the good of all Earth as his motivator.

To be honest, it was a breathless, extraordinarily bold move on the part of the regime, one that would be debated, wondered over and cursed for decades to come. The Valance family had no real connections or power and it was clear to all concerned that their son might well indeed come to wonder over, and even regret, the machinations which had put him at the helm of the *Roosevelt*.

But, none of that mattered to Alex Valance at that moment for, in that one, delirious instant, he was the captain of the solar system's most frighteningly advanced war machine, and there was room for but one glorious thought in his mind—

mine...

Other, more rueful thoughts, would come later.

Man has created any number of destructive forces from TNT to thermonuclear bombs, but none are more potent, more volatile and more unpredictable than a shipload of long-isolated sailors mixed well with large quantities of alcohol. Behold the crew of the Spacecarrier "Roosevelt" unleashed upon an unsuspecting alien world in...

SHORE LEAVE

"It is upon the navy under the Providence of God that the safety, honour, and welfare of this realm do chiefly attend."

Charles II

"God help us all."

Anonymous

THE HUMAN SAILOR'S FIST SMACKED AGAINST THE SIDE OF THE Embrian's head for the fifth time, making a loud and juicy sound. The noise seemed to please the sailor mightily; the Embrian, not so much.

"Keep it up, Noodles," shouted a much taller sailor, also human, one dressed in much the same uniform as the other. "We'll crack this coconut yet!"

The two sailors were part of the upstart human fleet from that far end of the galaxy into which most reputable races did not bother to venture. It was a fearsomely cluttered area, one filled with debris from the great space wars of the elder races, all of whom disappeared so long ago. The whole place abounded with black hole snares, meteor whirls, nebulae pits, all manner of mines and traps as well as system-wide sargassos of wrecked armadas just waiting for the chance to befoul modern travellers.

Of course, the Embrians being heelstomped in The Cold Bone Cellar—which by the way neither contained a particularly gelid temperature, nor found itself situated beneath the surface—did not care what race the sailors were, nor where they were from. They only wished for respite from the heelstomping and the continual thumping of their conga-like heads. Luckily for them, the unmistakable sound of approaching law enforcement began to filter through the riotous din enveloping the tavern at that moment.

"Rocky," cried out Noodles, he of the keener hearing, "sounds like the shore patrol." Holding off his next punch for the moment, Chief Gunnery Officer Rockland Vespucci cupped a hand to his ear, confirmed his friend's assertion, then shouted;

"Men of the Franklin—time for a strategic withdrawal!" To which Noodles, more officially known as Machinist First Mate Li Qui Kon, added most vocally;

"Run and live!"

Tossing the soldiers, sailors and officers from the other ships with whom they had been brawling into a central pile, the sailors in question assumed a semblance of a formation, heading for the back door on the run as they sang;

> "Oh, we're the boys of the Franklin,
> We fly in outer space,
> We wipe our asses with moonbeams,
> We know how star dust tastes.
>
> "The boys of the fighting Franklin,
> The best ship in all the fleet,
> Say a single word ag'in her,
> And we'll pound ya 'til yer meat!"

When the military police did arrive they seemed in a particular lather, one not quite in line with a simple barroom bare-knuckler. The MPs were, as was standard at any port where different cultures docked together, a mix of the five great races of the Pan-Galactic League of Suns. That meant, of course, there were no humans among their numbers, which is why those warbling the thirty-some odd verses dedicated to the virtues of the Fighting Franklin were so quick to make their exit. And, with their usual precision, within only five blocks at top-speed exit, the group of some twenty-seven original roughhousers had split up into some eleven groups of two and three, all eleven striving mightily to pretend not to know one another and to move in opposing directions.

Now calmly walking through the streets, Rocky and Noodles assumed the innocent pose of two guileless gobs out for a stroll in an exciting new port of call. And, to be fair, they were very good at doing so. Indeed, so shamelessly naive did they appear, the grifters, hoodwinks and typical

SHORE LEAVE - C.J. Henderson

bottom leeches one found in any such hub city allowed them passage, feeling it beneath their dignity as thieves to go after pigeons so utterly tender.

"I don't think we should have run for it until we found out if that place validated parking."

About to give out with a snappy rejoinder, Rocky suddenly noted that he and his partner were being followed by four rather large and singularly dangerous-looking Danierians—pasty, bulbous beings known far and wide for their quick tempers and all-around lack of social skills. Noting that they had been noted, the quartet began to pick up speed, not slowly, but switching from a quick walk to a supersonic lurch with one quick *whoosh*.

This motivated the sailors to take the opportunity to test their land-legs by cranking their own mobility up to the ultimate, racing down one oddly shaped back alley and then the next. By this point the Danierians could no longer actually be seen due to the great, bilious dust cloud their pursuit was raising. Availing himself of this advantage, Machinist First Mate Li rummaged through his pockets, examining one discovery after another until coming across a temporal spanner bar.

Setting it for what he imagined were the appropriate amount of seconds, he tossed it down in front of himself and Rocky, kept moving forward, then nodded with appreciation when he first heard the tool, normally used for re-aligning warp engines, "klik" back into standard reality, then heard the expansion field open just in time to trip up their pursuers. The welcome sounds of beings falling against one another and the somewhat harder surface of the street, as well as the unwelcome ozone-frying smell of shots being fired, came to the sailors, bringing a laugh to their lips as well as added speed to their retreat.

Finally, several blocks and random turns later, the two slowed down, picking up their conversation where they left off. Assuming the Danierians were simply part of the house security for the house they had helped make so less secure, they put the creatures out of their minds as Rocky asked;

"So, Noodles, tell me, exactly what did you park that you wanted a validation for?"

"It's the principle of the thing," responded the machinist. "Storage of future information."

"Where do you get these ideas," asked Rocky. "I swear, you're the kind of guy who proposes polkas for national anthems."

"And you're the kind of guy who steals miniature aliens when running out of a bar instead of a couple of spare bottles." Needless to say, Rocky

Everything's Better With Monkeys

was indeed puzzled by his friend's comment. Not that part about the bottles. No, the gunnery officer was certain Noodles had managed to palm two or three fifths on his way out the door. That would certainly explain the slight "klinking" sound emanating from his duffle.

Indeed, it was the part about stealing aliens—miniature or otherwise—which had him perplexed. Scratch his head as hard as he might, Rocky could not remember a single instance of doing such. Questioning Noodles on the subject only brought the equally inscrutable rejoinder;

"Don't look at me, *I* certainly didn't steal them."

Rocky's confusion only lasted another moment, however, mainly because at that point the gunnery officer followed the assumed trail leading from the end of Noodles' directional finger to the objective being speared by such action, namely the nine small fry following behind the pair of sailors.

"You crazy git," shouted Rocky. "I didn't steal them. They're followin' us. And," he added, after taking a closer look, "I don't think they're small aliens."

"You think they're human?"

"No, goddamnit—I don't think they're human. I mean, I don't think they're small aliens." Scrutinizing the troop now standing still behind them, obviously ready to start moving once more as soon as the sailors did, Noodles said slowly;

"I don't know... they look small and they look like aliens to me."

"I don't mean they're not small aliens, I mean yes, they're small, and yes, they're aliens, but I don't think that's all they are."

"What else could they be?" Noodles looked the silent contingent over again, then asked, "Robots?"

"Not robots—why is everything robots to you machinists? No, I think they're kids."

"Who cares if they're kids—why are they following us?"

"I don't know."

"Then, you should ask them."

"Why me?"

"Because, I spotted them first, you're closer to them, and I don't like children or small aliens, unless of course they're robots." Against such thunderous logic, the gunnery officer found himself without choice. So surrendering, he dropped down on one knee and asked;

"All right, who's the ring leader here? I want to know what you bunch are doing followin' us. Com'on now... speak up."

One plump melon of a creature dressed for all the world in what seemed to be a scouring pad stepped forward and announced in the squeakiest voice either sailor had ever experienced;

"We grateful orphans. Follow you to happy safety. We know you kind kipkips. Not sell us to be chowder."

After a painful amount of conversation with the alien, who did indeed turn out to be a child, the two sailors learned that the nine tykes, all of different species, were orphans purchased from a galactic state home for a Representative Brummellig'ic for the purpose of being turned into a type of outer rim gumbo. Somewhat suspicious, Noodles used his com to check what the orphan they nicknamed Melon had told them. When he looked up from his labors, Rocky threw an all-encompassing;

"Well?" at him to which Noodles replied;

"Like always, translation between Earth Basic 9.8 and Pan-Galactic's a bit rough, but the little zucchini might have something. There is a Representative Brummellig'ic on planet right now, and he's got enough power to keep all information about himself off the low class bands. The kid's right, though. I found a mention of him on some kind of society page—he is throwing a big party tonight."

Rocky and Noodles looked suspiciously, then sternly, then helplessly at their new litter. Finding no recourse there, they walked away several paces, then looked at each other, lips pursed, eyes narrowing. As one they turned and stared down at their three-times-three tag-alongs, and then turned back to look at one another again—lips tighter, eyes down to slits. Finally, on the verge of choking and going blind, Noodles offered;

"This can't be happening to us…"

"I know; we ain't had shore leave in sixteen months—"

"We don't know anything about taking care of kids…"

"And this Brummellig'ic creep, he's certain to have a lot of muscle—"

"It's not like we can go to the authorities…"

"No, no—even if there weren't no spotter cams in that bar we just helped redesign, they'll be lookin' for everything in blue and white to invite in for a chat—"

"MPs will only be worse…"

"Even if we weren't in trouble, guy like this Brummellig'ic could have people bought off anywhere. If we was to even talk about this to anyone, if word got back to him—" Rocky drew a finger across his throat, with an accompanying dreadful sound to get his point across. Rolling his eyes, mostly in fearful agreement, Noodles said;

"This is not fair..."

"I know that," agreed Rocky. Turning his head, he stared as hard as he could at their nine new companions, trying to ignore their pathetic demeanors and large imploring eyes--those that had eyes, of course. Turning back to his friend, he whispered;

"Elvis Corkin' Presley, all I wanted was to drink and fight, dance some with beautiful girls, see a couple shows, do a little gamblin'... not play nursemaid."

"You're absolutely right. This is not our responsibility. By Buddha's Mint Julep, for all we know, maybe they sell orphans all the time to make into bouillabaisse out here. We're not home, you know."

"And another important factor," added Rocky, his voice dropping to an even lower, more conspiratorial level, "we're a lot bigger than they are—"

"Our legs are longer..."

"We could most assuredly run much, much faster than them—"

And then, the one that looked like Shirley Temple, if Shirley Temple had been the offspring of a seal and a geranium, started to cry. She had a beautiful crying voice, not—that is—one melodious to listen to, but one perfectly designed for fetching sympathy. So utterly loud, shrill and trembling was it that windows began to open, and even passing motorists started coming to a halt. With the speed of politicians placing blame, the pair of gobs emptied their pockets, searching desperately for something they might just happen to have on their persons which would placate a caterwauling alien five-year-old.

Luckily, Noodles just happened to be in possession of a 9/10s galvanized securing bolt which caught little Shirley's eye. Throwing out a purple tendril, she snagged the five-point-eighteen ounces of steel and happily began chewing. Wiping perspiration from their now freely beading heads, Rocky with the edge of his tallywacker, Noodles with his bucket cap, the two shrank against the closest wall as the oppressive reality of their situation began to dawn on them.

"You know," said Noodles, his eyes now constantly scanning for authority in all its varied guises, "we're in trouble."

"Oh, ya think? Listen, Edison, we gotta start cogitatin' on what we're gonna do here." With that statement, Rocky turned to look over the kids. Noticing they were near a type of public park, he rounded up their reluctantly-accepted charges and got them all off the street and out of the main public view. Finding an alcove large enough to house them all, and discreet enough that they could talk freely, he posted Noodles at the leafy entrance to keep watch, positioned the children on the ground, then sat down in front of them and asked;

"All right, let's figure some stuff out. First off, how many of you understand what I'm saying?"

Melon screeched out a reply detailing that he, Shirley and three others whom the gobs immediately nick-named Curly, Snip and Poodle could understand basic humanspeak. The others, whom they designated Bubbles, Fork, Creepie and Poindexter, did not speak anything close to Earth 9.8, but Snip could apparently translate for Bubbles and Creepie, Creepie could then straighten out Fork, and Poodle could get across enough to Poindexter to keep him in the loop. With this established, Rocky immediately explained the buddy system, telling the group that if things were going to work at all, everyone was going to have to help everyone else. And at that point, Shirley asked the question that sent our boys from merely falling over a cliff to rocketing over it.

"What things are going to work?"

Her question could be taken in any of a hundred ways, and both swabbies felt the twisting knife of each possible one. Cutting through the selfishness of their desire to throw away their paychecks on dice, dames and drinks, her query focused the small fries' plight perfectly—abandoned by Rocky and Noodles, the nine of them were bound for a soup pot. Boiled alive with celery and onions to feed the decadent rich.

"Noodles," said Rocky of a sudden, "if you'd like to take off now, and go back out to have some fun, I'd be real understandin' of such an action."

"What," responded the machinist, "and let a loose propeller like you get our kids baked up into won tons? No way I'm going anywhere, you crazy wop."

The gunnery officer smiled. All right then, he thought, it was settled. They would help the kids. But, the back of his mind questioned, help them to do what?

A quick interrogation gave the gobs the following facts. The kids had all come from the orphanage. None of them had anyone on the outside to whom they could turn. The beings who were going to sell them to be soup were to meet those wishing to make them into soup at the Cold Bone Cellar. The merry disruption caused by Rocky, Noodles and their shipmates had rendered the kids' sellers unconscious, giving them the opportunity to escape along with the still conscious combatants. The buyers had been the ones they eluded outside the tavern.

"All right," declared Rocky. "We gotta get off the street, and back to the ship. We get these kids to the captain and he'll make sure they're taken care of." Melon and the other English speakers looked a little worried, but Noodles added;

"No, the captain's a good egg. Honest. He'll protect you all. But," the machinist indicated with several complicated eye movements both the idea of direction and extreme distance as he added, "it's a hell of a long way back to the ship. You got any ideas on how we're going to get there?"

"Actually," answered Rocky, his face rearranging itself into a mask of lopsided smugness, "I think I do."

"This is ridiculous," muttered Noodles. "This is something they only do in cartoons."

"And tell me what part of today hasn't been a damn cartoon, would you—please?" Looking over the pair's three new companions, the gunnery officer added;

"Besides, I think they look pretty good."

It had to be admitted, for a totally outlandish and completely improbable kind of stunt, their nine charges did look "pretty good." To shorten a frenzied search through numerous clothing stores, plus a great deal of pushing, guessing, prodding, a bit of cutting and sewing and some emergency work with baling wire and extra strength duct tape, what the sailors had done was stand the kids one atop the other, taking into account their different shapes and abilities, then dressed them as adults. The results made them—especially when attempting to walk—appear more like drunken zombies, but they looked far less like children, and for the moment, that was good enough for the boys.

"So now," whispered the machinist to his partner-in-absurdity, "what do we do next?"

"We get inside somewhere where we can find some guys we trust. Then, with some help on our side, we get back to the ship, get the kids placed somewheres where they won't get fricasseed or barbecued, and then we try to get back to enjoying ourselves."

"And where exactly would we be able to do that?" Staring across the street at a garishly lit nightclub, one promising gambling, female companionship and beers from across the galaxy, Rocky pulled at his chin and answered;

"Yeah, where indeed?"

SHORE LEAVE - C.J. Henderson

Moments later, the five were crossing the street, three of the quintet bouncing and rocking as if they were in a quake zone, the other two attempting to hold them together while talking loudly about how ashamed they were of their friends for drinking to excess. This continued up the stairs of the entrance to Ping's Dingled Showplace, through the doors, and down the stairs into the main ballroom. Following a waiter to a table for five, the oddly moving party waddled along as best they could, all of them gratefully collapsing into their chairs.

Instantly Snip began wailing because, as best the gobs could figure out, either Poodle was standing on his face, or Creepie had farted and the duct tape holding the two of them together had begun to melt. As quickly as it could be managed discreetly, the sailors got the kids as comfortably arranged as possible, ordered two pitchers of Gullyfoyle Malt Liquor, three of SweetSweet BugJuice, and then sat back to peruse their surroundings.

Ping's, at least at first glance, seemed a perfect place for the swabbies and their charges to try and get their bearings. If nothing else, every table received a complimentary revolving platter of treats, one with enough variety that it held something all the kids could ingest. The fact that the club was dark enough no one at the other tables would notice the extra hands, tentacles, flippers, claws and so forth extruding from the three non-humans at their table was certainly a bonus.

Beyond that, it seemed like the kind of place where people were only interested in those at their table, or what was going on up on stage, which at that moment was an act labeled as Tina Dillfreb and her Titanic Tower of Terriers. Feeling somewhat secure for the first time in some forty-nine Earth Standard Minutes, the swabbies began to relax. And, after finishing their first pitcher, Rocky and Noodles found themselves as relaxed as house cats on a hot day. Finding the kids content with their BugJuice, assorted treats and the ever-toppling tower of dogs on-stage, they were just about to begin planning a strategy when suddenly the already dark interior went positively ebony.

The darkness lasted but a moment, and then a bright orange spot focused on the center stage. In that brief moment Tina and her hounds were removed along with all of their props and one embarrassing accident, and replaced with startling efficiency by a Golblacian Master of Ceremonies. Drumming up a more-than-deserved round of applauds for the departed Dillfreb and associates, the creature best described as a seven foot blue/green penguin then dropped its voice to a lower, throatier range, and said;

Everything's Better With Monkeys

"Now, gentlebeings, all you flippers and floggers, you squasheads and bipeds, everything out there with the strength, enthusiasm and moral turpitude to do so, let me get you to make some deep, loving tribal noise for the seductive, the lovely, the incomparable, Miss Beezle Uvi!"

A pink shot of butterfly lights were sent dancing through the white spot framing center stage. All the orphans made appropriate "ouuuuuhhh-hhhhhh" sounds, except, of course, for those stuck in the middle of their costumes. At least, for that moment. Responding to the appreciative sounds of their fellow tureen escapees, those in the mid- and bottom sections of the costumes abandoned their stations to congregate around the center pole of their party's table and peek out from under the tablecloth.

As they did so, the curtains began to part and the orchestra began to warble, all of it timed to both the movement of the lights, and the entrance of a creature so entrancing, so curvaceously shimmering, so delightful in movement and gesture that Rocky would have fallen out of his chair and out onto the main floor if Noodles had not fallen over at the same moment, the two of them smacking into each other, then propping each other up as their insides dissolved into jelly. The darkness hid their antics, of course, as it was meant to do, keeping all eyes focused on the approaching Uvi.

Strolling calmly toward her spot, the singer moved her charmingly antique voice amplifier to what apparently served as her mouth, and in a slow, sultry voice began to release the lead-in lines of her song to the already raptured audience.

> "When intelligent beings first went into space,
> And met creatures from another race,
> It was, of course, one of those great, historic finds.
>
> "The galaxy didn't worry so much about war,
> Intolerance wasn't even brought to the floor,
>
> But...
> There was one...
> Burning question...
> On alllllll... inquiring minds...

And then, the house lights blazed up, whites becoming yellows, pinks becoming reds; the band shifted from a quiet respectful background accompaniment to a raucous blast of hot horns and sibilant strings, and Uvi hit her mark, threw back her head, and in a voice higher, louder, stronger, and twice as shot through with promise as before, belted out;

SHORE LEAVE - C.J. Henderson

"What is *that*, and *where* does it go?
Should it be inserted, fast or slow?

"Does it like to be licked?
Does it like to be grabbed?
Does it like to be twirled?
Does it like to be stabbed?

"Oh, just *what* is that, and *where* does it go?"

Bouncing off each other, their heads banging together like empty spittoons, Noodles and Rocky at first found themselves instinctively trying to cover the ears of their many charges. They gave off on this futile endeavor for, first off, they had far too few hands, second, they did not have the slightest idea where most of the orphans' audio organs where positioned, and third, to be perfectly honest, the childish tittering coming from all their charges, except well, of course, for Poindexter, cued them that they were far too late to protect this particular interstellar nine from the facts of life.

That being established, the swabbies looked at each other helplessly for a moment, then simply surrendered to the obvious and went back to enjoying the show. All of this happening within a handful of seconds, they had their chins firmly placed within the palms of their hands, their elbows on the table, and the sappiest of grins plastered on their faces as Uvi hit the second go-round, belting out;

"Oh, what is that, and what does it do?
Is it there for both of us, or just for you?

"Does it get much bigger?
Does it reach out and scratch?
Does it remain a solo, or
Can you grow a batch?

"Baby, *what* is that, and *what* does it do?"

At this point, alarms were going off back aboard the gobs' ship in the medical bay, alerting the dreadnought's physician-on-call that two shore-leavers were close to coronary arrest. With the flip of a few switches and the studying of the resulting readouts, however, the doctor ascertained the two were merely comfortably seated, staring at a choice piece of stimuli.

Everything's Better With Monkeys

Yearning to be fifty years younger, he mentally wished them both luck and cancelled the alert. All in all, a good thing, for the meter readings were only going to get worse.

As that stanza ended, the Dingled Showplace Dancers joined the club's star on stage, backing her up for a repeat of the chorus, making all the appropriately rude gestures of licking, grabbing, twirling and stabbing, while Uvi kicked up different sets of heels, mesmerizing the crowd with the way she could move her many and varied appendages with such flawless synchronization, all of her coming together just in time for her to re-enter the center spot and warble;

> "Tell me, what is that, and how does it feel?
> Like the mushroom we first saw, or some eventual eel?
>
> "When our races met,
> I thought it was just another find.
> Now all I can think of is,
> Your place or mine?
>
> "Oh lover, just *what* is that, and *how* does it feel?"

Noodles set about "shushing" the orphans, whose giggling had attracted the attention of more than one waiter. Rocky, in the meantime, could offer no assistance. Alien in every way as the singer was, he simply could not tear his eyes from her—the green parts or the purple. And, it had to be said that his utter intoxication with the singer had little to do with the woes of Earth navies of elder times. His ship was one of the most modern in the fleet; its compliment was completely integrated with members of both sexes.

No, Rocky's problem had nothing to do with not having seen any females for too long a time. The particular sailor's problem was that he had never seen anyone like Beezle Uvi—anywhere, ever—except in certain dreams, the dates of which he still marked the anniversaries of with a boyishly wistful fondness. Thus he did not even notice when Noodles slipped from his seat and fell to the floor with the kids, his eyes locking with Uvi's as she sang;

> "The cosmos is shrinking,
> The boundaries are changing,
> And I think my pelvis is in...
> For a slight... rearranging!

SHORE LEAVE - C.J. Henderson

"And so I challenge...
Our greatest scientific minds...
To somehow find an answer...
To that one burning question...
That IIIIIII...
Just have to know...

"Oh, just what is that...
And where, oh *where* does it gooooooooooooooooo?"

The full regular house lights went up then, and applauds thundered from the audience with a power so overwhelming some of the chorus girls were forced to take a backward step, or slither, or whatever. Rocky's own hands were contributing a massive amount of the audible appreciation, as were Noodles'. Melon, Poodle and Curly were in for a round as well, Bubbles, Snip, Fork and Creepie were all wrestling over the last items on the appetizer tray; Shirley, having finished her bolt was working on a corner of the table, and Poindexter, well... you know.

What startled Rocky, Noodles, their menagerie and most of the occupants of Ping's Dingled Showplace, however, was what happened next—an event so unexpected, so unprecedented, that the *Galaxy Today* reporter permanently stationed in the club would have written it up and sent it across the waves immediately if the shock of it had not sent her stumbling backward into an unfortunately extremely large and heavy ice sculpture. What stole the breath, ability to speak, and common sense from those gathered was the fact that, defying precedent, good taste, and well, common sense again, Beezle Uvi had left the stage and was walking for Rocky and Noodles' table.

"L-Little buddy," stuttered the finest gunnery officer in the fleet, "I-I-I d-do believe she's... comin' this way."

"You might be right," agreed Noodles. Ducking his head under the table, he hissed quick orders to the orphans, getting them to reassemble into their pretend persons before the singer could reach them. Doing his best to help, Rocky stared forward, attempting to keep his eyes from falling out of his head, rolling around on the table and growing their own tongues with which to blast wolf whistles.

"Mind if I join you?"

"Geezzzz," asked Rocky seriously, "do I look that foolish?" Uvi giggled, an undulating action that made several seemingly unconnected body parts shimmy. Signalling her favorite waiter to bring her a Cosmic Laugh, she

20   Everything's Better With Monkeys

turned and focused her attention on Rocky. After he introduced Noodles, she pointed a finger, moving it from one of them to the other, asking;

"You're human, aren't you?"

"Ah, well," Rocky answered honestly, "yeah—last time I looked."

"I've read about humans," she admitted. "Heard a lot of good things."

"Gosh, I don't know what to say," responded Rocky. "I don't even know what species you are. Not that that matters or nothin'."

"I was impressed by that attitude," Uvi admitted. "You stare with such charming hunger. Tell me, are you myopic, or were you just enjoying the show?"

"I don't want to seem forward or nothin'," the gunnery officer said, "the show was okay and everything, it's just, there's somethin' about you, ma'am, somethin'... and I know this must sound crazy, but it's like I'm fallin' in—"

"Ix-nay on the ov-lay alk-tay," hissed Noodles, poking his pal hard in the ribs. Rocky turned, mightily disturbed for having been interrupted at that particular moment, but then, he saw what the machinist had noticed. All around the club, police officers and MPs had begun to take up positions. Worse yet, the quartet of Danierians they thought they had left in temporal disruption had somehow gotten themselves undisrupted.

"Great jumpin' jackasses," blurted Rocky. "How could they *all* have found us—at the same time?"

"A good question," replied Noodles. "Rhetorical, I'm hoping?"

"The cops," asked Uvi, "those Danierian creeps? They're *all* looking for you?" When two forlorn nods were given her as answer, the interstellar diva asked the galaxy's most popular one-word question;

"Why?"

The swabbies took turns filling Uvi in on what had happened to them since leaving the Cold Bone Cellar, one explaining this or that section while the other looked to the orphans, seeing if there was any way possible they might be able to get all nine of them out of the boiling pan and away from the fire once more. Hearing everything the pair had to say, the singer asked;

"So all you want to do is get these kids to your captain to help you protect them?" When the boys nodded sincerely, Rocky tying Poodle's shoe for the fifth time, Noodles wiping what he hoped was Creepie's nose, Uvi's facial area seemed to melt with genuine affection. She was just about to speak when a whistle was blown from somewhere in the back. Leaping to his feet, praying there were more sailors within earshot than he could see, Rocky bellowed;

SHORE LEAVE · C.J. Henderson

"Pie fight—Franklin style!"

And at that moment, chaos exploded throughout Ping's Dingled Showplace. From twenty different spots, pastries, dinner plates, flower pots, beer mugs, chairs and anything else not nailed down was seen flying through the air, most of the flight plans registering an authority figure's head as its destination. As per standard Franklin tactics, the second fusillade was launched at the lights. Clutching Rocky's wrist, Uvi shouted;

"Grab the kids and follow me."

The sailors did as ordered, scooping up their charges and following the singer onto the stage. As their fellow sailors, and quite a number of innocent patrons, fell into a pitched battle with the police and MPs, Noodles noticed that the Danierians were still heading straight toward them. Reaching the up-stage side of the curtains, Uvi pointed out her dressing room, telling the others to meet her there. When Rocky protested, she hissed;

"This is my world; I can deal with them—go!" Then, turning to the chorus line of Dingled Showplace Dancers, she shouted;

"Rubes rushing the stage, girls—make them sorry!"

Giggling, the chorus girls waved Uvi on, then prepared for battle. Dropping the curtain on the heads of the Danierians, they then wandered from lump to lump, flattening them with heavy objects to what looked like heads and kicks to what looked like groins. In her dressing room, Uvi held out bundles of clothing to both Noodles and Rocky ordering them to get into them immediately. The pair protested, but she shouted back that they had no time to argue, and unless they had a better plan than hers, that they should simply shut up and do as they were told. Pulling his jersey off over his head, Noodles mumbled;

"I think she may be related to the lieutenant." To which Rocky responded;

"Awwww, just shut up and help me adjust my bra."

"Is that what that is?"

"I think so—for like maybe, three?"

Pulling, pushing, and experimenting, the two managed to get themselves dressed in only a handful of minutes. Checking themselves over in the room's full length mirror, they did make better females than the kids had made adults, but not by much. In the meantime, Uvi and her wardrobe assistant had removed the last remaining scraps of the kids' disguises and replaced them with new ones. Having cut apart several throw rugs and her own fur coat, the orphans had all been converted into what could pass for dogs if the inspection was not too strenuous. Looking again in the mirror, down at the kids, back to the mirror, and back to the kids, realization hit Noodles' mind.

"I get it," he exclaimed. "We're supposed to be Tina Dillfreb and her Titanic Tower of Terriers."

"Machinists are so smart," cooed Uvi. "I'll bet you know about robots and everything." Noodles beamed at the mention of his favorite topic, barely noticing the sour look Rocky was throwing his way. Getting in front of the pair of gobs before anything could come of it, either, Uvi said;

"All right, now we're going to just march out there right past them all, just a big happy bunch of girls and canines, right everybody?"

Rocky and Noodles agreed, as did Melon, Shirley and the others as translation spread through the pack. With the last pseudo-terrier nod, Uvi opened the door and the lot of them poured out into the hallway. The diva led the way, throwing her ample self in front of the first curious eyes of authority they met. A slight chill ran through her as she saw the enormous extent to which curiosity was running that day.

Flipping the "flirt" switch within her head, the singer sauntered, doing the best she could to attract all license-to-hurt attention to herself. Rocky and Noodles, doing their best to herd the orphans along, trying at the same time to maintain a light and breezy falsetto chatter, followed behind, keeping their all-too-stubbly faces averted from the police, military and otherwise, filling the hallway. As they approached the exit, they found two disagreeable officers arguing with one another.

"I don't understand the problem," growled the one. "We know they're from an Earth ship—the Franklin. You should have the bio-reads of every-one from that tub by now."

"But sir," answered the other, "I keep trying to tell you—we checked every registry in port. There's no ship, Earther or otherwise, called the Franklin in dock. The closest name is the Felkinsku, but that's a Saurian wine merchant freighter, methane breathers." As Rocky and Noodles smiled to one another, the superior of the two officers growled;

"And what do you, ah... ladies, find so funny?" Trusting his chances at making female sounds better than Rocky's, Noodles cocked his wrist limply and tittered;

"Ohhh, you big, strong man, you—I knew there was someone out here just dying to take me to dinner. Rocklina, be a dear and take the puppies out on your own. The general here has eyes for me."

Taking a good look at the eye batting, lip pursing Noodles, the officer blanched, practically knocking his underling over in his haste to clear a path

SHORE LEAVE - C.J. Henderson

to the door. Sticking his nose in the air with as offended an attitude as possible, Noodles sniffed appropriately, then followed the others out the door. Once outside, Rocky laughed;

"Didn't know you made such a good dame, little buddy. I'll have to keep that in mind for those lonely nights once were back out in the black." As Uvi hailed a passing cab, Noodles glared at Rocky through his eye makeup and snarled;

"And I'll be certain to let everyone on board know this new fact about you. There are more than a few members of the crew with enough 'alternate' wardrobe choices to keep you happy for years, I suspect."

"Bet they're all machinists, too."

The pair were about to contemplate taking things a step beyond the playful when a cab willing to risk nine hounds stopped for them. Piling inside, the kids all giggling with glee as they threw themselves onto the floor, doing their collective best to bark in their nine different accents, Uvi gave the driver a destination then turned to the boys. Settling her various appendages around her, she asked;

"Not that I'm not grateful, but why is it those two at the door couldn't find your ship?"

The swabbies smiled once more. As Rocky's laughter attracted Fork and Bubbles who both piled into his lap, soon followed by most of the others as he started tickling and growling at the first pair, Noodles explained;

"Our ship is really The *Roosevelt*. But, those what named her never said which *Roosevelt* she was named for. You see, back on our planet, there were two great men, Franklin and Theodore *Roosevelt*. On ship, there's those of us that say she was named for Teddy, and others who insist it was Frank. So, whenever we hit a new port, we Teddies cause as much trouble as we can pretending to be Franks, and then they do it to us." The machinist laughed shortly, then added;

"I guess it sounds a little stupid."

"Whether it is or isn't, it saved your bacon back there."

"They got bacon on this planet," asked Rocky with the mention of his favorite dessert. About to answer, Uvi suddenly went silent as her eyes caught sight of something out of the back of the cab. Squinting to make certain of what she had seen, she turned around to the driver, shouting;

"Triple the meter if you can outrun what's coming."

"What you are seeing and I am seeing," the driver asked, his fingers already implementing a speed shift, "this thing we are seeing, it is coming for you?"

"It's coming for 'us,' darling, and it's probably coming with the idea of shooting first and talking about it later. So unless you were thinking of jumping out at the next corner..."

"Your meaning is clear, good lady."

Turning around as one, Rocky and Noodles got a gander at what Uvi and the driver had already seen. As the cab blasted forward, nearly doubling its speed, Noodles offered;

"Make that quadruple—I've got money, too."

"Me, three—and I want to live to spend it," added Rocky. "By the blessed blue suede shoes of the King, what's goin' on around here?" Looking down at their charges, Noodles mused;

"Must be one damn good soup they were going to make." Rocky glared at his partner, who shrugged his shoulders, protesting;

"What? I'm just saying..."

Further talk was obscured as the first of the Antagonizers let loose a shot which tore large sections of street up behind their cab. The ships were a matched pair of Danierian design, a fact not lost on anyone in the cab. After a few more shots were fired, each barely missing their vehicle, the driver said;

"Luckily these are some very bad shots, yes?" Shaking her head, Uvi replied;

"No such luck—they're herding us."

Rocky and Noodles looked at each other grimly. Both the machinist and the gunnery officer knew she was correct. Rolling up the crushed silk sleeve of his blouse until the tattoo of an anchor on his upper arm showed, Rocky said;

"Well, little buddy, I'm thinkin' this is it."

"We all have to go sometime." The pair nodded one to another, touched fists, then Rocky shouted to the driver;

"Great ready to slow enough to let us jump out. We're gonna try and stop those mugs." Uvi started to protest. The orphans all started to squeal. The driver hit the brakes.

"I didn't mean for you to come to a complete stop, ya boob!"

"No sir, I am certain you did not," answered the driver. "But, I am thinking that they did."

Following the directional path of the cabby's pointing digit, the swabbies found their path blocked by more firepower than that possessed by many small planets. The Antagonizers rounded the same corner, saw what awaited them, and attempted to break off pursuit. One was vaporized,

SHORE LEAVE - C.J. Henderson

the other was sent crashing into a billboard advertising the great deals to be had at Lapine's Luxury Liquors. Poking his head out of his hound disguise, Melon asked;

"Is this where you jump out to save us, Rocky?" Staring forward into the oncoming armada, the gunnery officer asked;

"Noodles, can we improvise some weapons here?"

"What were you thinking," asked the machinist. "Wet towels? Pictures of their ex-wives?"

And then, the approaching ships came to a halt, the lead cruiser actually dropping to the street. As all in the cab watched, a panel slid open in the side of the personal dreadnought, and a figure in a business suit came out onto the extender reaching for the ground below, one surrounded by more than a score of heavily armed soldiers.

"Kids," said Noodles. "You go on and make a run for it. We'll hold them as long as we can."

"Yeah," added Rocky sourly. "That should give you two, maybe three seconds."

"If they're lucky," said Noodles with a grin. Smiling back at his partner, Rocky nodded, and then the two reached for the door handles, ready to do their best, when Melon suddenly shouted;

"Daddy!"

It was some time later when everything had finally been straightened out. Sitting in the offices which had been given over to representative Brummellig'ic and his staff, Rocky and Noodles, finally back in regulation dress, sat quietly at attention as their captain, as well as Caldo Bippdi, the mayor of the port town, and the representative tried to hash out all the particulars.

"So," said the captain, hoping to nail the whole thing down, "if I have this correct, you, Mr. Brummellig'ic, slipped on-planet quietly for an inspection, looking for signs of Danierian mischief." When the big alien nodded, the captain continued, saying;

"But, unknown to you, the Danierians, having discovered your plan, kidnapped your son's class while on field trip. They were attempting to force you to turn a blind eye to their chicanery, when my boys here caused a diversion that allowed the kids to escape their captors."

"A diversion?" Mayor Bippdi began turning an array of exotic colors, several which drew appreciative "ahs" and "ohs" from the former orphans.

26   Everything's Better With Monkeys

Before he could continue, however, representative Brummellig'ic cut him off with a wave of his hand, saying;

"Yes, captain, you are correct on all counts. And, please, Mayor, all damages will be taken care of by my office."

Noodles and Rocky smiled at each other upon hearing the representative's pronouncement. Still sketchy on some of the facts, however, Rocky asked;

"You'll forgive me, gentlemen, and all, but I was wonderin', Melon," he called out to the ringleader sitting on his father's desk, "why'd you give us that story about orphans and soup and all?"

"An idea of one of my officers," answered Brummellig'ic. "The children have been taught this cover story. You see, most species in the galaxy would sell their own mothers for a box of mints. We've found that whenever someone is lost, if they claim to be running away from us, most anyone who finds them will turn them into whomever they say they're running away from expecting a reward."

"Yes, Mr. Vespucci, Mr. Kon; it seems you two have done great things for the human race, intergalactic relations-wise. Wouldn't you agree, representative?"

"It's rare we of the inner circle of the Pan-Galactic League of Suns get such an opportunity to measure a race's true worth," said Brummellig'ic to the captain. Turning to the gobs, he said, "You two might turn out to be fine examples of humanity, or tremendous exceptions, but you have given the league something to think about."

There was more chatter back and forth after that, but it was the usual circular palaver of politicians. Finally, even that was cut short as the rest of the high-powered parents of the supposed orphans forced their way into the meeting to reclaim their youngsters, and to shower Rocky and Noodles with praise, well-wishes and gifts. Seeing Uvi waiting in the outer office, Rocky left Noodles to soak up any remaining goodies, hurrying out to the diva.

"So," he said, a trifle nervous, "they kept you here, too?"

"No, you silly," she said, her voice still delightfully in full possession of all the gunnery officer's faculties. "I was waiting for you." Rocky blinked hard, barely able to believe his ears. Smiling as wide as humanly possible, he answered;

"Oh my, I know I'm just a mutt, and I don't know how we could, er, I mean, what we'll have to, ummmm... I'm just sayin' I don't care about nothin', not so long as I can be with you."

SHORE LEAVE - C.J. Henderson

"Oh," said Uvi in response, her voice a thing filled with apologetic surprise. "I'm sorry—I get so comfortable in this thing I forget I have it on."

And, so saying, office Beezle Uvi of Earth Intelligence slipped out of her bio-infiltration suit, revealing all one hundred and fifteen pounds of green eyed, red-headed, well-proportioned loveliness which was the real her. Quickly explaining that she had been placed onworld in preparation for representative Brummellig'ic's inspection, she explained that she had spotted Melon in Rocky's care, and had moved in to recover him.

"Everyone was on alert. Normally I would have just stunned you and Noodles, taken the children into protective custody, and you two would have been taken away, but..."

"Yes," grinned Rocky, "but what?"

"Well, you do have such nice eyes..."

And then, the two came even closer together. Eyes closing, they were just about to kiss when suddenly, the door slammed open and a Embrian came in at a run, shouting;

"Mayor, mayor, big trouble! There are human sailors tearing up another tavern. Much fighting, much damage!"

"What ship are these from," growled the mayor, to which his aide answered;

"The Theodore."

"Oh well," sighed the captain. "There goes all that good will."

Representative Brummellig'ic scowled, but then Melon laughed, and his father laughed back. The other parents went back to hugging their children; Noodles asked the mayor if he had ever thought of using robot police; Uvi and Rocky finally kissed.

And outside, the port sirens shrieked in glorious futility as the boys of the "Theodore" continued their mayhem.

Sugar-saturated baked treats have been blamed for nearly everything, from cavities to childhood obesity. But no one dreamed they could be the focus of a galactic conflagration, until the crew of the Roosevelt went in search of...

SPACE PIRATES COOKIES

"Dignity does not consist in possessing honours, but in deserving them."

Aristotle

"AVAST, YE FILTHY SWABS, FIRE AT WILL—BLOW THEIR CRINGING HIDES to the red flames of Perdition!"

The snarling character exhorting his men onward to gleeful murder was certainly a colorful sort. From the button-down cuffs and epaulets of his woolen frock coat to the tricorn hat he wore jammed under his bubble-shaped space helmet, he gave new meaning to words such as "curious" and "outlandish." Or perhaps "goofy." Especially if one considered his diamond eye patch, blood-streaked cutlass, or the robot parrot sitting on his shoulder.

"Awk—*buzz/klik*—pieces of nine, pieces of nine—*zzzkt*"

The wholesale slaughter of innocents raced across the decks of the bizarre, seemingly wooden, apparently wind-driven spaceships, until finally a blood-soaked member of the pirate crew, the internal organs of several alien species hanging from his uplifted fist bellowed;

"They're beaten, Captain, sir."

"Of course they are," the peg-legged, eye-patched master of the human buccaneers pointed at the cringing members of a variety of other species huddled pitifully at his feet, shouting drunkenly at the top of his lungs;

"Because we're from Earth, and we fights dirty!"

Pulling a pistol from his pink silk sash, the drooling, comic opera pirate captain first scratched his posterior with its muzzle, then turned and jammed it against the head of what appeared to be a Lupnicki courtesan and pulled the trigger, scattering her brains across the deck of his ship. As his human crew laughed at such a morbid entertainment, the captain took a bow, then belched, the noise of it echoing inside his helmet so severely it bugged out his rheumy eyes—or at least, the visible one.

"Captain, sir," a wildly excited voice sounded off to the right, dragging all attention in its direction. "We *found* 'em!"

And, as all breaths were held in rapt curiosity as to which "'ems" had been found, two of the largest buccaneers, one a bare-chested black human with sharpened teeth, the other a pig wearing a vest, Hawaiian skirt and a graduation mortarboard, dragged an over-flowing chest into sight as the captain exclaimed with a vulgar glee—

"Space Pirate Cookies!"

And then, pirates from all over the ship rallied around the treat-laden chest, grabbing boxes of cookies, smacking one another in the head so as to steal each other's bottles of milk, and spitting voluminous amounts of crumbs as they sang;

> "Space Pirate Cookies—
> There is no better treat—
> Nothin' we like better to eat—
> So blippin', krippin sweet.
>
> "Space Pirate Cookies—
> All filled with blood and cream—
> Every bite's a dream—
> You can hear the ingredients scream!"

At that point, the gingerbread, shortcake-stuffed buccaneers began indiscriminately raping and murdering their captives as well as one another, dunking handfuls of cookies in blood and brains, and swallowing them whole while continuing to warble on about the joys of rapine slaughter and dessert treats until finally a harsh and disgruntled voice cried out;

"Turn that crap off!"

The voice making the demand was a deep and rumbling one, issuing forth from the lower diaphragm of Chief Gunnery Officer Rockland Vespucci, more commonly known as Rocky, of the good ship *Roosevelt* out of Earth. Standing a strapping 6' 2", when he could stand that was, Vespucci was considered quite a charismatic individual, well... among members of his own species, anyway. And, of course, when he was sober. At the moment of his outburst, he was certainly among members of his own species, but he was just as certainly by no means sober. Neither were the other members of the *Roosevelt*'s crew gathered around him, however, which is, really, what nearly started the Earth's first intergalactic war in the first place.

"Hey, didn't you hear the man," echoed Machinist First Mate Li Qui Kon, better known to top notch wire-and-screw jockeys everywhere as Noodles, "cut that feed or we'll show you a belligerence that will shake your miserable Pan-Galactic League of Suns to its butter-side-downed core!"

"Give in to the inevitable," squeaked the bartender, a mountain of a being with a tiny voice so wildly disproportionate to its size it caused even creatures of its own race to blink in confusion. "It's just a commercial. See, look, it's already back to the show."

The bartender was indeed correct—the Coronian singing star, Nell Char Yllier, was already back on the screen, warbling something about forgetting one's troubles and being happy, surrounded by a half dozen female dancers doing their best to look bubbly and carefree despite their tightly-binding costumes. So wonderful were her tones, and so dazzling the steps of her strapped and restrained troupe that the sailors were almost ready to turn down the thermostat on their tempers and go back to the well-revered, age old nautical pastime of complaining about something rather than doing something about it when the bartender made his fatal mistake.

In truth, the fellow could not really be blamed for his error. If the sailors in question had been Golblacians, or Fogelites, or Embrians (well, if they had been Embrians, there would not have been anything to worry about in the first place—but back to the point) he would have known what to do. The veteran suds-and-sours jockey had stood his station for several decades, and knew the flare-to-violence levels of every race from Andrewns to Zyganirs. But, the upstart human race came from that far end of the galaxy into which most reputable species did not bother to venture. They were too new, too unpredictably odd. And so it was, in an attempt to facilitate their arrival back at a place of pleasant, wallet-emptying drunkenness, he uttered those fateful words that began the entire incident which would come to be known as Darkest Black Glibsday;

"Look, how about a round on the house?"

And that, that tiniest of mistakes, was the beginning of it all.

Everything's Better With Monkeys

"Damn aliens," muttered Rocky, holding his throbbing head while sliding down a wall outside the bar. His voice a mumbling slur decipherable only to those of equal inebriation, he added, "No damn respect. Tramp all over a guy's... ummmm, ah... dignity. Yeah, that's it. It ain't right."

"You, you, ah yeah, you..." Noodles attempted to answer, directing his index finger aloft, at first shaking it to help make his point, then holding it steady because the motion of its waving back and forth had begun to make him seasick, "you know it, pal."

"Always puttin' down humans, juss, juss be... because they've had their damn club for, for what, what—how long?"

"A thousand hundred million and six years." Rocky eyed Noodles for a moment after his outburst, then replied;

"I thought it was seven."

"Must've been a leap year."

Both sailors nodded to each other, continuing their monumentally slow slide down the wall they had chosen to help prop up, neither speaking again until they felt cold, alien concrete beneath them. Settling in, their near-numb fingers feeling about to make certain they could not fall off the sidewalk, the two took deep breaths, sighing in relief over having made it to their seats without injury. Then, feeling secure, the pair settled in to venting their righteous fury at the Pan-Galactic League of Suns and all its members.

This captured their limited ability to focus for some time. Normally the pair had a quite high tolerance for the liquid stimulants of other planets. Indeed, the *Roosevelt* had made port at some seventy-five different worlds, and Rocky and Noodles had tied one on with a vengeance on seventy-eight of them. But, Fadilson was a new world to those plying the spaceways out from the Sol System, and thus possessed some gray areas.

For instance, no planet in the League was known to possess a higher oxygen concentrate to its atmosphere than Fadilson. This fact was made known to the men and women of the *Roosevelt* before disembarking, of course, but was happily ignored as irrelevant by swabbies and officers alike. The place also was known for the odd fact it had a house of worship and a tavern on every street, no matter how large or small the town. Temples had not interested the swabbies all that much, but after finding out the planet's one other interesting geographic fact, they had decided to find every bistro, lounge and cocktail-building establishment in town.

Alone and in bunches, the crew had managed to make great progress, uncovering many interesting cabarets such as Tibric's Treacherous Taproom, the Sum Zero Saloon and Noodles' personal favorite, the Alehouse

SPACE PIRATE COOKIES - C.J. Henderson

of the Gods. Of course, that was mainly because the bartender was a robot and machinists are notorious fans of artificial life forms, especially the kind employed at the Alehouse, which could not only mix every drink in the known universe—from a Thurmian Gargleblaster to a HeyDiddleDiddle-on-the-Rocks—but which could do so while shelling peanuts, washing up the dirty glasses and reciting Vogon poetry for those not buying what it felt was sufficient quantities of intoxicants.

All had seemed well, and the *Roosevelt*'s crew were by and large having a fine time, until that is, they came across that which was to change the course of human destiny—the phenomenon known as Space Pirate Cookies. The treats were a new product, one released in between shore leaves for the sailors of the *Roosevelt*. By themselves they seemed innocuous enough little dunkables, and to be fair it was not the cookies that had put the crew out of sorts. It was the advertising used to make them a household word from one end of the galaxy to the other which humanity-at-large found so completely off-putting.

Space Pirate Cookies came in a mind-boggling vast variety of flavors—they would have to. The snack pastries that came in the cute, human-shapes the galaxy was growing to adore—but for all the wrong reasons—had to be appealing to the one hundred and eighty-five different races officially registered as protectorates of the Pan-Galactic League of Suns, as well as to the five founding races, of course. And that was simply to be able to capture a decent slice of the galactic market share.

As cookies went, they were tasty enough. Not as creamy as the Feezba Chip Pouts of Breniki 7, or as crumblicious as those mouth-watering bursts of joy, the wondrous Velpin Grooblie Drops, nor did they even approach the delectable chewiness of the Archway Mouthful of Frogs, still they had their audience, and that, once again, was because of their advertising.

Space Pirate Cookies were "okay," taste-wise, but the trillions of beings who were doing their bit for intergalactic consumerism were doing so for one reason—they loved the commercials. The adverts had funny songs, colorful characters, and they pandered to the latest racist impulse sweeping the galaxy—mistrusting, fearing and generally hating those upstarts from Earth.

Now, do understand, humanity had not acted at all inappropriately when its first starships penetrated the outer confines of the Sol System, ready to explore the vast and foreboding unknown, only to find a cosmos awaiting them as neatly explored and subdivided as an English country garden. They were disappointed, of course—no great expeditions filled with peril, no staggering challenges laden with fabulous adventure awaited them. It was a surprise, to say the least.

More over, those who had labored and trained all their days to be the new Magellan or Columbus found instead that fate had relegated them to being more the new Ralph Kramden or Willy Loman, bus drivers and traveling salesmen rather than explorers. All races ran up against this obstacle when first they met the League, but humanity confused the Pan-Galactics because never before had a species ever seemed so, well... disappointed. Reaching the League meant an end to disease and hunger. Promise not to make war on any member or protected race, and access to the wealth of the galaxy's scientific knowledge was bestowed freely—at, of course, carefully regulated and competitive prices.

Earth had received instructions on how to repair all the damage it had done to itself, as well as cheap, renewable energy sources, cures for most ailments, directional transmitters for talking to God (it confused humanity to no end that when asked what the one true faith was He seemed to favor the Libertarians) and well, just all manner of wonders. What they lost, however, was that indefinable quality of self-determination, the chance to find these things for themselves. Willing to take the goodies, especially considering that there was no in any way, shape or form, sensible alternative, still it meant the party was over. All had been delivered, wrapped in a tidy pink bow. There was no more.

And so, as they sat staggered and blinded, drunker than a charred and steaming Benjamin Franklin when he belched;

"I tied a key to the end of a string and did *what?*"

Rocky and Noodles fell into a sorry, self-pitying depression of epic proportions. Both had left home to explore the cosmos, to be the men with the first sets of eyes to see vast and amazing unknowns, to fight great battles, to live lives of excitement and challenge. Sadly, to date, their greatest challenge had been to find a snack with the light and salty corn-goodness of Fritos ten million light years from Earth. It was not the kind of test-your-limits-to-the-utmost challenge either of them had had in mind when enlisting.

"I'm tellin' ya, Noodles..."

"What?"

"Did you want somethin', little buddy?"

"What?" Scratching his head, a gesture that took most of his available energy, the machinist said, "you said you were telling me something—"

"Was it important?"

SPACE PIRATE COOKIES - C.J. Henderson   35

"I don't know," answered Noodles, his tone one so over-reachingly depressed that the sound of it caused a nest of nearby rodents to question the meaning of it all and then ultimately take their lives rather than face the all-encompassing despair that had taken root in their souls. "But then, is *anything* important anymore?"

And, with hearing those words, Rocky was struck with a wild and impossible scheme one would have thought too insane even for him. Sitting forward so quickly he actually bounced his eyeballs off their protective membranes, causing himself a moment of temporary blindness, the gunner coughed up three taverns' worth of assorted liquors, the remains of two meals and a claim stub he had been searching for all weekend. Wiping his mouth on his sleeve, an action he was hoping would not damage the fabric, he blurted;

"Noodles, all them Space Pirate Cookie rats do is make fun of humans, right?" When the machinist nodded in agreement, practically passing out from the exertion, his pal continued.

"It ain't bad enough we get into space and find the whole place is just one big Levittown, but these guys, I mean... those guys, I mean, I just wanta..."

Rocky made unconscious motions of strangling some living thing, his eyes shining with a light bright enough to guarantee he found such an idea splendid. As he did so, his mind played for him the seemingly relentless advertisements for Space Pirate Cookies he had been forced to endured since making port. The videos showed the men of Earth as savage monsters, as vicious thugs bereft of morals, honor, common sense or even acceptable table manners. Their implication was that all humans were rapacious, murdering thieves and that the universe was better off without them. And, to be fair to the gunnery officer's mounting temper, he would not have been nearly as incensed if he had not noticed a marked change in the non-human population of the town.

The natural prejudice many of Earth felt the member races of the League harbored against humanity was in full evidence. Everywhere the sailors went, beings from all races were ready to point fingers, jabber about fearing the eventual hauling of their keels now that Earthers had arrived, and laughing hysterically at their supposed wit. In the first ten or twelve taverns they visited, the swabbies were able to keep their wits about them. But, as the juice of the grape, the wheat and the chocolate-and-caffeined caramel beans worked its usual magic, self-control had begun to evaporate.

36   **Everything's Better With Monkeys**

Once Rocky had reached the sidewalk, it had been boiled into non-existence.

"So," asked Noodles quietly, the aroma of his buddy's eruption prodding the machinist on toward his own vesuvian impersonation, "what is it you wanta do?"

Noodle's response to his question gave the gunnery officer's mind a reason to focus. What did he want to do? Obviously, he thought, from the delight his hands were having pretending to choke the life out of something, mayhem would have to be involved with any future actions designed to brighten his mood. But, what kind of mayhem? Against what or whom? And on what kind of scale? And, as his rage and frustration worked together to find answers that, although not intelligent or even remotely logical might still give some sort of "6" to the "3+3=" rattling about within his head, suddenly a smile, one both peaceful and sinister spread across Rocky's face.

"Noodles," he said, the wild gleam in his eyes suggesting nothing but trouble, "I know exactly what I want to do."

"It doesn't involve more drinking, does it?"

"Nope," answered the gunner. Struggling to push his way back up the wall, "I think we've downed just the right amount."

"For what?"

"We, little buddy," announced Rocky, back on his feet, his hand extended toward his friend to help him regain his own, "are going for a ride." Swallowing a deep breath, Noodles took his friend's hand, then grunted and wheezed his own way to an almost upright position, asking;

"Where?"

"To wherever the hell it is they make those damn Space Pirate Cookies."

Feeling a greatly unwanted wave of sobriety racing for his pickled brain cells, the machinist blanched, staggering back several steps to where he could hold onto the wall for support. Coughing with choked surprise, he finally was able to get control of himself sufficiently to say;

"Wait a minute, wait just a minute. The only way we could find them would be with the ship's computers. And, if we found them, the only way we could reach them would be with the ship. And, and, and... ah... the captain would, I mean, I'm thinking, ah... he would never let us..."

And then, Noodles' eyes cleared so rapidly the force of them opening in surprise knocked the machinist backward, bouncing his head off the wall against which he had so recently been resting. Stunned by what he had just realized, he shouted;

"You, you—you mean, you want to steal the *Roosevelt*! Steal her, and take her out of orbit, and then, take her out and find these cookiemakers and use the power of the United Earth Navy to blast them into chocolate chips! Yes—that's what you're saying—right?"

"Yeah," answered Rocky, grinning like an ape that had finally figured out the difference between a salad fork and a dessert spoon. "You want'a?"

"Did the Buddha drink Mint Juleps?"

And thus the whole mindless tragedy began.

Captain Alexander Benjamin Valance was not a happy man. For one thing, he had fallen asleep with his legs and arms in a tangle so overwhelmingly complete that all four of his appendages had been almost completely without blood since he had stumbled into his bunk. For another, at two years, eight months, fifteen days out from Earth, he had put up with the wacky, infantile and just plain brainless stunts of his crew longer than any reasonable man should have been asked to tolerate.

He had suffered the endless nonsense of their infighting over whom the *Roosevelt* had been named for—Franklin or Theodore. He had bailed them out when they had shaved the sacred monkeys of Templeworld. He had made the appropriate excuses and restitutions when they had conned the guards of the Pen'dwaker Holding Facility into allowing them to transform the prison into a gambling den (for a mere 18.3% of the gross) for their Intergalactic Crap Shoot of the Millennium tournament. He had even found a way to smooth things over when they had sponsored their infamous inter-species mixer where they introduced the debutante daughters of the leading politicians of the Pan-Galactic League of Suns to the bears, cows, pigs and chimps they were transporting to the Inter-Galaxy Zoo on Chamre XI.

Indeed, it was his weariness of riding herd on the compliment of Earth's sharpest minds and broadest backs that had caused him to do something he had often dreamed longingly about, but not once acted upon during all of his two years, eight months, and fifteen days at the helm of Earth's mightiest warship. For once, after making port on Fadilson, Valance had decided he could use a little shore leave himself.

Everything's Better With Monkeys

"Captain... what are you doing here?"

Yes, for once he had walked down the gangplank with the rest of the first wave heading offship with no thought more foremost in his mind than getting thoroughly and utterly polluted. Trained to explore the stars, prepared to take the greatest of risks, to dare the spectacular, brave the unthinkable, he had been the first to take a ship in the Great Dark, and thus the first human being to find out the game was completely and utterly over.

"This is my bunk, you know," mumbled the groggy Valance. "I do sleep here."

As sick of a military career without a trace of military action within it, no new peoples to meet, no trade routes to open, no tensions to either alleviate or to put down with a vengeance as any being could be, the captain had finally given in and taken solace within the bottle, the stop-gap solution to naval despair since the first aquanauts anywhere had piled into a canoe with beers and spears and set off to finally see just what the hell was around the bend.

"Bu..." the ensign stopped in mid-conjunction, the mixture of trepidation, terror and relief to be found on his face completely unreadable to the vastly hung-over captain of the *Roosevelt*.

"Did you want something, sailor?"

The man stood shaking in Valance's doorway, unable to answer. After only a few seconds, however, despite the crushing weigh of his hangover, the captain's well-trained senses began to pick up clues as to what was going on. The ensign working at gathering his wits before him was excited beyond any reasonable point—which meant something unreasonable had happened. The lad also was obviously afraid of something.

The back of Valance's mind rebelled at such a thought. Young to be a captain, especially of the Earth's first Dreadnought class starship, still he was a cool and competent commander, one who felt in his heart of hearts that the only thing his crew had any legitimate right to fear was him. Part of his mind immediately moved to dismiss such self-centered thinking, but then he stopped himself, realizing that was exactly what was going on.

"Sailor," muttered Valance, holding one hand over his eyes to keep them from spilling out and rolling about on the floor, "what's going on?"

"We did a bad thing, captain."

And with those words, Alexander Benjamin Valance removed his hand from his eyes, fixing his gaze upon the hapless ensign. Throwing himself to his feet with an effort which made the labors of Sisyphus appear to be nothing more than a game of shuffleboard, the captain quickly worked his way past the nerve-tingling pain of his sleeping limbs, around his need for fresh air, a shower and something in his stomach with a lesser alcohol content than rocket fuel. Steeling himself for whatever horrible truth he was about to learn, his mind raced in a thousand directions at once. What, oh what, had Vespucci and Kon done this time?

"How bad?"

As the ensign started to speak, Valance felt the need to sit down. As he continued, the captain felt the need to lie down. By the time the junior officer finished, Valance was contemplating ritual suicide. Deciding the high command would turn to voodoo to reanimate his carcass just so they could disembowel him themselves, however, he chose against hari kari. Not, that is, that he had decided against bloodshed—he just saw no immediate need for it to be his own.

"Captain on the—*captain?!*" The yeoman who had begun to automatically announce Valance's presence realized what she had done, did a double-take, then shouted, "Captain on the bridge! The *real* captain, you monkeys!"

Rocky turned to see Valance's formidable presence filling the doorway. Holding his head, still suffering from the night before, the gunnery officer said weakly;

"Captain, sir... huh... we, ah um well..."

"I take it you didn't know I was on board when you decided to take your little jaunt. Is that what you're trying to tell me as you continue to sit in *my* chair, Mr. Rockland?"

"Ah, yeah," responded Rocky, still seated. "Actually, it was, sir."

As Valance continued to stare at the gunner, from the sidelines Noodles made hand motions indicating that perhaps his friend should maybe get out of the captain's chair, perhaps salute, or at least try to quit passing gas. Noticing the machinist's animated pantomimes, he asked;

"Geezzzzit, Noodles, what'ya want?"

"He's trying to suggest that it might be a good idea if you got the hell *out* of my chair, you peanut-brained imbecile!"

Somehow catching the meaning of the captain's more direct suggestion, Rocky tumbled forward out of the ship's command center, crashing against the equally hungover navigator. Valance debated having his seat fumigated, but decided on just letting the air purification system deal with the remains of the gunner's bad evening. Despite what all the ensign had told him, the captain needed to hear what had happened from the source.

"Tell it, Rockland. And don't leave out any of the good parts."

Honest and heartfelt apology cascaded from every pour as the gunnery officer explained how their current situation had come to pass. He related the entire crew's outrage over both the Space Pirate Cookie advertisements as well as the greatly heightened edge of discomfort said ads had created. Privately Valance understood his crew's irritation over these points, having experienced them himself the day before, but he kept the information from showing as even a sympathetic glint in his eye. Instead, he merely snarled;

"Yes, go on."

Rocky did. In short order, despite his brain's continual refusal to remove the floating stars and polka dots from before his eyes, or to stop his teeth from itching, the gunnery officer told the whole, embarrassing tale. He sketched out his and Noodles' talk on the sidewalk, and then their subsequent trip back inside the tavern to gather together all the available *Roosevelt* crewmen they could find. He told of how their idea had gone over like an offer of ice cream in Hell, how every swabbie they could find, and even a few of the locals, rallied to the idea of stealing the ship, finding the location of the Space Pirate Cookie factory, and then sending it to that place where offers of ice cream were looked upon so favorably.

When the captain asked how they were able to countermand the *Roosevelt*'s layers of security codes, to pilot the ship without his executive clearances, and to reach deep space (like any spacer, he had known they were in the Great Dark from the moment he awoke) without Earth Command Authorization Releases, Noodles took over the explanations, getting an able assist from Technician Second Class Thorner and Quarter-master Harris. Remembering immediately how that pair had engineered the replacement of the Grand High Exalted Poobah of the Pan-Galactic League of Sun's acceptance broadcast for his new term in office with Richard M. Nixon's "I am not a crook" speech, he pushed the machinist to skip the details. After all, how they got to the Great Dark really was not all that important. What they had done since they got there, however, that was a different story.

"Well, sir," hemmed Rocky, getting ready to throw in a few dozen haws in the proper places, "drunk as we was, we got pretty single-minded. Since these cookie makers are a company, it wasn't all that hard to get a fix on them."

SPACE PIRATE COOKIES - C.J. Henderson

"Any normal person would never have been able to get a swing at their vector," added Thorner. "With the ship's access to trade lines, though, we were able to nail it pretty quick."

"I'll be certain to mention such in your next efficiency rating," answered Valance drolly. Getting back to Rocky, with eyes steely and hard, he said, "so you and your hyenas managed to steal the ship and get her into the Deep. I imagine we're on a full speed charge toward wherever the buccaneer bakers are located—correct?"

"Aye, sir."

"And just out of curiosity, you slackjaws couldn't have kept this information a secret, could you? I mean, it wouldn't be possible for us to just turn around and get the blazes back to Fadilson without anyone knowing about your little escapade, would it?"

"I'm afraid not, sir."

"No, no, of course not," agreed Valance with an angry sarcasm. "But indulge me, lieutenant, just *why* can't we do so?"

"Well, sir," stumbled Rocky, suddenly wishing he had taken his mother's advice and joined the priesthood, "you see, after we got on-course for the cookie factory, we thought maybe we should make an announcement about it..."

"Certainly," growled the captain. "What could be more natural?"

"So we sent one out, ah, over the official bands..."

"Of course you did."

"And basically, well... in the name of the Earth... ah, we declared war on the Space Pirate Cookie Company."

Silence filled the room with a noticeable pressure. The captain stared at Rocky for a long moment, unmoving. Unblinking. Then finally, with all present subconsciously holding their breath to the point of bursting, Valance reacted. Breaking off eye contact with the gunner, he tilted his head downward, looking at nothing specifically, and then began to laugh.

At first it was a simple one-note noise, as akin to humming as anything else. But, after only a handful of seconds, it expanded, becoming a loud and raucous thing, one so jocular and merry one could not help but join in. All across the bridge, semi-sober sailors began to chuckle, then guffaw, eventually falling into the knee-slapping helpless state of full-blown hysterics which had seized Valance.

"You declared war on a cookie factory?" The captain had to choke his question out in between bursts of merriment. Caught in much the same dilemma, Rocky answered;

"Yes, sir. Full scale."

"You announced this over the spaceways, of course?"

"Oh yes, sir, captain. Full intent. Full disclosure. Full speed ahead."

"And the League," answered Valance, his revelry tapering off just a touch, "and Earth High Command, they've made their positions clear—yes?"

"Oh, yes sir," howled Rocky, only seeing the humorous side of his answer, "they both pretty much want us dead."

"In fact," interrupted Noodles, chiming in as if actually in a hurry to get hung along with his pal, "the League is still on hold."

All laughter stopped at that point as completely as if each of the merry-makers had been slapped in the face with a wet porcupine. His mood crystallizing into a thing severe and frightening to behold, the captain snarled;

"You've had the League on hold all this time? Are you all out of your goddamned—"

"Sir," shouted Thorner, the large man's booming voice refocusing everyone's attention on their far-from-finished hangovers, "the League demanded to talk to you, refusing to believe you weren't on board. We send Brodsky to check your cabin so we could tell them with cleanslate assurance you weren't on board—that we did this all on our own."

"But that, um..." added Harris, the first to recognize the irony of their situation, "that didn't... work out for us, sir."

"Ya think," growled Valance. The captain lowered his vision once more, his mind racing desperately. He had to speak with the League, had to find a way out for his crew, and for the Earth. His head throbbing, eyes burning, bones melting, he gave the high sign to communications officer Feng to patch him through to the League connection. Making an audible gulp, the young woman depressed the correct switch, and the face of the Grand High Exalted Poobah of the Pan-Galactic League of Suns appeared on the forward monitor.

"Captain Valance," the Telrecian known as Merli Acirde said coolly, "I'm told you are not presently aboard the *Roosevelt*. Pray tell, from where are you transmitting?"

"Good to see you again, too, your Poobahship. If you don't mind, I think I can explain this whole mess so everyone can just go back about their business."

"Correct me if I'm wrong," answered the Grand High Exalted One, "but I believe I am already in possession of the facts. Your drunken crew, from your warship, with you on board, sent out a legal and binding confirmation of hostilities against member citizens of the Pan-Galactic League of Suns.

SPACE PIRATE COOKIES - C.J. Henderson   43

Is that not the case?"

Valance froze his first, second and even his third responses within his throat. He knew he was playing a high stakes game, and that more than his own safety or satisfaction had to be considered. He also, however, was suffering from a hangover so stupefying he actually needed to remind himself to breathe every so often. Feeling he had regained a fraction of his self-control, he began;

"It wasn't a serious confirmation, your Bigness. The boys, they've just—"

"Please, Captain, allow me to 'slice to the pursuit,' as you humans say. I have a speech to prepare for tonight's annual League dinner, so allow me to be brief. You and yours have committed the highest of crimes. Whatever your infantile reasons, the fact is you have given me clear justification to release the Pan-Galactic armada to pursue, hunt down, and blow your ship out of the deep. After that, it will track a course to your home system and obliterate every mote of human influence."

"You, you," stammered Rocky, his eyes wide as saucers, "we was just on a tear. You can't do that."

"Ahhhh, Mr. Rockland, how glad I am to see you amidst the doomed." Preening like a coyote that had just eradicated the last roadrunner from the surface of its world, the Grand High Exalted Poobah of the Pan-Galactic League of Suns added;

"And since you seem to have forgotten with whom you are dealing, I shall remind you. I am the combined will and final voice of civilized space. I can do whatever I want. I might not be 'a crook,' Mr. Rockland, but I'm a very patient, and vengeful being, and if there are gods in any heavens, they will arrange that the news of your destruction be brought to me during dessert so that they both might be made all the sweeter."

And with those words, the main bridge monitor went black. The crew of the *Roosevelt* present within command remained silent, all waiting for Valance's orders. To a man, despite their varying degrees of alcohol-induced suffering, each one of them despaired their actions. They had not only doomed their home world and all the planets, satellites and asteroid settlements it controlled, but worse, they had disappointed their captain. After a terribly long silence, Valance broke the hideous quiet, asking;

"What's our heading?"

"Ah, actually, sir," answered Noodles, "we're still headed for the Space Pirate Cookie factory at full tear."

"Good." As those around him gave their captain a quizzical stare, not certain what he was up to, Valance pulled down a great, cleansing breath through his nostrils, exhaled, pulled down another, then announced over the ship's speakers;

"Men, I'm not going to bother with accusations or recriminations. Quite frankly, at this point I don't care what got us here. To be perfectly honest, I'm as sick as every one of you over how Earth has been treated ever since we got out here. In fact, I believe our pal the Poobah's been waiting for something like this since long before our boys Milhoused him."

Rocky and Noodles grinned at each other, both as pleased as if they had just won a lifetime supply of bacon—thick-sliced and Canadian. As the rest of the crew began to perk up around them as well, Valance barked;

"All right, these spudboys want to start some shit, I say, bring it on. If they think the human race is a dog they can simply tell to roll over and play dead, I say we go Perryrohdanic on their asses and show these silk breeched Betties how we do things on our side of the tracks. How about it, men of the *Roosevelt*, who's for blowing the living hell out a cookie factory?!"

And with those words, and a fantastic deal of unrestrained cheering, the finest ship in the great Earth exploration fleet went to Top Turbo Thrust and sailed forth toward destiny.

"For the last time, you four, are you absolutely certain you want to do this?"

Valance stared at the almost sober quartet before him, trying not to let his inordinate pride show through. If any of them were to realize how he felt at that moment, he knew there would be no talking them out of their suggestion. As they all assured the captain they were as determined as ever, Thorner stepped forward, offering;

"Look, captain sir, it just makes sense. We're the ones that got this all started."

"Hey," shouted Rocky, "you and Harris were just the first apes me and Noodles come across. If anyone gets the credit for endangering all of humanity, it's gotta be us."

As the four began arguing over how little each of the others had contributed to the coming destruction of the human race, Valance barked an "at ease" at them, then said;

"All right, we'll play it your way. We're just a hair out from the asteroid complex where they make these damn cookies, so let's make certain we all understand each other. You four are going to take a dropship in, get inside and blow the place. That will keep the armada coming this way, looking for the *Roosevelt*."

The sailors all nodded, hands unconsciously checking their sidearms. Knowing time was precious, Valance wrapped things up quickly, saying;

"In the meantime, the rest of the crew and I will doublelight it back to Earth. With the League blocking all transmissions, the only was we can warn them is in person."

"Five minutes to drop." As the five all looked at Yeoman Feng's image on the console, the captain affirmed her message was received and understood, then turned back to the sailors before him. Pursing his lips for a moment, knowing he had time for only the shortest of goodbyes to the men before him whom, in all likelihood, he would never see again, he said;

"Gentlemen, it's been a pure, goddamned honor."

As Valance's hand shot upward, Rocky, Noodles, Harris and Thorner all snapped to attention, getting their own hands to their helmets a split-second before the captain's reached his forehead. Valance saluted, his men returned it, then they turned and piled into their dropship. As they did so, Valance pointed toward the skull and crossbones freshly painted on its bow, calling out;

"Nice touch."

"They wanted pirates," answered Harris, "we'll give them a few."

And, in only minutes the *Roosevelt* was but an echoing speck fading from sight. At the helm, Thorner moved them with all due haste toward the bakery complex hidden in the asteroids ahead. The instant they were far enough away from the *Roosevelt* for minimum safety, the Dreadnought's great protonic engines roared and the ship disappeared down a parabolic chuckhole toward home. Wordlessly, the quartet inside the extremely re-cently renamed good dropship Buckets o'Blood moved into the asteroid belt, drifting in toward the already visible complex.

The cookie factories, warehouses and staging areas were enormous, some of the massive ovens covering hundreds of acres. Landing in the shadows of several brobdingnagian syrup towers, the assault team gathered their explosives, record cameras and infiltration tools and exited the Bucket O'Blood, then headed for what appeared to be a little used side entrance to what they hoped was the main administration building. Even before landing, the swabbies had agreed that destroying the lair of the company's "suits" would best achieve their goals. Or, as Thorner had put it;

"It's not like we've got anything against the bakers."

"You try one of their Little Taste of Andromedas?"

46   Everything's Better With Monkeys

The others had smiled at the tech's dry humor, Harris noting that it was not half as dry as the cookies in question, a bon mot which brought a needed chuckle to them all. After that, however, their mission had become a strictly business affair. Twenty minutes after the tiny spot of humor, the quartet had made their way inside what indeed turned out to be the administrative headquarters of the Space Pirate Cookie Corporation.

As the team moved upward through the building, they were struck with the ease of their passage. True, they had been forced to duck and cover several times as various office types hurried down one hallway or another, but for the most part their journey from the outside to the main offices of the company proceeded without interruption.

"I'm thinking," said Harris, "fun as it's been playing pirate, if we do actually kill anyone, it would be like admitting these cookie bastards were right about Earth. You know what I mean?"

Indeed, all of his fellows knew exactly what he meant. The same notion had been plaguing the rest of the swabbies since they had launched from the *Roosevelt*. Making a nasty face, Rocky said;

"Don't you just hate guys who take all the fun out of everything?" The others chuckled, but realizing their time to act was tight, Thorner offered;

"Look, we have to do something. So, why don't we just march in on their meeting, tell them to clear out, and then blow up their damn corporate HQ without hurting anyone or even burning up any of their damn cookies. If Earth's gotta go, let's help her go with some class."

Everyone agreed, all except Harris who asked if they could not, please, let the Little Tastes of Andromeda burn. After that, knowing they were but a doorknob's turn away from making their room reservations for Valhalla, the quartet entered the main offices of SPC/Co., only to find the surprise of their lives.

"Humans," cried out one of the aliens joyously around the conspicuously large table taking up most of the meeting room. "Is this perfect or what?"

"Come in, brothers, come in," shouted another, one attired in such a shiny, multi-layered garment it had to be assumed he was the biggest of the wigs present. "'Tis fitting indeed for humans to be here at our moment of triumph."

"Ah, yeah," said Rocky. "But, er... which moment was that again?"

"The moment when we bring the repressive, stagnating dictatorship of the accursed Pan-Galactic League of Suns to its collective knees." As many

SPACE PIRATE COOKIES - C.J. Henderson

around the table thumped and whistled at what they obviously approved as a fine sentiment, Noodles asked;

"Huh, I know why we might want to do such a thing, but that would mainly be because of you guys. No offense, but, why would you want to do it?"

"Because," snarled the obvious ringleader, "the League has been lying to everyone for millennia. The galaxy hasn't been completely explored—shaz'bot, most of it is still unknown!"

"What?" The word echoed from one swabbie to another.

"It's true," said an alien garbed in only slightly less shiny layers, obviously a vice-president. "I used to be an aide to that Telrecian bastard, Merli Acirde. "The five 'great' races have been conning every new species they've found since forever. They pull their patented 'here's some goodies' bit with every slogbrain that pulls itself up out of the ooze, then intimidates them into just becoming another consumer outlet. Stay home, put your feet up, let us take care of you."

"You mean," said Rocky, his voice as filled with wonder as his heart was throbbing with hope, "there's still worlds to find out there?"

"There's a million of them—a billion," shouted the vice president. "And we're all going to have our crack at them as soon as we bring down the League."

"Nifty," answered Thorner. "How you gonna do that?"

"We member races of the resistance, we build SPC/Co. for one reason. Sorry about picking on the Earth and all, but you play to your audience, you know?" As the sailors all agreed the fellow had a point, the alien continued, telling them, "the Space Pirate Cookies that were sent to the League's big five homeworlds were filled with a responsive nano-explosive. When our grand high exalted poobah gives his speech in a few minutes, his voice will resonate with the nanites built into each cookie. Even ones digested six months ago will have left enough traces behind to ensure anyone who's eaten one will be blown to smithereens. Acirde will no sooner begin his speech when he along with billions of the oppressors will die—and then, the galaxy will be free to find its own destiny once more!"

As the alien VP panted from the exertion of his speech, smiling with a decidedly wild-eyed glee, the swabbies looked at each other. They knew they and every other human was safe, that only beings from the Pan-Galactic's big five, and perhaps a few snack-hungry tourists to their worlds would be affected. If they were to simply congratulate the corporate revolutionaries around the table and sit back and wait, their troubles, as well as Earth's, were over.

48   Everything's Better With Monkeys

All they had to do was approve the deaths of billions. Something the grand high exalted poobah, Merli Acirde, was happy to allow. As the men of the *Roosevelt* looked around the room, noting just how many guards were actually stationed within its confines, Thorner muttered;

"Hey, Mikey-boy, you had your cameras rolling the whole time?"

"As per procedure," answered Harris. "Think maybe I should send out a broadcast?"

"You know," said Noodles, his fingers casually slipping the binding clasp on his sidearm, "that's probably a good idea."

"Okay, boys," added Rocky in a tone as serious as a barium enema, "let's show these half-wits what it really means to be a goddamned human being."

And then, pistols were freed, triggers were pulled, and bodily fluids yellow, green and vermillion ran across the decks of corporate piracy.

"That's certainly an exciting story, Captain Valance."

The Galaxy Today reporter gushed, her excitement over being close to the first actual hero the known universe had seen in ages causing her reproductive juices to bubble with the excitement of the Trevi Fountain. As she beamed and Valance continued to spin the story he and his men had cooked up, said men turned from the monitor broadcasting the captain's interview to one another, clinking their bottles and glasses one against the other.

"Well, gentlemen, I think we pulled this one outta the fire rather nicely."

To point out that Rocky had somehow become the undisputed master of understatement would have been as uselessly redundant as sending a gallon of unleaded to the heart of the sun. But then, he could be excused, considering the circumstances. Quartermaster Harris' broadcast had been instantly picked up by the League's armada, which had responded in a traditional manner by homing in on the signal, then sending in a thousand League Marines to "pacify" the situation.

The soldiers, having seen the images being sent from the SPC/Co. boardroom targeted the corporate officers and their minions, arriving just in time to save the four humans who, to be fair, had made excellent use of the element of surprise, but who had also run out of time. Merli Acirde was stopped before he could broadcast his speech, and was also immediately stripped of his rank and put into confinement pending an investigation.

SPACE PIRATE COOKIES - C.J. Henderson   49

Now, it was true everyone paying the slightest attention knew the League was merely playing for time, trying to maintain their position as Kings of the Mountain. And, again to be fair, everyone with any reasonable understanding of how such games were played, knew that the League's iron grasp on the affairs of the galaxy might have been relaxed, but that they would by no means be swept away by events.

"Still," mused Noodles, reaching for a ninth, frosty cold Woodchuck Ale, "it's nice to know that we shook things up a little."

"A little?" Thorner spat a swallow of his Great Balls o'Firepower cocktail across the table, then shouted, "we struck away the chains shackling the oppressed of the universe!"

"We also worked it so the captain came out a hero, taught the galaxy what it means to screw with the human race, and kept ourselves alive long enough to enjoy it all," said Harris. His feet on the table, hands behind his head and seven inches of a nicely-fired Avo Uvezian hand-rolled clenched firmly between his teeth, he added;

"Not bad for a bunch of upstarts from the armpit of the universe, eh?"

"Not bad at all," agreed Noodles. "This means we're all going to get to do what we signed up to do in the first place—explore the Cosmos. Be the first beings to set foot on strange, new worlds. To seek out new life, and new civilizations..."

"To boldly go," shouted Thorner, his eyes filled with glee, "where no space pirates have gone before!"

All raised their drinks, saluted one another, then drank deeply once more. Noting Rocky's unusual silence, Noodles asked him the reason. Looking a bit sheepish, the gunner answered;

"It's nothin', really. We liberated all those cookies before we left the factory—right?" When all agreed, Rocky said, "Well, I've just been tryin' a bunch of 'em. And, interestin' enough, you know what I found?" When the others inquired, he told them;

"These Little Drops of Andromeda, they really ain't that bad."

All three of the gunnery officer's shipmates made quite caustic responses, but Rocky heard none of it for as they shouted their jibes the great protonic engines of the *Roosevelt* were brought on-line, and the finest ship in the great Earth exploration fleet went to Top Turbo Thrust and finally sailed forth, as it had been aching to since it was commissioned, to boldly search for drinks where no man had gotten drunk before.

Bridging the gap between Earthlings and alien races depends on more than the mere mechanics of communication; it requires an open line from the heart. That's why...

EVERYTHING'S BETTER
WITH MONKEYS

"What a piece of work is a man! How noble in reason! how infinite in faculties! in form and moving, how express and admirable! in action, how like an angel! in apprehension, how like a god! the beauty of the work! the paragon of animals!"
William Shakespeare

"Were it not for the presence of the unwashed and the half-educated, the formless, queer and incomplete, the unreasonable and absurd, the infinite shapes of the delightful human tadpole, the horizon would not wear so wide a grin."
F.M. Colby

THE *Roosevelt* WAS THE FIRST OF THE LONG-AWAITED DREADNOUGHT class, a single ship stretching for nearly half a mile, inconceivable tons of metal and plastics, crystal and biomechanical feeds brought together from Earth, the Moon and the asteroids that, when ultimately combined into an end product, became something unheard of—something utterly incomprehensible. And thus... so the thinking went... unbeatable, as well.

She was, in the end, a sum far greater than her parts. The *Roosevelt* was known as "the cowboy ship," for it had been that cocky gang of rocketeers known as the Moonpie Cowboys who had built her. They were the wildmen of the mightiest nation in the system's Advanced R&D Team, and it was their spirit that infested her—as well as programmed her still, not-quite-understood artificial mind.

The *Roosevelt* was the opening number of a new kind of show, the all or nothing-at-all first born of the Confederation of Planets—big, because she had to be. The first ship with functional energy shields, she needed room for the massive protonic engines essential in powering such revolutionary devices. And for her thousands of attack aircraft, hundreds of them merely hanging off her sides. And for her extensive guns, her big guns—the whisperers and the pounders—and all her hundreds of thousands of missiles and bombs.

She was the solar system's first spacecraft carrier, a mobile prairie outpost, a relentlessly strong, self-determining fortress in space. Capable of housing as many as 10,000 sailors and marines, the great ship was meant to explore the galaxy, to chart the universe, and to bring prestige and riches to the human race in general.

But, that had been when that particular track meet had thought it controlled the only runner on the field. Reaching the edge of the system's outer planet's orbit, the *Roosevelt* was hailed, in English, Spanish, Dutch, Jamaican and eighty-three other standard languages, by a small, obnoxiously shiny craft commanded by a small, and equally obnoxious alien life form that was all too happy to deliver its news.

The quite unexpected messenger announced to the finally-capable-of-interstellar-traveling human race that this accomplishment had gotten them an invitation to join the awe-inspiring Pan-Galactic League of Suns, an organization of worlds begun by the Five Great Races. It was an announcement that, essentially, the party was over before it began, that all the planets worth anything were all sewn up, all intelligent species discovered, all franchises in all the marketplaces possible well-established and even better protected.

The news came as a crushing blow to the adventure-craving crew of the *Roosevelt*, and for their first two years, eight months and fifteen days in space they showed their resentment in many a creative and colorful manner. And then, suddenly, all the rules changed. Thanks to that first, bold human crew in space, the entire galaxy discovered the League was a sham, that their claims to have everything under control were simply so much eye-wash, and that there was still plenty of unknown universe out there, teaming with mysteries and excitement—enough even to satisfy the collective curiosity of the crew of the *Roosevelt*.

Within weeks of that revelation, more than a dozen trans-galactic federations had begun to struggle into existence, including the *Roosevelt*'s hometown group. Once made up of only six of the Earth's neighboring planets, because of its pivotal role in pulling the Pan-Galactic wool from the galaxy's eyes, the Confederation of Planets had already expanded to a

EVERYTHING'S BETTER... - C.J. Henderson

membership of some seventy-eight worlds, proving quite nicely the old adage that everyone does, indeed, "love a winner."

Which is why the crew of the *Roosevelt*, one fine galactic star date, from its stalwart captain down to the lowest chef's assistants and protonic bolt tighteners, was in a rousing, near giddy mood. They had started their space-bound careers in defeat and through a luck understood by only the most perverse of gods had rolled it over into unbridled victory. So recent had their triumph been that, truthfully, most on board were still at a loss for words when it came to explaining exactly how their good fortune had come about.

"I'm tellin' ya, Noodles," announced Chief Gunnery Officer Rockland Vespucci, more commonly known to bartenders and military police officers across the galaxy as Rocky, "there ain't nuthin' that's gonna trip things up for us again."

"Incautious words," answered the aforementioned Noodles, better known to top notch wire-and-screw jockeys everywhere as Machinist First Mate Li Qui Kon. "As Confucius said, 'he who stops watching for falling fruit will be first to get bonked by an apple.'"

"So, we just reinvent gravity."

Both sailors turned at the sound of a new voice indicating their being joined on the observation deck. As they did so, Technician Second Class Thorner and Quartermaster Harris came into view. As Noodles took exception with the tech's off-handed comment, accusing him of not taking theoretical physics seriously enough, Thorner spread his meaty hands wide, answering;

"Hey, it was just a joke. But com'on, really, look at the way things have been cruising for us. Earth is out in front. We've got the edge. It's our game from now on."

"I've got to agree," chimed in Harris. Taking a deck chair, he leaned back, putting his hands behind his head as he added, "Fate keeps lobbing us softballs, and we keep knocking them out of the park."

"He's right, little buddy," added Rocky. Grinning from ear to ear, staring out into the vast black, Rocky cavalierly added, "Criminey, it's almost enough to make a guy wish for some trouble."

And, it was at that moment that Fate, as she so often does when those bound to her decrees begin to act as if they had somehow negated her sway over their existence, chose to prompt the commander of the good ship *Roosevelt* to broadcast an announcement.

"Attention, this is your captain speaking. We've just received orders to proceed to the Kebb Quadrant to begin negotiations with the inhabitants of the planet Edilson. More information will be zimmed to us shortly, but we're to make best possible speed, which means, ladies and gentlemen, it's time to once more bend the fabric of space and time and be on our merry way."

"Edilson," asked Harris, "where in the wonderful world of color is Edilson?"

"And so it begins." All heads turned to the latest voice to join the conversation. As they did, one of the thinnest individuals to ever muster enough soaking-wet-weight to make it into the Navy added;

"The MI boys are just beginning to appreciate galactic rotation. Which meant that mudball was absolutely destined to hit our radar."

The speaker was Mac Michaels, a balding, bespectacled razormind out of the science division. As the others continued to stare at him, scratching their heads, he spread his hands like a high school math teacher about to share the wondrous joys of algebra as he said;

"Right now Edilson is nowhere, a low rent piece of real estate totally off the charts. But, if you calculate the rotation of the galaxy's set pieces, four hundred years from now, it's going to be in the veritable center of everything." Noting the group stare of complete lack of comprehension slamming at him from every angle, Michaels sighed, then added;

"It means that those who are far thinking will want to strike an alliance with Edilson now, so that when the time comes, they'll have an ally situated smack in the center of everything."

Michael's words made sense. Earth was expanding, making friends and teammates everywhere its representatives went. Enemies as well. If the Confederation of Planets was to maintain its presence, to continue advancing in power and prestige, let alone to be able to handle itself in the political and economic arenas of the universe against the likes of the Pan-Galactic League of Suns and others, this was just the kind of advanced cogitation they should be pursuing.

And, as the gobs headed off cheerfully to their various posts, their pride in the planet of their birth swelled. They came, after all, from a forward thinking world, one clever enough to send them off to negotiate with a solar system that would not really be worth having as a pal for centuries. That, they knew, whistling merrily as they took up their duties, took foresight. It took brains.

If they had possessed the brains to realize just how much desperate luck they were going to need to survive their upcoming expedition, however, they might have thrown in a few prayers in between all the whistling.

EVERYTHING'S BETTER... - C.J. Henderson

"All right then," growled Captain Alexander Benjamin Valance, as he reached for what was to be the first of several large drinks, "tell me someone has discovered something to explain whatever in hell *that* was."

The *Roosevelt* had arrived at the Edilson Well far in advance of the time required for their diplomatic team's meeting with the planetary council. In their best dress uniforms, the captain and his senior staff along with the ship's resident diplomatic officers had disembarked, prepared to put the Confederation's collective best foot forward. "An unmitigated disaster of incalculable proportions" was the phrase one might use to describe their meeting with the Edilsoni who came to greet them—but then, *only* if that one were trying to put the best spin possible on the most unfortunate encounter between dissimilar species since the Log Cabin Republicans first came across the D.A.R.

"Ahhh, if you're willing to consider some non-sanctioned information, sir..."

"Meaning?"

"Meaning," answered Valance's aide in a slightly lowered voice, "data acquired from outside official circles." When the captain only stared, the look in his eyes indicating his aide should just simply speak, the woman cleared her throat, then said;

"I did a records swap with a Chambrin starsweeper a few months back. Running a search through those files, I've managed to pull up some records from a couple of freelance Embrian traders who passed through this sector a few years ago—Iggzy and Cosentino Shipping."

At first, everything had seemed swell. The planet's inhabitants turned out to be an semi-amorphous life-form. Neither male or female, the Edilsoni could, with some difficulty, stretch and remold themselves into any manner of shapes if they desired. Normally, however, they were rubbery, blue-skinned watermelon-shaped folk who walked on three appendages roughly two to three feet in length. The melon of them—their torso as well as skull—was surrounded by three tentacle-like arms, as well as three eye-stalks, their disturbingly large mouths sprouting from the center of their heads.

"And what did these shippers report?"

The captain and the others, of course, were no strangers to aliens. They had encountered all manner of varied life forms since hitting deep space, and not once had any of them so much as raised an offending eyebrow at anyone or thing they had met. Not when they had watched the Georgths groom each other and subsequently devour their findings, or when they labored to decipher the language of the Mauzrieni, the only race in the

Everything's Better With Monkeys

galaxy to communicate through farting. But the Edilsoni, they... well... they were different.

"Their report tallies pretty much with what we just crashed through." As the aide read through her findings, the captain and his diplomatic squad fell further into the abysmally deep funk they had brought on board with them. For a while they had been able to hold onto the hope they had simply not understood what had been happening. But, sadly, they had.

The planet Edilson possessed a singularly peculiar make-up. Much of it was formed on unstable rock. Not the kind given over to earthquakes— or edilsonquakes, if you would—but the kind that produced the type of environment found in Earthspots such as Japan or Yellowstone National Park. Edilson was, in short, one great big steam-manufacturing ball, and due to its odd rock formations, anywhere the steam leaked out, it filled the air with various streams of continual sound.

Over the millennia, the Edilsoni had cultivated these passage ways, giving their planet an unending steam-driven soundtrack. They filled vents with crystals and cymbals, fashioned all manner of horns and harmonicas, even planted bamboo-like reeds where the steam could leak through, making music in every corner of their world. Of course, as one might imagine, this had more of an effect on the population than to simply dress up their days.

"There's no doubt about it, sir," said the aide hopelessly. "The Edilsoni sing and dance to make conversation. It seems they can't even understand races that simply 'talk' at them. In fact, they distrust any species that isn't comfortable doing so."

"Distrust?"

"Yes, sir," said the woman absently as she continued to read from the stream crossing her handscreen. "Seems they even went to war with one of their in-system neighbors when they stopped up the steam vents on the grounds of their consulate here."

Captain Alexander Benjamin Valance found himself as close to despair as ever he had been since taking command of the *Roosevelt*. "Why," he thought, imploring what gods might be left in his ever-shrinking corner of the galaxy, "do these things keep happening to me?"

This was worse than when his crew had shaved the sacred monkeys of Templeworld. Or when they had conned the guards of the Pen'dwaker Holding Facility into allowing them to transform the prison into a gambling den for their Intergalactic Crap Shoot of the Millennium tournament. Or even when they had sponsored their infamous inter-species mixer where they introduced the debutante daughters of the leading politicians of the Pan-Galactic League of Suns to the various bears, cows, pigs and chimps they were transporting to the Inter-Galaxy Zoo on Chamre XI.

It was worse than when they had stolen the *Roosevelt* and declared war on a cookie factory, more disastrous than when their pie fight had clogged the ship's protonic engines with strawberry, pineapple and cheesecake filling along with graham cracker crumbs, whipped creme and rhubarb. Of course, such nonsense could not imper the performance of such mighty machines, but it did play havoc with Admiral Morey's white-glove-and-I'm-not-kidding inspection.

It was, in his opinion, worse than anything they had ever done before and most likely would do any time soon. Because, quite simply, for once his insane-as-a-flock-of-dice-addled-cephalopods crew had not done anything. He had no one upon whom he might cast the blame for this one. For once, Captain Alexander Valance was as stuck as stuck could be, with no options in sight.

"So," he said weakly, looking for a third highball while turning to the others in the room, those others besides himself responsible for getting the most important treaty in the history of Earth signed, "who's got any really bright ideas?"

The thundering lack of enthusiastic response did not surprise him greatly.

"Tell me again," asked Noodles, not at all certain about the wisdom involved in what he and Rocky were attempting, "why is it we're stealing a shuttle craft and heading for the surface?"

"Look, little buddy," answered the gunnery officer while he gave Quartermaster Harris the high-sign that they were ready to launch. "The captain is tied up in knots about his meetin' with these beachballs down below—right? Now, it seems gettin' these mugs on board with the Confederation is a big deal and so, I was thinkin', if we could crack whatever the big problem is, we could kinda make up for some of the little improprieties we've... well, you know..."

"Getting ourselves court-marshalled would probably add some small ray of happiness to the captain's otherwise present dismal outlook."

"You machinists, you're always so gloomy."

"That's only the machinists who run around with Italians."

Everything's Better With Monkeys

"Look," replied Rocky as he eased the shuttle out the side bay doors while Technician Second Class Thorner kept the perimeter radar jumbled so they might avoid detection, "we're a couple of clever guys. We figure out how to smooth things so the Confederation beats the League and all the other bozos to signin' up this bunch and we'll be spendin' the rest of our days sittin' around swimmin' pools."

"With cleaning equipment," responded a particularly glum Noodles under his breath. He did not bother to argue further, though. Once Rocky had made his mind up on something, it was rare the machinist was ever able to talk him out of it. The reasons why he went along with said schemes were many and varied.

First, he liked Rocky and did not want to see him end up in more trouble than he could handle. Second, he was fairly certain the gunner had saved his life during one of their many drunken escapades, and so he felt a certain amount of obligation on that front as well. He also had to admit Rocky had a point. The *Roosevelt* on the whole would be in for tough times if Edilson decided to take a pass on joining the Confederation of Planets. Lastly, however, he went along with his pal's crazy plans usually because it just always turned out to be more fun doing things his way.

"Machinists are a dull lot," he thought, keeping the notion as quiet within his noggin as possible. He would never admit to such a thing, of course. If questioned on the verve and vigor of his profession, he would point to the many fine activities he and the rest of the ship's tool jockeys enjoyed, from their shipwide Call of Cthulhu LARPs and their free-style origami fold-offs to the week out of every year they lived for, their Sexy Robot-Building Competition. Privately, he feared Intelligence Officer DiVico's assessment, "I've seen lead foil that was snappier than the average machinist," might sadly be true.

Regardless, it was but a matter of minutes after take-off that the pair of gobs found themselves loose in the capital city of the planet Edilson. After walking about more or less aimlessly for a half an hour, confident from their observation of various street signs and cafe notices that Edilson to Pan-Galactic to Earth Basic 9.8 translation was more or less working fine enough, Rocky approached a passing rubbery watermelon of an Edilsoni and asked;

"So, what's the story around here, chief?"

Bending back and forth so that all the eyes ringing its head could scrutinize the individual addressing it, the random citizen decided it had no idea what this bizarre new species wanted and, doing its best to make a motion with its shoulderless body that would translate to an alien as a confused shrug, it went about its business. The gunner gave his buddy a look meant to convey his mixture of confusion and annoyance, then tried again with the next native to pass by. The results were the same.

After that, both sailors tried to communicate with the locals, trying this or that different idiom, working to keep their questions as simple as possible in case their problem was merely some translation difficulty. Nothing helped. Eventually, having been working on questioning a large flow of Edilsoni moving toward a stadium of sorts, they found themselves having been moved along with the flow to where they were indoors, awaiting some sort of performance. Frustrated, but hoping whatever was about to be presented on the field before them would give them some sort of clue, they managed to purchase a container of what seemed to be fried, bacon-flavored grass, and two milky fruit drinks which came in a kind of squeeze-bag affair. As they settled in, an announcer came out onto a small side stage and sang an introduction.

Since it seemed that all that he was introducing was the formal presentation from some alien world or the other to the Edilson government, the need for a tune-filled introduction struck the two humans as odd. When it turned out the aliens making the presentation were Danierians, Rocky and Noodles both began to titter with amusement. Bulbous, dour, and as exciting as a panda in fishnet stockings, the boys chuckled over how utterly awful the following would have to be.

"Danierians are gonna try and get these guys' attention," scoffed Rocky. "Now this, I'm glad I'm here ta see."

The chief gunnery officer's joy was short-lived. As he and Noodles finished off the last of their Crunchy Goodness snack pack, a troop of some four hundred Danierian warriors, outfitted in full battle gear, marched onto the field from three triangularly situated entrances. Flags unfurled, horns blaring, drums setting down an impressively unshakable cadence, the troopers met in the center of the parade ground, shouting out in their lumbering cadence as they began to file into formation;

> "Denieria, it is our home,
> That roasting world, so far away,
> Denieria, its red sky and foam,
> It's the best, on *any* day."

Looking first at each other, Rocky and Noodles then began to scan the crowd around them. Unlike their attempts to communicate with the Edilsoni on the streets, the Danierians were getting through to the natives. Indeed, as their simple forward marches began to intertwine, the crowd began tapping their tentacles to the martial rhythm.

"We're here to tell you about our world,
How splendid it is, to live in peace,
With Danierian banners, everywhere unfurled,
And all strife and despair made to cease."

"Noodles," asked Rocky, "is this as bad as I'm thinkin' it is?" When the machinist nodded in agreement, his partner answered, "Yeah, I was afraid of that."

"The galaxy is filled with lies,
Other races present intentions, but disguise
Their true meaning,
There's no gleaning,
What, oh what, is an innocent race to do?"

Rocky shuddered, thinking he had a good idea what was about to be suggested.

"Face front! And join
The United Coalition
Of Danierian Worlds.

Be a member of the winning team,
It's a lone and vulnerable planet's
Dream come true!

As the marching and singing continued, Noodles was struck by how the Edilsoni were responding to the ever-more-intricate step-pattern the warriors below were developing. With every intricate side turn, with each spin of their weapons and the tossing of banners from one team to another, the native inhabitants gave out with more and louder appreciative whistling noises. And then, the warriors offered up their next-to-final chorus;

"Others offer chaos,
We bring rules,
Those who turn down order,
We slaughter as fools!"

EVERYTHING'S BETTER... - C.J. Henderson   61

Eliciting cheers from every corner of the arena. As the Danierian Dress Guard broke into an even tighter, and it must be said rather snappy (well, snappy for Danierians) close order drill, chanting "Go Denieria" on every left step, the Edilsoni began singing to one another and performing a variety of three-legged jigs which left the two sailors both astounded and, it had to be admitted, a touch frightened.

> **"Submit to our will,**
> **It's for your own good,**
> **Don't wonder if we kill,**
> **Just do what you should."**

"Little buddy," whispered Rocky, "I'm thinkin' we'd better get back to the *Roosevelt*. The captain's gonna wanta know about this."

"He's not going to want to know it," answered Noodles, reaching for his bag o'juice, "but he needs to."

And with that, the swabbies returned to their borrowed shuttle craft, even as the Edilsoni picked up the admittedly catchy chorus of "Submit, Submit, just do it," sending its singular message wafting out over their capital city in all directions.

"So," asked Rocky quietly, "just how much trouble are we in, captain?"

"Vespucci," sighed Valance heavily, "you only did what you did for ship and country, and you did good, so let's just say you two have a bit of credit in reserve against your next knuckleheaded shenanigan—all right?"

"Sweet deal, sir."

At that point the *Roosevelt*'s commanding officer moved into as high a gear as his hangover would permit. With confirmation of the true nature of Edilsoni communication in hand, as well as intelligence on how effective had been the Danierian's singing and marching negotiation, he dismissed the two gobs while ordering a channel opened to Earth High Command at once. Quickly outlining his overwhelmingly insurmountable problem, his desperate honesty was rewarded with the worst type of military logic.

Since his was the only ship in the area, the mission was still his. And, since he was the ranking officer, he and his diplomatic staff would simply have to dance and sing their way into the hearts of the planetary government and win the day. In the meantime, while Valance and his command staff were reduced to trying to form a not-completely-painful-to-listen-to barbershop quartet, Rocky and Noodles headed for the galley to wash down their planetside snacks with something a little more substantial than milk juice.

"Listen," said Noodles, after finishing his fourth tall and frosty mug of something-more-substantial, "you know, I wonder what the captain's going to do."

"Not our concern," answered his pal. "Hey, we're heroes for once. Little tiny minor heroes, sure. But, considerin' the esteem we're usually held in around here, I'll take it."

The machinist nodded non-commitally. Rocky was right. The two of them had pushed their luck within the bounds of Navy regs to an extreme not seen since a drunken Admiral Chester William Nimitz had attempted to steer an aircraft carrier up the Venetian canals in search of a combination pizza parlor/chianti distributor/bordello he had been assured by Enrico Curuso was "really primo." Still, it was not in the machinist's internal make-up to simply allow nature to take its course. Running his finger around the inside of his mug to get the last delightful bits of foam, he licked up the delicious residue, then said;

"So, you think the captain can handle things?"

"Well, sure," answered Rocky automatically. Draining his own mug, he added with an equal lack of thought, "the captain's aces. Ain't he got us outta every mess we ever got ourselves into? He don't ever need any help—he's always got the answer."

"Not to be contrary, Rock, but... if the captain didn't ever need any help, then he wouldn't need a crew."

It was not so much Noodles' words, but the tone with which he delivered them that caught the gunnery officer's attention. Squinting hard, as if that might instantly negate the effects of his own eight tall portions of more-substantial, Rocky finally answered;

"You mean, you think the captain maybe can't handle singin' these guys into the Confederation?"

"Do you remember his trying to teach Christmas carols to those kids back on Embri?" The gunner shuddered at the memory, his fingers unconsciously reaching up to his ears to see if they were bleeding.

"So," asked Rocky, fairly certain he knew the answer he would receive, "you're sayin' that ah... you want us to steal a shuttle on the same day we already stole one shuttle, and then use said shuttle to head back down to the planet so we can interfere with the most important mission the *Roosevelt* was ever given?"

"Yeah—you want'a?"

"Hey," answered the gunner, grinning from ear to ear, "does the Buddha drink Mint Juleps?"

"Isn't that usually my line?"

"Ahhhh, tell it to the board of inquiry."

"Oh yeah," laughed Noodles. "Good thinking."

And, with no other pints of more-substantial in sight, the two swabbies got down to planning their course of action.

In all honesty, Captain Valance would never have believed it was possible for four people to sweat so intently. Indeed, the puddle growing around his feet, as well as those of the *Roosevelt*'s intelligence officer, her diplomatic attaché and the ship's doctor was spreading with such vigor it left the Edilsoni to wonder if the human contingent might not actually be melting. To be fair, the makeshift quartet had tried their darnest, calling upon the spirit of a thousand long-sung sea chanteys to aid them in their hour of desperation.

Sadly, though, King Neptune had not seen fit to shower them with any such bounty. In fact, it had to be admitted that their feeble attempts to harmonize had failed so miserably that the Edilsoni's visceral reaction to their singing was the only thing that kept the aliens from noticing how utterly terrible the humans' lyrics were. Finally, when the four paused for a breath at the same moment, although it was obvious they had only covered a third of their points, the Edilsoni prime minister practically fell over his podium as he leaped forward to interrupt, asking if that concluded the Earth Confederation's presentation. Valance was just about to throw in the proverbial towel, considering losing the planet and his commission favorable to provoking interstellar warfare, when suddenly a shout was heard from the back of the amphitheater.

"If you kind and noble Edilsoni will permit,
I'd like to step up, while you sit...,"

As Valance stared in disbelief, he saw Machinist First Mate Li Qui Kon actually doing a handy little two-step, making his way in between the central two rows of spectators down toward the staging area where he and his fellow officers had been dying by inches.

"And discuss with you the ramifications,
Of inter-galactic political integrations."

Reaching the captain and his officers, Rocky urged them to vacate the stage, telling them in an exaggerated stage whisper;

"Don't worry, sir. I think he knows what he's doin'."

"But Vespucci," answered Valance, "singing and dancing... a machinist?"

"With all due respect, a *Chinese* machinist, sir."

"There are species descended from fish and bugs,
Others that crawled up from oozing slugs,
Some came from birds and some from rats,
Insects, clams, giraffes and bats,"

"Chinese moms, sir," added Rocky. "How'd he say it? They expect their kids to... well, they have to be a credit to their family."

"And they're all fine, in their own way,
But they're kind of singular, I must say,
Bred for a certain uni... form... ity,
They lack that one human odd... i... ty."

"Mrs. Kon, you see..."

"The thing that makes us the ones to choose,
That quality that guarantees you never lose,
It's our single greatest facility...
Our hard-won, irritating..."

"Un... pre... dic... ta... bility!"

"She wanted an entertainer in the family."

And then, at a hand signal from Noodles, waiting in a lurkercraft hidden in the clouds, Technician Second Class Thorner began their free-air music broadcast, as well as sending down a blinding purple spotlight, illuminating the machinist in an iridescent glow as he warbled—

EVERYTHING'S BETTER... - C.J. Henderson

"Oh, everything's better with monkeys,
We're the best bet in the show,
I'm certain you're getting a lot of offers,
But trust me, simian's the way to go."

While Noodles spun around, setting himself up for the next stanza, Rocky caught the captain's ear once more, telling him;

"Five years of tap and jazz dance, six of voice training, and apparently two years of piano which, from what he says, were a really serious mistake."

"Yes everything's better with monkeys,
They're curious, funny and true,
They'll stand by your side, go along for a ride,
And they'll make sure you get what you're due."

As Noodles went into a complicated dance routine, one that seemed to Rocky he had seen in a revival of "My Fair Lady" the two of them had been lured into by promises of a different type of entertainment, the gunnery officer and his captain began to notice that the crowd was responding favorably to the performance. Indeed, those who had been previously fleeing from the caterwauling of Valance and his officers actually seemed to be returning to their seats. While the captain dangerously tempted Fate by allowing his hopes to rise from actual imprisonment to a simple court-martial, Rocky sent the signal to Mac Michaels up above with Thorner to both turn up the music and begin the fountain of lights display. As the crowd began to "aaaaahhhhhhhhh" in synchronized harmony, Noodles went into his big finish.

"Yes, we earthlings, we make mistakes,
We've got our bad eggs, who will always disgrace,
We spill our own blood, and we're not always smart,
But the one thing I can assure you is...
The human race has... got... heart!"

And then, in that instant, even as the entire ship's company of the *Roosevelt* Machinist's Saturday Evening LARP Society surrounded the stage, decked in full costume from their upcoming Bambi versus Godzilla extravaganza, accompanied by all the final entries in the Sexiest Robot of All Time competition, all around the stadium Edilsoni began to jump up from their seats. Unable to restrain themselves, the rotund aliens began humming and dancing, slapping tentacles, spinning on their mouths, and in short throwing themselves with total abandon into the fierce joy of Noodle's song.

> "We're not perfect,
> We don't claim to be,
> Hell what do you expect?
> Twenty thousand years ago,
> We were all still monkeys!
>
> "But you can trust me, you can trust that fact,
> 'Cause even after all this time,
> You throw crap at us,
> And I guarantee...
> We'll throw it right back!"

The captain, of course, could only be overjoyed by the obvious shift in the average Edilsonian attitude toward humanity. But Rocky was set to wondering. He had seen the response the natives had shown the Danierians. They had gotten into the rhythm of things, had seemed ready to sign on to the program, so to speak. But, the reaction to Noodle's presentation was overwhelming. The aliens were actually dropping down onto the stadium grounds and rushing the stage, eager to join the machinists' newly forming macarana formation.

> "But we'll stand at your side,
> We'll be there at the end,
> We make lousy dictators,
> But we make really good friends.
>
> "Yes, everything's better with monkeys,
> The bad ones mixed in with the good,
> So, show a little trust, but keep your eye on us,
> And everything—
> I'm saying just everything—
> Will work out, as it... sshhhoooouuuullllddddd!"

And in that moment, as Noodles dropped to one knee and delivered the greatest display of jazz hands since Bob Fosse starred in "The Al Jolson Story," the long unfathomed secret of the Edilsoni came to light. Although the race *could* communicate through speech, they were *actually* a telepathic species, one bound by a hive mentality. As the native population cheered, not just there in the capital city's stadium, but across every continent, in every corner of the planet, their human guests' minds were suddenly filled with billions of voices, all of them sharing in the wonder that was the unquestionable uniqueness of the human race.

"Do you get it, Vespucci," shouted the captain, straining to be heard over the multitudinous ringing within his mind, "the Edilsoni have rejected every offer that's come their way because no one else has ever opened up completely to them!"

"Jimeny," answered Rocky, still a little befuddled over exactly what had happened, being distracted as he was by coordinating the start of the *Roosevelt* fireworks display, "I didn't think his song was that good."

"It's not the song," cried Valance, tears streaming down his face as an utterly alien race's reflected understanding of the true nobility of the human spirit washed through his mind, "it's not the song."

What happened over the next few days became somewhat of a blur in the intergalactic news items out of the Kebb Quadrant, the official reports sent from the *Roosevelt* back to the Confederation, and to be honest, in the minds of most of the ship's crew. That last, however, had more to do with the planet-wide party spontaneously thrown by every individual on Edilson than with any deficiency in the human ability to comprehend the situation.

Distrustful of aliens who masked their true intent, the Edilsoni had turned down every offer of alliance over the two hundred years since first contact. Understanding better than any others the upcoming importance of their world, they had kept communications open with all, dangling the hope of eventual alliance with one world or league or whatever to keep any one of them from invading.

"Four hundred of your years," their prime minister eventually sang to Valance, "is not a great deal of time, galactically speaking, but it did give us some room in which to maneuver."

They had responded as well as they had to the Danierians because, vicious and cruel as that race might be, at least they were honest about it. Their warriors had held nothing back emotionally on the field, and for once someone had shown the Edilsoni true intent. Luckily, as the prime minister was happy to admit, someone else had come along and done the same who had something better to show.

The surprise hit of the negotiations, or whatever one would call the drunken insanity that had transpired on Edilson, had been the trio of Thorner, Harris and Michaels who had taken to the stage in their dress kilts to not only sing the Scottish ballad, the Blue Ribbon Song, but to show off the fact that the Edilsoni were not the only sentient beings around who walked on three legs. Valance had been mortified at first, but the riotous response of the natives to the spontaneous gesture had been so positive the captain had been given no choice other than to return to attempting to drink the prime minister under the table.

In the end, the Confederation of Planets got the wished for deal with Edilson. Valance was showered with praise from Earth Central which he translated into as much shore leave and good favor as he possibly could for his crew. The next issue of the Monthly Newsletter of the Grand Gaggle of Confederation Machinists tripled in size and, once the ship's doctor had been able to synthesize enough Hangover-B-Gone, the crew of the *Roosevelt* had been able to finally remember how to break orbit and set a course that did not skew to a basanova beat.

Heroes all, loved and admired by an entire world, showered with gifts, the men and women of the *Roosevelt* set off for whatever the universe had in store for them next. The Edilsoni could tell the earthlings were reluctant to leave, and yet somehow eager to be on to whatever came next, and loved them all the more for it. But, beyond that display of all-too-human confusion of purpose, beyond everything they had heard and felt and learned of the gorilla-spawn who had won their hearts, there was one single moment that gave them greater insight than any other.

Being a collective species, having no actual experience with the idea of male or female, sons and daughters, or any of the other mammalian building blocks of individuality, nothing revealed more to the Edilsoni about their human visitors than when the prime minister met privately with Noodles. Asking the machinist what boon he might ask for his part in that which a united Edilson believed was the cementing of their security for the next four centuries, offering him anything the wealth and might of an entire planetary treasury might secure, the sailor asked if he might send a real time message.

Yes, Noodles explained, he could send notes to Earth via the *Roosevelt*, but because of the distance they could take months, sometimes *years* to reach their intended destination. He did not want to send anything exceedingly long, he told them, just a few words. Understanding his request, touched to the core of what he had thought until meeting human beings was an emotionless heart beating within his breast, the prime minister not only agreed, but without the machinist's knowledge, he sent his own note as well.

EVERYTHING'S BETTER... - C.J. Henderson

Which is why, while the U.S.S. *Roosevelt* broke orbit and headed back out to their next destination in the stars, on the planet Earth, at 12/17 Seloon Street in one of the quieter corners of Canton, China, Mrs. Xiu Yue Kon received two messages. One that read;

"Thanks, Mom."

And a second that read;

"Yes, good Earthwoman, thank you, indeed."

We tend to gravitate towards those deities that fulfill our personal needs, whether for structure and discipline or forgiveness or a vehicle through which the joy of life can be expressed. But who are our Gods to the inhabitants of other worlds? Do we bring our Gods there with us? Or are they already waiting when we arrive?

A MEAL FIT FOR GOD

"It now appears that research underway offers the possibility of establishing the existence of an agency having the properties and characteristics ascribed to the religious concept of God."

Dr. Evan Harris Walker
Theoretical Physicist

"CORRECT STABILIZERS—BRING DRIFT BACK BELOW TWO DEGREES— now, mister!" The navigator of the Earth Alliance Ship *Roosevelt* sprang to her task. Despite the incredible nature of the ship's design and the sophistication of its state-of-the-art sensors, the *Roosevelt* had somehow accidentally blundered into a cosmic storm of unbelievable intensity.

"Still being dragged, Captain."

Of course, that the great battlewagon would somehow manage to find an uncharted storm system, one infinitely more severe than any previous encountered—anywhere, by any race—came as no surprise to her crew. The most forward-sailing of any space vehicle dispatched from its world since the beginning of galactic exploration, the *E.A.S. Roosevelt* had encountered more confounding, unbelievable and well, downright wozzlingly strange stuff than any human being had ever imagined possible.

"Reroute the auxiliary power reserve from the light motion cannon—do whatever it takes but get us straight-lined!"

Indeed, if the entire tally of intergalactic oddities the *Roosevelt* had encountered up until that particular star date were ever to be reviewed by the proper authorities back home, they would have no choice other than to conclude that the crew member who drew up the list must have been quite mad.

"The helm just isn't responding, Captain. We're still listing, shoving the needle close to six."

Yes, of course, the *Roosevelt* was the first Earth ship to leave the solar system. Hers was the first crew to come face to face with alien races, to walk on other worlds, to interact with unimaginable cultures. Still, space exploration, it had always been assumed, would be a thing of monotony, a tedium of cataloguing inert planets, charting the currents of the galactic undertow, clearing debris from what would become the spaceways of the only sentient race in the universe.

"There's no reason for any storm to be this powerful. Check for magnetic pulsing."

But, humanity had discovered that not only were they not alone in the universe, they were actually residents of a galaxy practically choking on a seemingly never-ending roster of other life forms. The activities of this cacophony of civilizations was overseen by the five great races comprising the ruling body of the highly esteemed organization known as the Pan-Galactic League of Suns. Or, should it be said, the "formerly," highly esteemed organization.

"Pulsing detected, sir. Strong mounting—seventeen to the fifth, and growing."

For, once the *Roosevelt* inserted itself into the actual workings of the galaxy, the League's stranglehold on things had crumpled. Within weeks the Earth-led Confederation of Planets had been overwhelmed with applications for membership. Never ones to not press an advantage, those in charge of the Confederation had dispatched the *Roosevelt* on one dicey mission after another, which is what had put the flagship of the Earth Alliance on a research mission in a centrally located section of the galaxy unexplored by any other race.

"Suggest a rotational vectoring, sir."

Not that no other race had ever sent a ship into the nebulous six-light-year across swamp of gas clouds and radiant shadows that hovered around the Milky Way's ground zero. Plenty had tried.

"Give it to me yesterday, Mr. Michaels."

It was just that none of them had ever returned.

At the order of Captain Alexander Benjamin Valance, science officer Mac Michaels keyed the controls in question, throwing The *Roosevelt* into a lateral come-about so unexpected a full third of the crew were thrown

A MEAL FIT FOR GOD - C.J. Henderson   73

against the nearest floor, wall or ceiling. But, despite the resulting overloading of the ship's medical bays, the maneuver had been worth it. Cracked ribs, broken fingers, scraped flesh, bruises, dents, dings, and lost blood aside, The *Roosevelt* found its way in between the competing solar winds and broke loose of the terrible current which had been thrashing it about so.

The instant the bridge instruments announced that control was back within the hands of the crew, the captain ordered an immediate reversal of their course. In seconds the *Roosevelt* was smoothly gliding once more through the darkness, backing off to a point safely away from the storm where the impossible manifestation could be charted, studied, and maybe even explained.

And, as one might expect, a great series of cheers, whoops, and unrestrained applauds went up from one end of the great warwagon to the other in praise of those who had once more pulled the crew's collective derrières out of the fire. Those currently performing essential duties, of course, continued to do so. But, any who could stop for a meal, a smoke, a round of drinks, or anything else that might take their mind off the fact they had once again cheated six kinds of death by the proverbial skin of their teeth did so with all possible speed.

And, it was that unadulterated burst of relief and good cheer which started the terrifying chain of events that followed.

"Okay, which one of you slobs wants a mouthful of poison?"

From the staggering amount of positive responses following the offer for seeming self-destruction, it appeared fairly obvious the woman in white carrying an over-sized tray was not actually offering death. Indeed, so fervent were the screams and pleas of acceptance even an alien visitor with the most inadequate of translators would be able to figure out that the crowd swarming about the relatively short chef had not the slightest interest in self-destruction—hers or anyone else's.

"The female does not actually offer the ceasing of life—yes?"

"No, no, sir," Captain Valance responded, torn between amusement and exasperation. "That's Chef Kinlock, and she's just kidding around with the crew."

The captain's guest was Thortom'tonmas, the newly installed ambassador from Daneria to the Confederation of Planets. The *Roosevelt* had the dubious honor of the ambassador's presence due to a brilliant idea hatched by one of the less competent members of the Alliance's public relations department. Since it had been agreed the new ambassador should be transported to Earth by a Confederation ship, it was decided such "advanced" thinking should be compounded by saddling their greatest ship with said "privilege." Then, the same genius decided that giving the *Roosevelt* a monumentally difficult task to perform on the way home would be the perfect vehicle for putting the war-like Danerians in their place.

Of course, what this obvious civilian had failed to take into consideration were the less self-congratulatory ramifications surrounding the idea of a high-ranking individual from the Confederation's greatest enemies being given a tour of the Earth's most advanced ship. Despite the nifty press release such news generated, carrying out such a stunt meant giving Daneria access to the Earth Alliance's most closely guarded military secrets, as well as a perfect opportunity to embarrass the hell out of the Confederation if they failed to complete their next-to-impossible task.

"Then what is she offering them?"

"You know," Valance admitted, "I don't actually know. Why don't we go over and find out?"

Even as the captain and Thortom'tonmas approached the gathering crowd, Kinlock shouted;

"Okay, back off, you decksliders. I think you all know who gets first dibs on this batch."

The batch, as all assembled could tell from the heavenly aroma wafting through the mess was comprised of the chef's galaxy-famous chocolate chip cookies. And the one of their number who was to get first pick they all knew could be none other than Mac Michaels, the science officer who had kept the *Roosevelt*, and by extension her crew, from becoming just another statistic concerning investigation of Sector 84-Af7, the nebulous swamp of gas clouds and radiant shadows they had recently escaped.

"Open up, Michaels."

Grinning, the *Roosevelt's* chief razormind stretched his mouth wide as Kinlock tossed a cookie high into the air. Everyone held their breath as Michaels moved forward, snapping at his target as it came into range. Amazingly, he snagged the treat in mid-descent, managing to snare it intact without merely biting off a piece and sending the rest to the floor—or worse, missing altogether.

"All right, you bilge nasties—come and get 'em!"

A staggering wall of cheers echoed throughout the mess and down the halls in every direction. The first tray the chef had brought with her from the

A MEAL FIT FOR GOD - C.J. Henderson

galley was emptied in less than a handful of seconds. No consternation followed, for ten more trays were brought forth by Kinlock's crew, the contents of which were more than enough to make certain everyone received one—even Valance and Thortom'tonmas.

And, while the two debated the merits of chocolate chip cookies to the ones known as A Little Taste of Andromedas, the favorite dessert treat of the Danierian Empire, at the next table over, where Mac Michaels had planted himself, a similar conversation had also begun. Holding the remaining half of his cookie aloft, nursing the treasure like a middle-schooler savoring his first beer, Michaels said;

"These are really the absolute best ever."

"Ohhhhh, I don't know," Chief Gunnery Officer Rockland Vespucci answered, known to pawn brokers and bartenders across the Confederation as Rocky. "My mom, she used to make the best canolis. I mean the cream was so rich, and she would use so many pistachios...."

"Awwww, that's nothing," Technician Second Class Thorner interrupted. "If you guys ever tasted my dad's koogle, well then...."

"Forget it," piped in Quartermaster Harris. "None of it can compare to the oatmeal raisin squares my grandma used to make."

And so the conversation ran up and down the length of the table, one sailor after another defending their families' or nationalities' favorite dessert treat. After a while, however, after Rocky noted that his best friend, Machinist First Mate Li Qui Kon, more commonly known to wire and screw jockeys and robotics enthusiasts everywhere as Noodles, had not joined into the conversation. When he enquired as to "why," his shipmate answered;

"Chinese families aren't big on fancy desserts. It's all orange slices and almond cookies and ginger candies—"

"Ginger candies," asked another crewman, "what are those?"

"A reminder as to why China will never be at the forefront of the dessert industry." As everyone chuckled over Noodles' quip, the machinist held up a hand, adding;

"Hey, but don't think Chinese can't cook. Any culture that can create the Monkey King must know something about filling a table."

When asked to explain his reference, Noodles told those assembled;

"Well, the Monkey King was a member of the Chinese pantheon, not a god really, but he mingled with the gods. He was the troublemaker in all the really good Chinese stories—"

"Like Loki for the Norse?" Intelligence Officer DiVico asked. "Or Coyote for the Native Americans?"

The machinist confirmed that the Monkey King was absolutely best described as one of the most mischievous god-figures ever, one who could just as easily work tirelessly for a noble cause as he might throw himself into tearing down an empire. Nigh invulnerable, monstrously powerful, and driven by a quirkier set of conflicting passions than a cocaine addict at a slow-dance marathon, he was totally unpredictable, and one presence no one—rich, poor, or somewhere in the middle *ever* wanted to see.

But, no matter what he was up to, no matter in what story the Monkey King was starring, sooner or later things came down to food. Simply put, the guy loved to eat. Noodles regaled his shipmates, and, through extension, the captain and his guest, with a seemingly endless list of the mouth-watering meals that the myths reported had been consumed by the mythic trouble-maker. Pies and pork, apples and ambrosia, shrimp, salads and sorbets, plus a thousand other dishes, each one more wonderful sounding than the one before it had all been consumed by the legendary simian.

Noodles made the Monkey King's typical menu sound so wondrous that after a while all those gathered at the table were driven by hunger to race off to the dinner queue. Even the captain and the ambassador felt their differently constructed stomachs growling viciously enough to follow suit. Indeed, the machinist had made the mounting list sound so absolutely magnificent that all within earshot had deserted the area to fill themselves a tray and get down to enjoying a meal on a more fulfilling level than simply hearing about one.

All, that was, except for the single crewman at the table who, if any of the others had asked, it would have been discovered had never before been seen by anyone in attendance. That sailor, or at least, what appeared to be just another sailor, the only being in sight to not take a cookie, instead kept to its seat, thinking. It did this for some time, finally making a decision after some eighteen minutes of contemplation.

After that it smiled, a very malicious thought filling its mind with a glee it had not known in centuries.

"By the blessed blue suede shoes of the King, what's in Hell is *that*?"

Noodles was even more surprised that his pal, Rocky. On their way to the galley for breakfast the day after all the swirling nebula excitement, they ran into a humanoid figure in the hallway that froze both of them in their tracks. It did not stand more than four feet tall, though size was not important to it. The thing had merely chosen a convenient height for walking the world of man.

"By the Buddha's mint julep, it can't be...."

The creature grinned at the two sailors from its perch atop a small but animated cloud floating in the middle of the hallway. It was a cumulus wispy thing, seemingly nothing more than steam, but still substantial enough to carry a passenger. The cloud, however, was not what was causing the swabbies' concern.

"Can't be what?"

The creature possessed a body short of leg and long of arm, one clad in a wardrobe of the finest Chinese silk—resplendent robes covered in delicate designs, stitched with thread made from the purest gold and silver. Its knuckles were hairier than many a man's dome, topped by a head with a simian face and eyes that saw men's souls as just so many leaves, pretty things that fell and dried and danced at the merest whim of the breeze. Barely able to speak, knowing that his mind could not possibly be correctly interpreting the data it was receiving from his senses, still did Noodles shout;

"Shiu Yin Hong!"

And at that gesture of recognition, the creature smiled, for despite all logic, it was indeed the great and powerful Monkey King which floated peacefully there in Connecting Corridor 17-L. Rocky and Noodles looked one to the other in a helplessness so utterly complete they could not have been more useless if they had just come across an eighteen-foot-wide breach in the hull or been asked to identify the capital of Oregon.

"What in the aurory, the borey, and the whole damn allus are we supposed to do with him?"

"How am I supposed to know?"

"Hey, he's your damn god of mischief."

It was not actually a fair piece of logic, but even Noodles had to agree it was the best they had. Deciding that not doing anything at all was probably the worst way to proceed, the machinist thought for a moment, then remembered what his father had told him about facing problems head on and always doing the most sensible thing in any situation—pass the buck. Sucking down a deep breath, Noodles asked;

"Hey-ah, so...how would you like to go and meet our captain?"

The look of sinister glee that filled the Monkey King's tiny eyes did not gift either of the sailors with encouragement. More than that, other crew members had begun to gather, their forward motion in either direction impeded by Shiu Yin Hong and his floating cloud. All were willing to wait a moment and let the trio pass. Well, almost all.

"What," cried out one of the ship's compliment of Marines, "the ever-lovin' hell is that thing?"

"Our best guess at the moment," Noodles answered, "is that it's a godling from Earth legends known as the Monkey King." The towering jarhead snickered. Llaughing as he pointed at Shiu Yin Hong, he said;

"You ain't foolin' nobody, Kon. That's just another one of your idiot robots. And a fairly stupid lookin' one at that."

Its head turning toward the Marine, the Monkey King responded with a quite authentic simian howl of derision. Jumping down from its cloud playfully, Shiu Yin Hong ambled on its bowed legs to where the Marine was standing. Putting out a paw as if asking to shake hands, the Monkey King smiled widely. As everyone in the hall laughed at the ludicrous sight—the four-foot-tall chimp-thing facing off with a six-and-a-half-foot marine—the soldier decided he had better places to be. And so, not wishing to look the bully, he stuck out his hand to simply shake and be on his way.

Shiu Yin Hong took the man's hand, and then with merely two fingers, twisted it violently, forcing the marine to his knees. The soldier screamed wildly, the pain he must be in obvious to all as they heard the bones within his hand snapping. Several thought about moving on the godling, but as each did the Monkey King turned in their direction, eyeing them with a malevolent glee which froze all in their tracks.

"Shiu Yin Hong—"

Turning toward the sound of Noodles' voice, not releasing the Marine's hand, the Monkey King focused on the machinist, waiting for him to speak. Forcing himself to remain calm, to not allow his voice to crack, Noodles said;

"We were going to see the captain—yes? I mean, if you want to play with this fellow, by all means...but I thought, surely someone as important as you would want to meet the most important person on board ship. Right?"

The simian form considered the machinist's words for a moment, then suddenly released his grip on the marine while letting out a piercing whistle. As he did so, the soldier fell backward into the bulkhead even as the Monkey King's cloud flashed across the hall and lifted its master up from the floor. Seated cross-legged, the god-thing then floated over to Noodles, its expression indicating he was ready to leave.

A MEAL FIT FOR GOD - C.J. Henderson
79

Reaching out to the nearest wall-com, the machinist routed a call to Valance, requesting a moment of the captain's time. When asked what he wanted, Noodles responded;

"Captain, sir, Rocky and I, we ahhhh, umm...we've got a god on board, sir, and he seems eager to meet you."

Alexander Benjamin Valance had endured quite a lot since assuming command of the *Roosevelt*—so much so that the brass back home considered him the one field officer they had who could be counted on to handle anything. Still, when he hesitated a full three seconds before responding to the fact that a supreme being of some sort wanted to come by for a chat, none thought it an overly long period of time before he could quite figure out how to make his mouth work once more.

"Oh, yes—of course you do."

Considering the notion he was aware that both Chief Gunnery Officer Rockland Vespucci and Machinist First Mate Li Qui Kon—the crewmen not only responsible for shaving the sacred monkeys of Templeworld, but for also conning the guards of the Pen'dwaker Holding Facility into allowing them to transform the prison into a gambling den for their Intergalactic Crap Shoot of the Millennium tournament (just two items on their ever-increasing roster of chicanery)—were involved, the fact he answered at all only proved once more to the crew how incredibly cool under pressure their captain really was.

Indeed, during their tour of duty together, more than one of the ten thousand men and women under his command had announced that Valance was the one man they would willing follow into Hell.

"Well, don't keep god waiting. Bring him to my ready room and let's see what he wants."

As news spread from one end of the *Roosevelt* to the other of what was happening, more than one of them found themselves wondering if they were about to get their chance to do so.

What Valance discovered "god," or at least the closest thing to one presently spending its time on any Earth Alliance vessel, wanted seemed to be to play an endless series of practical jokes. Shiu Yin Hong had shaken the captain's hand with a frank seriousness and then pulled his pants down around his ankles, caused bananas to rain from the ceiling by the thousands, and switched the ship's intercom from

80   **Everything's Better With Monkeys**

keeping the crew informed on daily goings-on to playing "I'm a Believer" non-stop.

And that was just his opening salvo.

Over the four days after he had first arrived on the decks of the *Roosevelt*, the Monkey King had filled the air with helium so he could laugh at everyone's voices, transformed much of the *Roosevelt's* electrical wiring into gelatin, and even fired the ship's devastatingly powerful light-wave motion gun several times simply to hear the clicking noises the final securing locks made as they bolted the weapon into position.

"I'm tellin' ya, Noodles," Rocky growled, picking himself up from the deck after having slipped on yet another loose banana peel, "I'm gettin' goddamned sick of this deity of yours."

"Mine," snapped the machinist indigently. "Do not blame that knuckle-dragging fleabag on me. His being on board was not my idea."

"I hate to argue with you, Li," Mac Michaels interrupted, "but you might be wrong about that." As Noodles turned to glare at the science officer, Michaels raised his hands, saying;

"Don't get me wrong, I'm not saying you wanted him here. But if I've doped things out correctly, *something* was going to be here, and it was you that gave it form."

"That is an interesting statement, officer." As the sailors turned, they found Ambassador Thortom'tonmas standing behind them. "Please elaborate."

"Well, sir, the captain had asked me to figure out where our intruder had come from. I suspected he wasn't the actual Monkey King because, as overwhelmingly powerful as his abilities supposedly are, they aren't the ones Machinist Kon here described to us at dinner the other night." As those listening nodded, Michaels added;

"Since that moment, however, immediately preceded the intruder's arrival, I brought up the galley cameras and studied it. Seemed too much of a coincidence to not be connected." As the heads all around him continued to nod, the science officer, clearly enjoying the spotlight, told the growing assembly;

"As I studied that moment when the Monkey King story was told, I noted one sailor at the table I didn't recognize. Not hard in a crew of ten thousand, but there was something in the way he was listening to Noodles talk that made me suspicious. So, I asked the computer to find a match among the crew and it couldn't."

A MEAL FIT FOR GOD - C.J. Henderson

"You mean..." said Rocky, only to then pause, scowl, then add, "okay, so what'dya mean?"

"I set the camera links to observation. First I had them follow him after dinner. Sure enough, right after he left the galley he found a private corner and transformed into the Monkey King." As the crowd made various noises of surprise, Michaels continued, telling them;

"Just wait. It gets better. I then turned the link to pre-trace the guy, to see where he came from. The cameras retraced his steps back to the moment when the storm ended. And, to make a long story short, 'he' isn't a 'he' at all."

"So then, like what the hell is he?" Thorner asked, two dozen other wide-eyed listeners letting it be known they were as interested as the technician.

"'He,' for lack of a better pronoun, is a ball of energy that—immediately following that nebula storm we barely survived—passed through a bulkhead, floated to the ceiling, observed those of us walking by for a while, and then just...congealed into a non-descript human guy."

"So," Harris asked, "what do we do now?"

"Now," came the voice of Intelligence Officer DiVico, "we get back to our duties."

Snapping his fingers, the security chief signaled two of his men to come forward, commanding them to escort the Danerian ambassador to his quarters, citing safety issues, "what with an unknown life form roaming the ship, and all." After that he suggested everyone else return to their duties while he hurried Michaels and Noodles off to see the captain. Forced to travel at a slower speed than he would have preferred thanks to all the banana peels still littering the halls, once in Valance's quarters, DiVico reported on all that had happened. After the intelligence officer had finished, the captain asked;

"So, Thortom'tonmas knows what we know about Cheetah?"

"I'm sorry, sir," Michaels responded, immediately accepting full responsibility. "I was telling some of the fellows, and the ambassador happened to walk by, and..."

"I know," sighed Valance. "I gave very strict orders that he be shown every courtesy."

"Still, we need to do some damage control, sir," DiVico said. "Perhaps it would be best if you outlined what your plans are for dealing with the intruder, so I know how you'd like me to move against it."

"Oh my God." Valance, Michaels, and DiVico all turned at the sound of Noodles' voice. "Shiu Yin Hong, whatever it is...it came from this part of space, where no ship has survived before. It came aboard the ship, it wanted to know what we thought God looked like, and it assumed the first version it heard about."

"We did pick it up in the heart of the galaxy," Michaels added. "The first ship to ever penetrate this area and make it back out in one piece."

"Maybe..." DiVico suggested, his voice an inch away from breaking, "maybe we were the first to make it to God's doormat, and...and now he's curious to survey his handiwork."

"Meaning," the captain added, "I thought I had my hands full with just the Monkey King, and now it seems like we might be playing host to the burning bush."

The four navy men stared at each other for a moment, none quite certain how to proceed. Realizing that whether he knew what to do or not that it was still his job to do something, Valance snapped;

"Well, nothing's going to get done with us standing around like a flock of flamingos. Michaels, get to a scanner. Find that omnipotent furball and let me know where it is. DiVico, you track down Thortom'tonmas and keep him away from our intruder."

As the officers hurried to follow their orders, Noodles asked;

"What about me, sir?"

"You?" The captain let the single word echo against the metal walls of his office, then said, "You're going to teach me everything I need to know about the Monkey King before this mess gets any worse."

It took the sailors some twelve minutes to find both the Monkey King, or at least, that entity presenting itself as the legendary Shiu Yin Hong, and Ambassador Thortom'tonmas. Confirming the captain's worst fears, however, they found the two of them in conference. Having put the clues of what had happened together while listening to Mac Michaels' explanation in the hallway, the Danerian had immediately sent his staff in search of the banana-breathed intruder. By the time Valance was alerted and arrived at their location, Thortom'tonmas had enjoyed a full twenty minutes with the intruder.

"I'm going to have to ask you to step away from the alien, ambassador."

"Oh, oh no," replied the Danerian, a sinister smile twisting his lips, "no, I don't believe I'll be able to do that at all."

As DiVico's security team stepped forward, Thortom'tonmas' aides moved to cut them off. Before either side could escalate the situation beyond words, however, the intruder clapped its hands together. Instantly a dazzling and somewhat itching force wall appeared around everyone in the area, immobilizing them.

"Ambassador," Valance shouted, "I don't think you know what you're dealing with here!"

"Oh, to the contrary, Captain, I understand my new friend, and what he wants, ever so exactly."

"And what the hell would that be?!"

"Why, Mr. DiVico," the ambassador answered. "The guise of Shiu Yin Hong was assumed by this most wondrous visitor to our galaxy because that god's particular demeanor suited him...to a degree, anyway."

The Danerian's tone sent a warning tingling through the nervous systems of all the humans present. Several of them had an idea as to what Thortom'tonmas was planning. None of them were pleased to discover they were correct.

"Every race has its trickster deities. The cruel jokester, the prank player, and worse. This Monkey King is a charming fellow, but...how would one put it, one limited in its scope. I've merely offered our friend...a greater opportunity to utilize its talents."

"Oh crap..."

"Such language, Mr. Michaels," the ambassador laughed. "But forgivable. All you humans offered was the tale of a mischievous godling who ultimately caused more trouble for himself than anyone else. I, on the other hand, have presented him with a more effective, hands-on, you might say, type of trouble-making supreme being—the Monkey King's Danerian counterpart—Saboth, the Unforgiving."

And, in an instant, the minds of everyone present were filled with Thortom'tonmas' description of the Danerian warrior god of laughter. Cruel and capricious, a monstrous blue giant possessed of a ravenous appetite for the cruelest of jests, the kind of being that would set a world ablaze merely so he might take a steam bath in its dying oceans.

"Our visitor is curious as to what this galaxy which he helped set into motion now has to offer. I have given him a clear picture of the weakness of so many of its races, the soft, mewling wretchedness of the shivering members of your Confederation."

"You're a lying sack of crap, Thortom'tonmas," Michaels shouted. "Why should he believe you?"

"Because," the ambassador replied, "our delightful Shiu Yin Hong does not have to blindly place his trust in anything anyone says. Have you heard him converse? Utter a single syllable? No, you have not. He knows I speak the truth because he has gone into my mind. As he learned of the Monkey King from your man, Pasta—"

"Noodles—"

"Whatever...so did he learn of Saboth from me!"

And for another moment, the room went silent. Still held in stasis by what appeared to be nothing more than a mote of the intruder's power, the crewmen of the *Roosevelt* struggled to find a way out of what they could all see coming. If the ambassador could convince the cosmic force in simian form before them to adapt the shape of Saboth, to take on the mantle of the warrior deity of Daneria, there would be no stopping their conquest machine.

The member races of the Earth-led Confederation of Planets were all well aware that the Danerian Empire was looking for an excuse to start poaching their worlds. Twice Danerian agents had tangled with the crew of the *Roosevelt* and both times had been handed defeats that astonished the odds brokers from Las Vegas to the Horseshoe Nebula. If suddenly they found themselves with the closest thing to God Himself leading their fleet, it was a safe bet they would no longer be worried about excuses.

As all human eyes turned toward the form of the Monkey King, all of them despaired. Although each of the sailors was certainly worried over the thought of their own all-too-possible demises, that was not the major concern of any of them. Instead, as a group they were far more focused on the thought that they had failed in their duty, to protect Earth—to maintain the peace, not only for their own world, but for all the members of the Confederation.

And, as the youngest naval officer to ever be awarded command of a dreadnought-class vessel allowed himself a moment of pure self-pity, he suddenly remembered what his mentor, Admiral Mach, had once said about every coin having two sides. Realizing that nothing was ever truly over until it was over, he shouted;

"All right, so monkey boy here got the full picture of all the fun he could have carving up the galaxy from your mind. Well, that's a two way street, pal." As Thortom'tonmas complained, Valance turned as best he could against the force of the stasis field toward the intruder and said;

"Okay, so you went to the core of that gasbag's soul and read what Danerians really think of the rest of us. Yeah, it's no secret they believe they should be running everything with everyone else either serving them dinner

A MEAL FIT FOR GOD - C.J. Henderson

85

or being it. But they're just one little race, and if you're reading my mind you damn well know there aren't very many that think much of them."

The ambassador bellowed in protest, but the captain ignored him, shouting to be heard over the Danerian;

"Look, all I'm saying is, before you start carving up the galaxy for those wiener schnitzels, maybe you should read the fine print in someone else's goddamned brain while you're at it."

"Whose brain, exactly, did you have in mind?"

And at that moment, even Thortom'tonmas went silent, for after his days of silence, the intruder had finally spoken. Valance studied his face, staring into the small, black eyes of the ape visage before him. In the seconds he had to make an answer, the captain knew he was being given one chance to counter the ambassador's offer. He was also well aware of the fact that he could hide behind no subterfuge, that no matter whom he picked, the alien force before him would know and understand his reason for selecting as he did.

"Hell," Valance thought, to himself as well as to the grinning shape before him, "you're probably reading my subconscious, too. You'll know more about why I picked whoever I do than I will. Well so, with that thought in mind...

"You want someone to represent the Confederation of Planets, okay— fine. I'll give you one. Rockland Vespucci."

From the utter despair to be heard in the horrified groans of the other crew members present, Valance could tell not everyone was as confident in his choice as he was.

"Captain, no disrespect intended, but like, you didn't fall in the shower or nuthin' recently, did ya?"

Valance smiled, willing to concede that the gunnery officer's question was not nearly as impertinent as it might have sounded to a board of inquiry. The captain had called for all to meet in the Roosevelt's main galley. It was the largest open room with seating on the ship as well as the place where the entire affair had begun. In attendance were all the sailors the intruder had dealt with so far, as well as himself, Thortom'tonmas, and his aides.

"No, Mr. Vespucci. I was asked by our new best friend here to pick one among us who might be able to give him a compelling reason not to manifest himself as the Danerian god of Whoop-Ass. Since he chose to appear to us as a devious trouble-making type, I decided to fight fire with fire."

"You ain't never forgiven me for our inter-species mixer when we introduced the debutante daughters of all the Pan-Galactic League's big wigs to the bears, cows, pigs, and chimps we was transporting to that Inter-Galaxy Zoo, have you, sir?"

"Sailor," the captain answered, "that's exactly the kind of shenanigan that's brought you here right now." Sighing heavily, realizing his mother was right when she had told him his never-ending stunts were going to catch up to him someday, usually then whacking him across his noggin with a large wooden spoon, the gunnery officer unconsciously rubbed the back of his head, then said;

"So, I gotta...what, exactly?"

"Our visitor is actually a part of the force which started the universe," Michaels said so matter-of-factly he made such utter outlandishness seem practically reasonable. "Apparently every once in a millennium it goes out into the galaxy to see what we've been up to, generally appearing as some sort of god."

"The Danerian ambassador," Valance added, "put two and two together and offered it the option of becoming their god of destruction. I need you to convince it that while on its current good-will tour it remain the Monkey King."

With hundreds of eyes focusing upon him, Rocky felt time shatter, the resulting debris of chronal forward motion splintering further as it fell to the deck throughout the room. For an impossibly long moment he simply stared, eyes unblinking, seeing nothing. All about him, no one spoke—did not even seem to breathe.

Within his brain, the gunnery officer floundered for a direction in which to move. Knowing the intruder could read his mind, his usual craftiness was useless. Whatever it was he might try to use to convince the god-presence to not enlist in the Danerian armed forces, it was going to have to be open and honest, free of subterfuge and, of course, utterly compelling. Convinced the captain really had never forgiven him, the gunnery officer put both hands on his belt, hitched it higher as if heading into high water, and then moved forward to where the Monkey King awaited.

"Okay, well there, ummmm yeah, okay..." he said, his mind scrambling for more words to heap on his less-than-overwhelming opening, "so, you're looking for a reason to not become this murder guy, right?"

A MEAL FIT FOR GOD - C.J. Henderson   87

"No," the intruder answered. "I am waiting to see if you can offer me something more attractive."

Rocky looked to his left, then his right, not knowing for what he was looking—not actually seeing anything. Rejecting a score of devious notions as they filtered through his mind, he finally turned both his palms outward, thrusting his hands in the Monkey King's direction as he admitted;

"Look, I got nuthin', okay? Crimminey, you don't even make sense to me. I mean, Christ on a crutch, why would you even consider killin' billions of people and stuff for Daneria?"

"See here—"

Thortom'tonmas had begun to protest, but the Monkey King raised his hand in the ambassador's direction causing the Danerian to go silent. The alien's eyes bulged as it tried desperately to force words across its lips, but it had been rendered mute, the words "you had your turn" ringing not only within its mind, but that of everyone else present as well.

"Why should I not?" Shiu Yin Hong asked. "Have you ever sat idle for centuries on end?"

"But they want you to *kill* people."

"Is that not *your* job, Gunnery Officer Vespucci?"

"No. No it is not." His eyes narrowing to slits, Rocky slid his tallywacker forward on his head, then growled, "My job is *defending* people." As the Monkey King allowed his own eyes to narrow, Rocky shouted;

"You're a god, you check our records. Read ol' Thor-ton-a-mass's mind, and you find me one instance where this ship, or any damn ship in our whole fleet ever fired the first shot. You show me a single time when we did anything except try and protect folks from the bad guys." Smiling, Shiu Yin Hong told Rocky;

"I know you have not. But, what is the point? Your lives are so brief, so overwhelmingly fleeting...if you save a million souls, and Thortom'tonmas' people slay just as many, what does it matter?"

Clambering aboard his floating cloud, the Monkey King floated forward and upward to where he was just high enough to stare down into the gunnery officer's eyes. His words coming out clipped and precise, his tone descending downward into gravel, he continued, saying;

"I have come forth to engage you all once again. I am intrigued by the Danerian's notion of spreading fear. What can you offer in return?"

Rocky held up an index finger, signaling he needed a moment. In every direction, men and women ground their teeth together, staring in quiet desperation. Sweat running across their foreheads, down their backs, the crew of the *Roosevelt* held their collective breath as the gunnery officer searched for an answer. Desperately, Rocky had gone back in his mind to the moment when the intruder had first learned of the Monkey King. Replaying the scene within his brain, he tried to determine why the god-presence had chosen Shiu Yin Hong over any and everything else it might have become.

His mind swirling, it dawned on Rocky that if the intruder could read minds, then it did not need to hear about the Monkey King to make a choice. It had access to every god ever worshipped throughout human history stored away in someone or another's subconscious aboard ship. No, he decided, it was something Noodles had said that intrigued it.

And then, suddenly remembering the one thing the intruder had not done that night that everyone else in the galley had, Rocky smiled, then called out as loud as he could;

"Hey, Kinlock, get your ass out here!"

And, as Valance wondered what a board of inquiry would say to an officer that allowed the galaxy to be destroyed out from under him, Head Chef Patti Kinlock, as far away from her home in Baltimore, Maryland as any cook ever had been, stuck her head out from her kitchen and shouted back;

"What in hell do you want from me right now, you double-dipper?"

"Dinner!"

Catching on to what his partner in chicanery had figured out, Noodles raced for the kitchen, pushing Kinlock back inside as Rocky indicated a seat at one of the tables, telling the Monkey King;

"Have a seat, your highness. 'Cause I think I got an idea on a much better line of work for you." As Shiu Yin Hong slid off his cloud and then clambered into the chair Rocky had indicated, the gunnery officer said;

"Look, you wanta wipe out solar systems and trash whole races for a buncha lardlumps like the Danerians, hey, that's your choice. But the way I see it, you helped create the galaxy or the whole universe or whatever, right? Seems to me your days of heavy-liftin' are over."

The intruder tilted its head to one side, eyeing Rocky with more intrigue than suspicion. Taking the seat next to it, the gunnery officer moved his hands before him, punctuating his words with a variety of gestures as he continued.

"You want to come out and see some stuff, sure—why not? Great idea. But why would you want to go back to work? That's just crazy. Seems to me

A MEAL FIT FOR GOD - C.J. Henderson   89

after building the universe, you wouldn't want to tear it down, you'd want to enjoy it."

"Enjoy it?" The Monkey King tilted its head in the opposite direction, then asked, "I know all it has to offer. I 'built' it, as you said. What is there for me to enjoy?"

"Good question, but I got an answer. That first night, back when you first listened to my pal Noodles tellin' about his people's old legends, you listened, but you didn't pay any attention."

Throughout the galley, hope began to blossom as one sailor after another figured out where Rocky was headed.

"While he was busy talkin', we were all busy doin' what any sensible person does when the universe's best chocolate chip cookies are served—we was eatin'!"

Then, as if on cue, the doors to the kitchen opened and Kinlock appeared once more carrying a tray almost as wide as she was tall. Behind came Noodles and a dozen kitchen workers, all similarly laden, walking carefully to avoid the endless litter of banana peels which despite the clean-up crews assigned to tackle that single problem seemed to be multiplying on their own.

Such considerations became meaningless, however, all conversation ceasing as the kitchen staff came forward and hints of shredded ginger and lobster meat intertwined with the aroma of peaches and peppers filled the air. As the intruder's eyes went wide with surprise, the opening scents were overwhelmed as more fought to supplant them.

In rapid order the delectable odors of celery and crab meat, bamboo shoots and coconut, oyster sauce and lotus root, freshly roasted cashews, pork ribs, baked apples, caramel doughnuts, broccoli with candied walnuts and beans with bourbon filtered throughout the room. It did not stop there.

As tray after tray was laid out before the Monkey King, the god-presence found itself overwhelmed by the sight of chicken wings crusty with barbecue sauce, pineapple melon cake, hard sausages graced with onions and mushrooms, seventeen different kinds of fish—nine of them steamed, eight of them fried—bean sprouts and hamburger heavily doused with black pepper, along with dishes of succulent beef, tender pork, crispy chicken and a basket of large, batter-dipped shrimp flash-fried so evenly one could eat them shell and all without even noticing the crunch.

As the Monkey King shuddered in gentle delight, everyone throughout the galley watched in rapt anticipation waiting for the intruder to reach for one dish or the other. Even as it deliberated, more trays appeared,

90   Everything's Better With Monkeys

ushering every conceivable dish for its consideration. Hamburgers and cheeseburgers, tacos, burritos and sushi. Lasagna heavy with cheese and roasted beef, pizza covered in pepperoni and anchovies. Chicken pot pies and roasted carrots sat side by side with bowls of grapes, tureens of New England clam chowder and Tutti-Frutti ice cream.

Running its tongue around the inside of its mouth, the Monkey King looked from one dish to another. Would it try the key lime pie or the beef stroganoff? The lobster newberg or the macaroni and cheese? Turning to Rocky, the intruder said;

"So, Mr. Vespucci, you've made your argument—yes?"

"Well, er...yeah. Pretty much. All I'm sayin' is, if you're like God, why would ya want to go back to work? If anything, you're on vacation. People on vacation are supposed to enjoy themselves."

"And what if," asked the god-presence, "if what I enjoy is, as you said, 'killin' billions of people and stuff?'"

Catching the scent of one last dish being brought forth from the kitchen, Rocky made a gesture with his hand to set the final tray down in front of the Monkey King. As Kinlock did so, careful not to let any of the perspiration coating her brow to drip into the steaming delicacy, the gunnery officer picked up a knife that had been laid out for the intruder and handed it to him, saying;

"I'm puttin' it to ya, chief, if you can take a bite of this and still want to kill someone, then you can go ahead and start with me, 'cause this is the best we got to offer."

Intrigued, Shiu Yin Hong reached out, grabbed up one of entrees before it and then popped it into its mouth. The intruder chewed for a moment, swallowed and then sat motionless for a nerve-wrackingly long moment. The Monkey King ran its tongue over the inside of its mouth several times, then in a motion too fast to follow, it suddenly scooped up its knife and thrust it directly for Rocky's face.

A number of crewmen shouted, many rushed forwarded, and then all of them saw that the blade had stopped a millimeter from Rocky's mouth, one of the entrees stuck to its end.

"Join me for dinner, Mr. Vespucci?" Laughing, a noise made from equal parts nervousness and relief, knowing he was in the presence of another jokester as wacky as himself, Rocky answered;

"Don't mind if I do, your highness."

And, pulling the over-sized sea scallop, dripping in butter, festooned with shallots, and wrapped three times around with several lengths of

A MEAL FIT FOR GOD - C.J. Henderson

thick-sliced, Virginia-cured bacon from the end of the Monkey King's blade, the gunnery officer took a healthy bite from the glistening morsel even as Shiu Yin Hong scooped up six more and a thousand hats were tossed into the air.

Dinner continued for several days, Kinlock continuing to prepare dish after dish until the *Roosevelt*'s pantry held nothing more than two bottles of oregano, half a pint of Wild Turkey liquor and a dozen strawberry-flavored Slim Jims. Thortom'tonmas was picked up by a Danerian cruiser at the ambassador's request after the Monkey King mused aloud that he wondered what a deep-fried Danerian might taste like.

Valance reported the entire affair to Confederation Headquarters, of course, receiving the orders to head for Earth so that the intruder might continue his culinary excursion and the *Roosevelt* could resupply its larder. And, as the dreadnought entered its home system, reaching the point where its crew could spot a dime-sized Jupiter through the observation windows, Alexander Benjamin Valance stood in his ready room, staring out into the void, making a silent prayer of thanks to the darkness.

"Captain, you wanted to see me?"

"Yes, come in, Mr. Vespucci." As Rocky entered Valance's private sanctuary, the captain continued;

"I suppose you've heard the rumors that they're going to pin a medal on you once we're back home?"

"Yeah, there's been some scuttlebutt floatin' around."

"Well, you deserve it."

"Beggin' your pardon, sir, but I probably don't." When Valance merely stared, the gunnery officer added;

"Awww, it's like, you know, I woulda never come up with any of that if you hadn't pushed me forward. I don't wanta come across as no suck-up or nuthin', but you always seem to know how to get the best outta all of us. Whoever it was passed over all them admirals and the such to put you in charge...ummm, like I'm just glad someone in the brass was thinkin' with their head outside their ass for once."

"You're always such a colorful guy," sighed the captain. "Aren't you, Vespucci?"

Then, before Rocky could answer, suddenly Noodles stuck his head inside the captain's doorway, announcing the arrival of Shin Yin Hong a moment before he floated in upon his cloud. Valance turned sharply, giving the god-presence a solemn look as he asked;

Everything's Better With Monkeys

"So, you're off now?"

"Yes, I have the restaurants of an entire universe to explore."

"Any place you're thinking of heading toward first," asked Noodles.

"How could I be so close to the Earth, and not visit—yes?"

"Wanta try a little more human-style cookin', eh?"

"I have always enjoyed the cuisine of your world, Mr. Vespucci." And, as the captain, Rocky and Noodles stared, not quite understanding, the Monkey King said;

"I am Shiu Yin Hong, as I have forever been."

And then, the four foot tall simian form faded from sight, reappeared for an instant outside the observation portal, then disappeared completely. After a moment of simply staring and scratching their heads, Rocky broke the silence, saying;

"So he actually was the Monkey King? And he was just jerkin' us around? Like some kind of test? Or..."

"But," interrupted Noodles, "he had Thortom'tonmas convinced he was going to be their war-god, and he acted like he didn't know what food was, and he..."

"The ways of the Lord are mysterious," quoted the captain. Staring out the window, Rocky said;

"God of mischief is right. Man, I think I need a little drink." Nodding in agreement, Noodles added;

"I need a lot of little drinks." Feeling generous, Valance said;

"I've got a couple bottles of Jack Daniels, Green Label, in a compartment—"

"Behind the picture of Admiral Halsey," said Rocky without thinking, "voice- activated lock box, responds to the first three lines of 'Jocko Homo' but only..." Realizing his mistake, the gunnery officer added;

"Ahhh, actually, sir, I think there's only one bottle left in there."

Valance grimaced, then smiled, thinking;

"What the hell, he's earned a moment. I'll let him get his medal...*then* I'll make him clean up all the damned banana peels."

The ability to communicate with your opponent doesn't preclude the possibility of violence, but it can make it appear the less attractive option. But only if the other side is listening.

OH WHY, CAN'T I?

"Sing, everyone sing;
Sing, everyone sing;
All of your troubles,
Will vanish like bubbles,
Sing, everyone sing."

Italian folk ballad

IT CROSSED THE EDGE OF THE GALAXY WITHOUT WARNING. WHEN IT arrived at a point where someone might notice, it was discovered there was no stopping it. Indeed, for those unfortunates in its path there was not even the possibility of understanding it.

The thing, of course, in the previous galaxies which it would have called home if it had possessed intelligence enough to do so, had consumed many worlds over the millennia—some containing sentience, some not. The entity, whatever it was, was not a picky eater. All it required for sustenance was matter in any form. Asteroids, comets, free-floating cosmic ice, galactic dust particles, oh, and planets. It did enjoy planets.

Round and large, filled with elements and all manner of goodness. Skies thick with water vapor, mountains covered with green, fields overflowing with scrub and vines and grasses. Oh, and oceans—how it dearly loved water. Brimming over with swimmers and plants and things somewhere in between the two.

Things that flew in the skies, that swam the seas, lumbered across the ground, these were delicious treats, like tiny grains of sugar sprinkled across an otherwise somber slab of oatmeal. The swallower of worlds loved their taste. It was only the sometimes aftertaste of certain rare planets which left it somewhat unsatisfied. All the screaming, the wailing and the panic, the fear and terror, those worlds crawling with higher life forms, those could be so disturbing—a nuisance, really.

But, it could overcome. It could endure. After all, in the shallow recesses of its stunted consciousness, it realized that one had to accept the good with the bad. The problem was, thinking creatures which, once consumed, upset its delicate balance. It did not enjoy their mental recriminations, their self-absorbed, overwhelming need to complain over their unexpectedly abrupt deaths.

But, what else was it to do, it wondered. Since the time of creation it had chewed its way across the universe, consuming life, assimilating the sweet and varied chemical composition of whatever might drift within its path. Not a being possessed of very developed cognitive skills, the thing let the piece of a thought pass—as it always did. Some planets were tasty and that was that, and some were tasty, but talked back to it the next day. It was the way of things. There was nothing to do but press on.

As the entity allowed itself to be pulled along by the currents of space, it threw itself into slumber. The swallower knew it would awaken, as always, when the next meal presented itself. And, with luck, by then the recently acquired, and highly annoying, four hundred voices screaming within its mind would be dissolved, and it would be able to feed happily once more.

"Could you repeat that, sir?"

Captain Alexander Benjamin Valance, commander of the Earth Alliance Ship *Roosevelt*, stared at the face on his com-screen. He knew he had heard the words correctly, realized there was little chance his equipment could be so selectively faulty as to be capable of distorting random words within a sentence. Still, there was a part of him that hoped such a thing was possible.

"I could sing your orders a cappella, captain, but it wouldn't change them any."

"No, sir," answered Valance, his tone crisp, if still the slightest bit dazed. "I'm certain it wouldn't. Although, it would make such moments more interesting."

Admiral Jeffrey Mach was shorter than many career officers who reached the Navy's upper echelon. He wore a beard always bordering on non-regulatory length, and understood that when you were sending the best and the brightest off toward almost certain doom, that allowing them a moment of near-insubordination was not only acceptable, but recommended. Pursing his lips to acknowledge Valance's comment, he raised one eyebrow as a warning against any further line-crossing, telling the captain;

"It might at that. Perhaps we'll get the chance to test your theory when you return."

"I do appreciate the admiral's highly optimistic use of the word "when," rather than "if.""

"I try to stay positive, captain. As you might wish to do yourself. Are there any questions?" Valance could think of several, but none he cared to voice. Rather than risk his superior's further displeasure, he answered simply;

"No, sir. I believe my orders were straightforward enough."

"Listen, Al... I know this is a raw deal. We should be sending a fleet, and we are. But well... you know politics... we have a responsibility to the Forgeen. They've already lost one world, we've got a treaty, and yours is the closest ship we've got. We just can't get anything else there in time, and we've got to get something in between their homeworld and... and whatever it is that's coming."

"I understand, admiral," responded Valance, meaning his words. "It's what we sign on for."

Both men stared at each other over their comlink for a moment. Separated by some twelve lightyears of space and two decades of age, still they both knew the elder no more enjoyed handing down a death sentence than the younger enjoyed receiving it. With a final salute, though, the pair broke their connection and returned to their respective tasks. Time. After all, was not standing still.

And neither was the horror making it way toward the Forgeen homeworld. Valance allowed himself a small sigh, then prepared to alert his crew to the almost certain possibility of their upcoming demise.

"Tell me I didn't hear what I thought I just heard. There's a pack of Delbickie's Frosted Pink Tobacco Chews in it for anyone that can convince me."

The speaker, Chief Gunnery Officer Rockland Vespucci, better known to his shipmates and pit bosses across the Confederation of Planets as "Rocky," had good reason to doubt his hearing. The shipwide announcement just made by his vessel's captain was enough to throw any swabbie for a loop. Possibly three.

Everything's Better With Monkeys

"To do so, even for the dubious joy of receiving a free pack of Delbickie's Frosted Pinks, would be to do you no favor. We all heard the same message, I do believe."

The words of Machinist First Mate Li Qui Kon, most often referred to by the rest of the crew as well as tube and wire jockeys everywhere as "Noodles," left his friend rolling his eyes as well as reaching for another beer. Pulling the remanents of the six pack of JingleTime Stout out of his reach, though, Technician Second Class Mark Thorner waggled his index finger in the gunnery officer's face, reminding him;

"Now, now, you know better than that. No depressants to be self-administered after a Stations 10 alert."

"Yeah," added Quartermaster Harris, knocking back the last of his Indiana HicUps longneck, "after all, when a to-stations call is that depressing, who needs to add on to it?"

"Hey," said Rocky, still unable to move himself out of his chair, more from depression than inebriation, "anything worth doing is worth doing right."

"Then perhaps," interjected Mac Michaels, one of the top Grade A members of the *Roosevelt*'s egghead division, "we might want to get ourselves squared away and attempt to meet this approaching nightmare with a touch of competence. I don't know, call it a change of pace."

"Hey, listen," snapped Rocky, his defensive hackles rising up of their own volition, "we're plenty competent, when it comes to dealing with things even a quarterway normal. But this, I mean... *this*... this ain't what anyone I know's gonna be callin' normal any time soon."

"He does has a point," admitted Thorner.

And, so did they all, each and every one of them. Around the mess hall, the gathering of suddenly no-longer-off-duty sailors began to push themselves up and out of their seats, preparing to throw themselves at their latest excursion into the unknown—a movement toward which none of them were looking forward. Of all the assignments ever handed to the *Roosevelt*, this was the most colossally unbelievable.

One of their allies, the mainly agrarian, and largely defenseless Forgeen System, had called for help. One of their outer planets, apparently, had been consumed. Not blown apart, not shredded, not sliced, diced, cubed or vaporized. It had been, the Forgeen ambassador swore, eaten.

A rambling, impossible space anomaly, a thing some fifteen thousand standard miles across, had floated into the Forgeen sphere of influence and wrapped itself around one of their worlds. The planet had been called Xiube,

OH WHY, CAN'T I? - C.J. Henderson

a place entirely given over to the cultivation of grains and marine life. It was a profit sphere, a world with very few inhabitants, every inch possible of its surface having been given over to agricultural commerce. When the unknown critter had finally unrolled itself, not so much as a spare set of atoms could be found of Xiube, its four hundred some growth specialists, weather functionaries, farmhands and the such, any of its twenty-seven billion sea creatures, its wheat, clover, bamboo, frill hedge, keblir vines, et cetera.

It was gone. All of it. Just as the Forgeen had said.

And now, the obviously not-yet-sated thing was on the move once more. This time headed for D'frok, homeworld of the Forgeen—a giant of a planet with some seventeen natural satellites, as well as four artificial ones. Every one of them packed with beings—some fifty-six billion residents all in all. Each and every one of them terrified out of their minds as their evening news programs did their best to grab ratings by endlessly broadcasting just how desperately hopeless their situation was.

Historical records, once cross-referenced against all those available from throughout the Confederation of Planets' one-hundred-and-fifty-eight members, revealed the creature to not be completely unknown. It had been discovered, in fact, after all available data had been culled, that the entity had been cutting its way across the galaxy in a somewhat straight line for several hundred standard years, apparently entering the Milky Way at, what the jokesters at Earth Alliance HQ referred to as, the "ass-end of the wrapper."

Chocolate-treat-related nonsense aside, this intel had left the rough and readies of the *Roosevelt* more than a touch apprehensive. First off, as big as their ship was, large enough to comfortably hold a complement of ten thousand Navy personnel, something over fifteen thousand miles across sounded at least a trifle bigger. Second, the facts at hand stated that this head chef for the interstellar house of wipe-you-out had been doing so for millennia, without the slightest interference. This meant that no space-faring race had ever been able to do anything about it in the past, except perhaps the precision military maneuver generally known as get-the-hell-out-of-the-way.

Hoping to be able to manage a slightly better showing, especially considering that not doing so meant death and destruction to quite a few innocent Forgeens, Captain Valance immediately set his maintenance and technical crews to making certain every weapon they had was up to standards. The pounders, the whisperers, even the forward particle

98 Everything's Better With Monkeys

accelerator affectionately dubbed "the lightwave motion gun" were all brought on line, every recoil circuit checked, each cross beam tested, every toggle oiled.

Sadly, what normally would have enough to draw the crew together in white hot comradery, was in this instance only heightening their tension. Up and down the length of the *Roosevelt*, its men and women were growing tense, frightened. Desperate.

It was hard to blame them.

They had been sent on a suicide mission, and everyone knew it. They were the stop-gap, the noble gesture. As whispers and murmurs ran along the great ship's grapevine, darkness filled the minds of its crew. The thing could not be stopped. Not by them. Not by just one ship, no matter how big. They were doomed, and they knew it. Hell, they were supposed to know it.

And with that knowledge came the creeping fear. It was one thing to be sent into battle against hopeless odds, the lone ship sacrificed to cover a retreat so the fleet could survive. That meant glory and an honorable death. But that was not where the *Roosevelt* was headed. They were headed down the gullet of a voracious, intergalactic paramecium. They were fish food, leftovers, the soon-to-be joke of the fleet.

Although, even that much they could have held out against. The *Roosevelt*'s complement were the finest Earth had to offer. They were tough, well trained, and ready to die for their world. But, many of them were wondering, was dying all they were being asked to do this time? What exactly, the question asked, was going to happen to them? After all, they were not being requested to simply be blown apart—no. They were being asked to be eaten. Dissolved, digested, rendered down to their basic atoms. What, nearly half the crew was wondering in less than half an hour after the announcement, did that actually mean?

What was this inconceivable thing toward which they were headed? Would it store their memories, absorb their souls, keep each individual consciousness prisoner within its vast, unknowable reaches? Would their minds be tortured throughout eternity, or would their bodies be used as fuel, an endlessly slow, painful dissolving which would leave them screaming for eons?

Like speculation, as they had encountered other alien situations since mankind had left its own minuscule corner of the galaxy, had been kept in check due to a welcome combination of luck and scope. So far, none of them had been asked to accept anything so mind-bogglingly fantastic or hideous. No creature met, no world uncovered, no race or life-form upon which they had happened defied explanation to such an extent as to be beyond comprehension.

Now, that had changed.

Now they had been ordered to throw themselves against some sort of impossible space vampire, a ravaging eating machine so spectacularly, sky-blotting large it could be seen while still in space by those it would consume. Now they were being asked to offer up more than just their lives—suddenly, their souls were in the balance. And, it had to be admitted, with that being the case the crew of the *Roosevelt* were not reacting as well as might have been hoped.

Valance included.

The captain forced himself to walk the corridor from his cabin to the bridge with a steady, casual motion. He would not betray the dread he was feeling, would not allow the creeping terror gnawing at the back of his mind to show in his face. That was his job, to rise to the occasion. To bear the burden of command. He did not assemble a false smile on his face, did not try to convince his crew he did not understand or share their panic. Such was too hard a mask to maintain, and unfair.

"One step at a time," he thought, nodding to each he encountered in the passageway. "Just take it one step at a time."

No, he told himself, his responsibility was to prove that it was possible to hold oneself together. Those he saw with moisture in the corners of their eyes he did not reprimand. Those he heard muttering prayers he did not chastise. They would snap to when needed. When it came time to fight, they would do so with courage. And when it came time to die, they would do so with honor.

As Valance glanced around the bridge, standing in the doorway without actually stepping inside for a moment, he set his mind in order. They were not coming back. There was no hope. Still, there were lives counting on them. Billions of them. And then, suddenly, something he had read as a child flashed through the captain's mind. It was some sort of fantasy story, men in loin cloths and wizards and the such. He could not remember the title, the author, even the name of the main character, but he did remember what was important—

"If it bleeds, it can die."

"What, captain?"

To the amazement of communications officer Feng, Valance looked at her and smiled. Giving her a jaunty tilt of his head, he moved to his command chair, ordering her to patch him through to the entire ship. When she responded that the channel was open, Alexander Benjamin Valance addressed his crew.

"As if I had to tell you, this is your captain speaking. A look at the latest projections shows we're going to be on top of this thing in less than an hour. So, I thought we should get our game face together."

From stem to stern, heads turned, attention was riveted.

"I know a lot of you are scared. Why not? It's a scary thing they've asked us to do. But, some of us have been scaring ourselves, and that, ladies and gentlemen of the *Roosevelt*, we do *not* need. Do you understand me, people? That is something we... do not... *need!*"

"Oh yeah," said Rocky, hope beginning to scratch its way through the depression which had settled in his chest, "the captain's goin' somewheres with this."

"Ahhh," responded Noodles, his eyes fixed on the speaker above their heads, "you think?"

"So this thing is big. So it's something we've never seen before. Every time we turn around we keep stumbling across things we've never seen before. That no one has ever seen before. But... nothing we've found so far has been able to stop us, so what is it that's making us all so certain this goddamned bacteria from Hell is going to be able to?"

Around the ship, nerves began to unwind, shoulders began to straighten.

"And let me remind you people of something, our orders were to stop this thing. Not to whine and moan, not to lie down and let it roll over us. Keep this in mind, ladies and gentlemen, nobody said you were supposed to *die* today—*nobody!*"

In the fighter bays, in the engine rooms—everywhere—sailors began to turn to one another, heads nodding, grins replacing despair.

"You were given a job... to protect fifty-six billion lives. Now, I don't know what a Forgeen looks like. I don't know what they eat, how they make love or what it smells like when they fart. But, I'm willing to bet they love each other. That they love their children. And, when that goddamned son'va bitchin' thing fills their sky, I'm willing to bet they're going to know fear."

Throughout the *Roosevelt*, fingers tightened into fists.

"Well, we're the only hope they've got. Maybe we can't stop this thing, but then, maybe we can. The simple truth is we won't know until our guns bark and the smoke clears. And if we can't kill it, maybe we can hurt it. Maybe we can change its mind, drive it off, get it to chase us somewhere else."

OH WHY, CAN'T I? - C.J. Henderson

"Captain's right," Harris said to Thorner, giving him an elbow to the ribs, "we were giving up without a fight."

"All I want to remind you people of," snapped Valance, "is that we have a duty, and that we have more than one way to fulfill it. So, grease the long rods, you monkeys. Check out your fighters, fire up the shields and swab the damned decks, because we're on a hunt, and we're going to throw everything we have at the enemy until its nothing more than an intergalactic pancake!"

From the rear mine launching facility, to the very tip of the forward shuffleboard tournament hall, a thunderous cheering burst forth from every throat. Some forty-three minutes later, the crew of the *Roosevelt* would discover whether or not their own personal spatula was big enough to do the job required.

The first sighting of the approaching creature did nothing much to help spread calm throughout the crew. As deep spacers they were accustomed to seeing massive things framed against the blackness of the void. But, these were always moons, comets, planets, stars. Rarely in their travels had they even come up against other ships much bigger than their own. But, the thing centered in the ship's monitors now was not a ship or any other kind of inanimate object. It was alive.

No one color could be attributed to it. Vast areas of the thing were a sallow purple, others black, red, green—more. None of the colors were vibrant. They surged beneath the beast's outer skin, pulsating, sometimes mixing one with another. None of the continual combinations did anything to improve the monstrosity's looks.

"Primary weapons in range, captain."

"Heat 'em," ordered Valance, "but let's just keep the array ready for now. We don't want to give away our entire hand right at the beginning." Turning toward his tactical unit officer, the captain gave the redhead a nod, saying;

"Send out a few teams, Acampora, mix the payloads. Let's see what this thing does."

"It's still a great distance off, captain," answered the woman. "They're only going to have fuel to get there and get back."

"That's all we need, lieutenant," snapped Valance. "They're not going out to mix it up against enemy fighters. They're dumping payload so we can assess from a distance. Now move 'em out."

Everything's Better With Monkeys

In only seconds some ninety fighters were streaking through the black, headed for the creature. The first wave in broke across a several thousand mile stretch of the beast, raking it with laser fire. The second wave went right up the middle of the same sector, dropping nuclear payloads. The last thirty ships strafed the outer edges of the sector, blasting away with combination missiles, dropping everything from napalm and shrapnel bombs to chemical and corrosive weapons.

As the ships turned to make their run back to the *Roosevelt*, Valance and Mac Michaels studied the data coming back to the ship from the various tagged sensors dropped during the attack. Pursing his lips, the science officer sighed hard, then said;

"Not even slowing down, sir. Speed and heading constant. Like it didn't even notice us."

Valance nodded. Silent. Tight-lipped. While he pretended to be concentrating on the forward screen, the captain darted looks at the rest of the bridge crew from the corners of his eyes. All of them were feeling the strain. He could see their nerves tightening. Knowing he had to do something quickly, Valance said;

"All right, much like we figured, light weapons don't have much effect on this gorilla. Let's up the ante, then. Whisper guns, mark central mass. Mr. Michaels, provide coordinates. Full beam dispersal..."

Sweat beaded across every forehead not already soaked.

"On my command..."

Everywhere, chatter ceased. Prayers were offered.

"*Fire!*"

The *Roosevelt*'s fourteen forward particle weapons sliced the darkness, varying rays of pink, green and yellow boiling through space. Striking in a ring around the seven hundred square miles of surface area above their target, the beams tore across the flesh of the beast, all moving inward toward the center of what Valance and Mac Michaels hoped was the creature's heart. And, while the devastating attack continued, before damage assessment could be made, the captain ordered;

"Pounder batteries, zero the mark. Battery commanders, commence firing!"

The pounders, the ship's planet busters, had been gathering projectiles during the entire race to head off their target. The pounders were normally used against orbiting bodies. The mass drivers would launch a captured asteroid or meteor at high speed toward a target, then let the planetary

OH WHY, CAN'T I? - C.J. Henderson

body's gravity take over, pulling the object in hard and fast. The resulting damage was usually catastrophic.

Their target this time, of course, was not a planet, but long range observation had revealed that due to its incredible size the beast did generate its own gravitational field. Whether or not it would be sufficient to cause itself damage—that remained to be seen.

"First volley within a hundred thousand miles, captain."

"Release the second volley."

As the next brace of pounders released their payloads, the first sped on toward their target. No one on the bridge broke the mounting silence as the initial salvo shattered the creature's personal atmosphere. The thing's gravity grabbing hold of the projectiles, their speed nearly doubled as the beast dragged them closer, embracing their promise of destruction.

"Second volley entering atmosphere—"

"Fingers crossed, everyone—"

And then, the thousands of tons of rock, ice and iron slammed into its target. Massive renting holes burst through the creature's outer skin, driving deep enough into the horror to release great, thousand mile arcs of fluid pumping madly. The bridge crew held their breaths, waiting for a reaction, and then, the second volley hit.

Michaels' science team had planned the attack to pound at what was hopefully the monster's most vulnerable spot. The fighters were sent in to attack its fringes, to draw attention away from the core. Then, after the whisper beams hopefully broke open the thing's flesh, the pounders were released to fall in two circles—the first broad, the second tighter, more focused. As the second volley struck, sending more geysers of blood and bile into the air, cheers went up across the *Roosevelt*. Taking no chances, however, her captain commanded;

"Half a job done is nothing accomplished. Mr. Rockland..."

"Aye, sir?"

"Fire the lightwave!"

Prepared since before the creature had been sighted, Rocky punched in the final three codes needed to begin the lightwave motion sequence. Deep within the *Roosevelt*, its massive protonic engines began to siphon off energy for the attack to come. The lightwave gun was the ship's most powerful weapon, but it was also its desperate last chance. Capable of disrupting the gravity of a gas giant, of collapsing an entire solar system's logical motion, it was humanity's ultimate weapon of mass destruction.

"Weapon ready, sir," snapped Rocky, his finger posed above its detonator.

The only problem was, once fired, the *Roosevelt* would not be capable of independent movement for several hours. The decision to use the lightwave motion weapon was never one made lightly. Indeed, it had never before been made in combat.

"Is target locked, Mr. Rockland?"

"Target is locked, sir."

Which meant, if the lightwave motion burst did not destroy the creature utterly, or at the least incapacitate it, then the Forgeen, and the *Roosevelt* along with its crew, were finished.

"Then *fire!*"

Valance's orders, it would later be determined, was given a mere 2.43597 seconds too late.

Even as Rocky's finger descended, at his observation post, Mac Michaels began to notice an odd reaction taking place across the surface of the creature. With the majority of the steam beginning to dissipate, his long-range sensors were finally able to send back visual images worth examining. As he did so, the science officer raised one eyebrow. That first was lifted due to perplexity. The second out of horror.

"Oh crap—"

Was all the science officer could blurt before the lightwave motion gun was engaged. As its overwhelming payload of destruction raced through the darkness, gobbling up distance at the speed of light, across the surface of its target, the creature's skin was mutating, bonding—rebuilding itself.

"All hands," announced Valance, his voice edged with both hope and doom, "brace for motion backwash."

The golden dazzle of accelerated light slammed into the monster with power enough to not only stop its forward motion, but to force it backward for the first time in its entire existence. However, that was all it did. As the impact flash faded from the screens, to the horror of the crew, the beast appeared unaffected.

"Mac," asked Valance with a still even tone, one desperate to shatter, "what? Give me a 'what?'"

"It, it seems to have... scabbed over, sir. The wound—the fluid release, we thought we hurt it, and we did. But it seems all we did was bring its defenses on line. Scanners indicate the scab is the density of adamantium, running a solid mile deep."

"And *that* was enough to stop our beam?"

OH WHY, CAN'T I? - C.J. Henderson

"It didn't stop it, sir. It deflected it. And, since the bonded area runs to around a depth of five miles around the impact point, well..."

"Yes, Mr. Michaels?"

"At least we know the thing works... ah, sir."

No one spoke. No one breathed. All any of the crew on the bridge did was stare at the screen, at the image of the terrible thing hanging in space. The living being that had just survived a direct blast from the mightiest weapon ever assembled by Earth science.

"It does seem to have stopped moving, sir," offered one of the sailors on long-range duty. "Perhaps we did more to it than we realize."

"And perhaps, Mr. Rennie, it's just trying to decide how to proceed," responded Mac Michaels, glowering at the ensign under his command.

"Well, goddamnit," snapped Valance, "then it's one up on us, because that's what we should be doing!" Not waiting for anyone to respond, the captain depressed his comlink and addressed the crew.

"Now hear this. We have apparently stunned the beast, but that is all. I have no idea how much time we have before it begins to move again, either toward Forgeen or us, but in that window of opportunity, if *anyone* thinks they have a good idea, *now* is the time to sing out with it."

For a moment there was no response to the captain's request. And then, Ensign Rennie, going as pale as a man could without actually fainting from blood loss, pointed toward the forward screen, whispering;

"Th-Th-The... it... it's moving."

As all eyes turned, dread etching them open, unblinking, bulging from the dawning realization that what they were viewing might possibly be the last thing they ever witnessed, all could see Rennie was correct. The thing was moving once more. This time, toward the *Roosevelt*. A number of the bridge crew began to tremble, several shed tears.

"*No!*"

As all heads turned, hope springing wildly into hearts across the bridge, Communications Officer Feng turned to her console and began flipping switches. Focusing both the *Roosevelt*'s messaging systems and translation programs into a tight beam aimed at the monstrosity beyond, she hit her transmit button, then sang;

"I don't want to die,
Although I'll admit we're beaten,
I'm telling you this from the heart—
No one here wants to be eaten."

"What in the wonderful world of color is she doin'?"

"Of course," said Valance, ignoring Rocky's question. "Of *course!*" Snapping his fingers, the captain shouted;

"She's the communications officer. She's doing her job—she's trying to communicate!"

"By singin'?"

> "We're sorry that we shot you,
> To see you bleeding made me sad.
> We want you to be our friend,
> Not someone who's all mad."

"She's not making up the best lyrics, sir."

"Who cares," Valance snapped at Michaels. "It's the feeling she's putting into them, the heart—listen to her. She's trying to explain us. She's—"

And then, the captain went quiet. Staring into Valance's eyes, Rocky whispered to Rennie;

"Oh yeah, that's the look. Here it comes."

Slamming his fist against the arm of his command chair, Valance let out a whoop of triumph. Ordering Michaels to patch all the ship's com systems into Feng's console, he broadcast to the rest of the ship;

"Yeoman Feng is attempting to teach fifteen thousand miles of angry space-faring Jell-o that sentient beings are worth something. She's looking to get through to it with song, the most basic emotional tool our lizard cortex ever created. Any of you that know how to sing, help her out."

And with those words, it started.

> "You must remember this—"
> "We all live on a yellow—"
> "Born free, as free as—"

From every corner of the ship, from the forward batteries to the mess hall...

> "Roll out the barrel—"
> "Moon over Rigel 7—"
> "Row, row, row yer boat—"

In a hundred languages, and five times as many keys, some ten thousand voices unleashed the story of humanity.

OH WHY, CAN'T I? - C.J. Henderson

"I am the very model of a modern major gentleman—"
"Fairies wear boots and you better believe—"
"We are the champions—"

They used light opera and heavy metal. They sang country western ballads, rock & roll and parodies. They sang of their homes...

"I'll take Manhattan—"

They sang of their hopes...

"To dream, the impossible—"

They sang of their loves...

"Oh, the yellow rose of Texas—"

And, none of it seemed to work. Relentlessly the horror moved forward on the ship, sliding ever closer, undeterred. Unforgiving. As the image of the nearing monstrosity began to fill the observation screens, voices by the dozens, by the hundreds were silenced. What, their owners' minds asked, was the use? It was over. They were finished. It was inevitable.

But, on the bridge, one voice did not fail.

Having given off trying to make songs up, Yeoman Feng reached into her past and pulled forth the one collection of notes and words that could stop any force thrown against it. Her voice small and trembling, she sang of need. She sang of hope.

Closing her eyes and filling her lungs, she sang of something that might be behind the moon, or beyond the stars. She sang of a place where there was no trouble, one she was not certain existed, but that could be found by happy little bluebirds.

And, although the bleeding, revenge-seeking creature approaching the *Roosevelt* had never before heard a human voice, did not know what a rainbow was, or why one might wish to go over it, something within its staggering bulk began to stir—to awaken.

To comprehend.

Then, Feng sang—

"Why, oh why, can't I?"

And, the entity which had only a few minutes earlier shed its first drop of blood, followed that sensation by shedding its first tears.

Everything's Better With Monkeys

It was some days later that Rocky and Noodles sat in a quiet corner of the mess hall with a few others of the crew, including newly promoted Lieutenant Feng. Knocking back another long gulp from his Ballards Bitters, the gunnery officer announced;

"I've said it before, and I'll say it again, ain't nobody gets to see shit like we do."

"Not very eloquent, Mr. Rockland," said Feng, grinning wide, "but eminently correct."

"So, Mac," asked Noodles, "you've got the captain's ear. What's the word? What are they going to do with our playmate?"

"You mean Caesar, that's what command's named the intergalactic fried egg that almost ate the *Roosevelt*—"

"And us along with it."

"Amen to that." Taking a swig from his own high voltage refreshment, Michaels added;

"Oh, you guys'll love this. Seems the Confederation of Planets cut a deal with it. Turns out swallowing down thinking beings gives our new pal psychic gas. But, it can't tell one planet from another. So, we're putting together a team that will simply lead Caesar across the galaxy, directing it to dead worlds, asteroid belts with no useable resources, comets that have become a hazard to navigation—"

"Hey," offered Harris, "they could take it to that sargasso of space junk that makes getting around our own system such a nightmare."

"Good call," answered the science officer. "First place they took him."

"You know, it's kind of sad."

"What do you mean, Feng?"

"What I mean is, Caesar was happy enough, millions of years, just floating along, eating anything that came his way. No worries... then—bang— he meets us, next thing he knows, he's like janitor to the galaxy."

"One day you're a god," observed Rennie, "the next you're just pushing a broom."

"The horror," joked Noodles. "The horror."

"Man," replied Thorner, "consciousness really *is* a bitch, ain't it?"

And, with that, the conversation turned to other things, as conversations always do. Some left the table, others replaced them. They did, after all, have duties to perform. Much like Caesar, and any other being the universe has ever known unfortunate enough to develop language skills.

Our strongest weapon in the face of other beings seems to be a display of innate decency. Newbie heathens we may be, but we continue to distinguish ourselves by simply demonstrating humanity. Can an ancient schism be repaired? Can war and bloodshed be avoided? And, most important of all, who's coming out on top when the Roosevelt is called in to judge the...

SPACE BATTLE OF THE BANDS

"Music hath charms to soothe the savage breast, to soften rocks, to bend a knotted oak."

William Congreve

"NOW YA GOTTA ADMIT, NOODLES, THAT WAS REALLY SOMETHING COOL."

The speaker was Chief Gunnery Officer Rockland Vespucci, and on a casual, or even close inspection it would have to be admitted by most anybody that he indeed had a point. The person to whom he had been making his point, however, Machinist First Mate Li Qui Kon, did not answer. At least not at first, which was also perfectly understandable. What they were seeing before them was not a sight oft' seen by anyone.

"Rocky," the gunnery officer's friend said finally, his voice a whisper as had been his companion's, "I see those understatement seminars the captain insisted you attend really have done the trick."

As members of the crew of the E.A.S. *Roosevelt*, the pair of swabbies had witnessed many of the most inspiring, dreadful, and even down-right goofy things the galaxy had to offer. It was a rare moment, however, when they managed to see something that combined all three emotions so completely as the one they were sharing at that moment. The *Roosevelt*, as the most advanced of all Earth's warships, was often times sent into

Everything's Better With Monkeys

situations merely to allow its admittedly awesome presence to be observed by others not in possession of such a presence. That particular segment of current reality in the ship's already grand history was another one of those times.

At present, the *Roosevelt* and her crew were on display in the Belthis System. More specifically, they were in orbit around Belthis Prime, one of the newest candidates for entry into the grand Confederation of Planets, of which the Earth was the big cheese. The *Roosevelt* was the ship responsible for exposing the Pan-Galactic League of Suns (the galaxy's former big cheeses) as somewhat of a fraud when it came to ruling the universe, and thus the ship had earned itself the job, desired or not, of being present at every official Confederation Entrance Ceremony that the Confederation could manage.

At this particular ceremony, those members of the crew not on duty were pressed up against the ship's various view ports, or at least crowding around a monitor with an external feed, watching as the Belthin Navy put on a display of their weaponry. The demonstration was part fireworks-show, part how-you-like-them-apples, but it was, nonetheless, most effective.

Out beyond one of Belthis' third moon, a wide range of target vessels had been arrayed for systematic destruction, and so far it had been in the parlance of the average fellow, "a hell of a show." The Belthin ships were knocking off their objectives one after another with an array of light beams which lit the ebony of space with a astounding splash of interwoven colors, and something else the crew of the *Roosevelt* could not quite believe.

Sound.

Yes, of course, they were all aware that sound could not travel in a vacuum. Travel? It could not even exist. And yet, somehow the destructive rays were slathering the area with not only color, but for lack of a better word, music, as well.

It seemed that Belthin science had, over the centuries, developed a defensive/offensive capability unknown anywhere else in the galaxy. And, on the *Roosevelt*'s forward bridge, it was that very factor which was the topic of conversation between the ship's captain, Alexander Benjamin Valance, her science officer, Mac Michaels, and a rather average looking Belthin, DixWix Plemp, Supreme Defulator for the Regime.

"You like our ships, yes? Impressive in their furious manner, are they not, hum? Magnificent in their ferocious demeanor, no?"

SPACE BATTLE OF THE BANDS - C.J. Henderson

"Absolutely," answered Valance, only being partially diplomatic by praising the event, "it is, I must admit, one of the most outstanding military displays I've ever had the privilege to witness."

"I have to agree," said Michaels, the all-around big-brained whiz kid of the *Roosevelt*. "This branch of defensive weaponry you folks have created has to be singularly unique in all the cosmos. I mean, I've certainly never heard of anything even *remotely* like it."

"It is very impressive," added the captain. And, to be fair, he was not just doing so to keep the oddly-shaped alien smiling. In fact, the human contingent actually had no way of knowing if their current could hosts could smile. The Belthins were basically a race of beings that resembled nothing else more than a stack of meat pancakes. They did not possess heads, persay, but heard and saw and spoke through a variety of slits located around the summit of their conical bodies. Their means of locomotion consisted of puckering their rounded base and then moving by tilting themselves back and forth as they wobbled along. Needless to say, the Belthins did not believe in stairs.

Most of them fell within the range of three to four feet tall with few exceptions. They were also quite a symmetrical race, the majority of them being almost exactly equal in their diameter to their height. Indeed, the ship's utility crew had been called upon to construct a platform affair for the Supreme Defulator to perch upon so he might be able to view the display along with Valance and Michaels as more of an equal—and without looking so much like some manner of pet waiting for one of them to take for a walk.

"Can you tell us anything about these systems, Defulator Plemp," asked Michaels in a clearly admiring tone. "Not looking to cart off your secrets, of course, but... oh, seriously... how did your people stumbled across such an astounding technology, or was it a conscious search? And, how long ago did they do so... or was it was it merely a lucky stumble? Did some Belthin visionary actually set out to unravel such secrets, I mean..."

Plemp formed a hand/arm-like appendage with a thought, extending it in a casual manner, gesturing with an impressively fluid bow that he would be most happy to answer such questions. The Defulator was not worried about revealing any of his people's secrets. As he explained, he was not scientist or even mechanic enough to give away any important points about their defenses. He was, however, a politician through and through, one dedicated to getting his race into the Confederation of Planets and thus ready to brag about anything Belthinian at a moment's notice.

"We Belthins are quite ready, willing as well, to discuss such things, yes? All our weapons have been developed, constructed, designed upon these lines over our centuries, hum? You understand, no?"

"You're telling me," asked Michaels, more excited than ever, "you have in-atmosphere weapons which work using this same basic technology?"

"All Belthin weapons work thus, you see? You follow? From the slightest personal protector, to our deluxe line of planet smashers... yes? All are music to the ears, no?"

Valance and his science officer did not hesitate to agree. The Belthin weapons were extraordinary, both in that they possessed devastating power, and yet did not use very much energy at all to create their devastation. And, unlike the old style nuclear weapons of Earth, they were an utterly clean source of destruction which left no undesirable residues or contaminants behind.

"Very long time we possess these principles, yes? But, to use in space, new this is for us, you understand? You follow? Did not need—did not know there was need, did not suspect, hum? You are with us, no? You—"

"Captain," interrupted Lieutenant Drew Cass, the weapons officer on duty, "we've got three unknowns approaching the display sector. Running silent."

"Confirming silence is intentional, sir," added Iris Feng, the communications officer, "identical requests sent out in Earth 9.8, Belthin, and Pan-Galactic—no response."

"Defulator Plemp," asked Valance, "any idea whose ships those are?" Puckering violently, swelling to his full extension of some four feet, three inches, the supreme ruler of Belthin shouted;

"These are known, yes! Enemies! Hostiles, you understand? You know? You—"

And then, the weapons fire began, and the darkness of space exploded in flame.

The intruders had struck with ruthless precision, knocking all of the remaining Belthin drone ships from orbit, but carefully avoiding all vessels, including the *Roosevelt*, which might carry any living beings. Only after they had destroyed the segment of the local remote fleet putting on the weapons display—shattering their meteors, liquefying decommissioned satellites, et cetera—had they then answered Feng's broadcasts, asking permission to address the Confederation representatives.

SPACE BATTLE OF THE BANDS - C.J. Henderson

DixWix Plemp had objected to the taking place of such an activity most strenuously, but Valance had ignored the Defulator and readily agreed to it. Partly because it was standard Confederation policy to do so and, partly because the unknown intruders—whoever they were—seemed to possess the exact same technology as the Belthins down to the last note and flicker.

Although they used it in a quite unorthodox manner.

"All right, everyone," said the captain as they waited for the invaders' representatives to be ushered to the ship's diplomatic chamber, "if we could bring this little meeting to order—"

"Again, Captain," squeaked Plemp from the lowest part of his conical body, "I must protest, yes? Most strenuously, most vehemently... most—"

"Most nosily, as always, eh, Plemp? Eh?"

And then, much to the surprise of the humans, as well as the consternation of the Belthins in the room, the contingent of invaders were ushered in, all three of them looking to be exactly of the same species as DixWix Plemp, himself. As most of the ship's personnel merely stared, Valance narrowed his eyes, glancing suspiciously at the Defulator as he said;

"Well, well, now here's a surprise nobody was expecting."

Actually, to state that the new arrivals looked to be exactly the same species as Plemp and his contingent was perhaps a hasty judgment. Oh, biologically there was little doubt they had dropped out of the same evolutionary tree at roughly the same time of day. But, somewhere along the line the Plemps of the universe had taken a decidedly right-hand turn while the newcomers' ancestors had certainly turned left.

"You are the high chief of the human contingent, eh," asked one of the invaders of Valance. Giving the alien a bit of a polite stare, the captain answered;

"To be exact, I am Captain Alexander Benjamin Valance, commander of this vessel, and main negotiator in this sector at the moment for the Confederation of Planets. And you are...?"

"Outraged, eh, that these pompous knobstuffers are at it again." When his comment went sailing past all the humans, the alien made a sucking noise, then said;

"I am Kleb, eh? Of Contingent Swy'ng. The other inhabited planet in this system. Eh? The one roundmound here likes to pretend doesn't exist, eh, hey?"

"Traitors, yes," snapped DixWix, the hue of his skin molding from purple to scarlet. "Renegades, hum? Promoters of vulgar indecency, no?"

"So spits the tightthrob," shouted Kleb. "Still choking to hit the loft notes, eh?"

And, at that point, the two aliens began screeching at each other in their own language, puckering toward each other with such vehemence that their individual aids had to move forward to restrain them. In seconds the negotiation chamber was filled with the high-pitched verbal violence of the two leaders, along with the occasional bit of mayhem when one or the other of them would manage to form an additional appendage which one of their seconds did not manage to snag. Once they began to hurl chairs at one another, however, Valance barked in his loudest someone's-going-to-pay-for-this voice;

"All right, you maniacs—that's *enough*! Might I remind you both that you are guests on this vessel. DixWix, if you want to bring your people into the Confederation, this display is not going to make your case. As for you, Kleb, I don't even know what you want, yet, but I'm either going to find out, quickly—and quietly—or the bunch of you can clear my line of sight and go make your case to join up with the Danerians! Have I made myself clear?"

"Exceedingly, eh." Kleb responded first, shifting the focus of his attention from DixWix to the captain. "Questions that are asked will be answered, eh?"

"With lies, yes," shouted the Defulator. "With deceptions, hummm? With—"

"With a touch of courtesy toward all," interrupted Valance, glowering at the aliens, "thank you. Now, since there seems to be a bit of hostility here, I think it best we separate the two of you." Turning toward his science officer, the captain ordered;

"Mac, get the diplomatic team assembled. Have them break down into two teams, one in meeting room alpha, the other in beta. Have security escort the Belthins, and our new-found friends here, to meet with our boys. I want this mess hashed out in no less than two hours." Turning toward the indistinguishable sets of aliens before him, he said;

"Back on Earth we have a custom when two parties don't agree with each other. We put them in two different rooms, ask them the same questions, and then compare their answers. It cuts down on the screaming, the posturing, and most importantly, the lying." As the leaders of both races began to rankle, Valance added;

"See what I mean about posturing? Now let me remind you, the Confederation is eager to establish a presence in this sector of space. So are the Danerians. I doubt either of you wants to find yourselves one of their

SPACE BATTLE OF THE BANDS - C.J. Henderson   115

servitor planets. So, why not indulge my little social experiment, for the sake of your races?"

DixWix and Kleb stared, if that was the right word, at each other with a rigid violence which made more than one crew member wonder if seats were going to take flight once more. After a moment, however, both leaders nodded sullenly and led their people off to the meeting rooms. And, once the area had been cleared, Feng asked the captain;

"Sir, where will you be if you're needed?"

"Somewhere where's there's liquor."

An hour later, Valance was regretting his decision to limit his intake to a solitary Saurian and Coke. Apparently, a pair of human hours was far less time than was required to get to the bottom of the dispute between the Swy'ngs and the Belthins. At least, to a bottom both sides of the argument could appreciate.

While the talks floundered on into their fifth hour, the captain met with several of his officers whose assignment had been to follow the proceedings and to be ready to brief Valance whenever he asked for an update. What they had to offer him during his fifth briefing did not vary in any substantial manner from his first.

The separate teams had established the basics fairly early. Belthis Prime was indeed the mother world in the system. There were Belthin colonies on several moons and major asteroids, and a thriving industrial presence on the inner-most planet to their sun. Swy'ng had been colonized only some hundred and thirty-seven to two-hundred and eighty-three years in their past, depending on which world's calendar was used.

As DixWix had revealed earlier, all major Belthin weapons were based off the same power source. Actually, most of what ran their cities, pumped their water, illuminated their homes, et cetera, originated in one variation or another of the self-same force.

Music.

Generations earlier, a Belthin by the name of Roget NemSem found a way to blend sound and light into an energy form. It became an almost self-sustaining source of limitless, inexpensive power—one created from blending musical notes with any available glimmer, flicker or glint to create a storage-ready form of energy. And, apparently, it had to be music.

And live music at that.

Random sound only produced limp, tepid power. When the age of recording came along, the utilities barons thought the moment had come when the musicians' unions would be broken, but such did not come to pass. Canned music, no matter how excellent the reproduction, could somehow not replicate the essential quality needed for high-grade, light-up-the-world, keep-the-wheels-turning energy.

Valance had been amazed to discover that this meant the grand mother ship of the Belthins contained an actual symphony orchestra. But, after some of the things he and his crew had seen since first hitting the wide ebony, he had arrived at the juncture where he was willing to believe just about anything. Being far from where he was willing to put up with anything, however, he pulled a coin from his pocket and tossed it into the air. Catching it, he slapped it onto his wrist, revealed the side which had landed upright to himself, then sighed;

"Damn."

"Lost the toss, captain," asked Feng.

"Well, it was either go have another drink or throw our guests together to try to hash this all out, with me riding herd on the whole proceeding."

"Going to be a dry night, eh sir?"

Valance grinned at his communications officer, nodded, then gave the order to move all their guests into one conference room so they might try and attack the problem of the Belthis system from a different angle.

"All right," snarled the captain two hours into the second round of meetings, "let's try and make something out of this. Surely there has to be some way the Confederation and both of you can agree to a mutual cooperation pact where you can just go on hating each other. I mean, can't there?"

Valance knew he had reached a limit to his patience if he was willing to propose such a thing. Yes, the Belthin System was important to the Confederation. They needed a base of operations in that sector of space, and they needed it to be Danierian free. Too many of the systems in which the Confederation had established a presence had a Danierian protectorate within it, or far too close by to give the kind of advantage either side desired.

But, the dislike between the two worlds was so intense, that no matter what the captain proposed, if one side said they liked it, the other turned it

SPACE BATTLE OF THE BANDS - C.J. Henderson

down, threatening to give the Danerians a corner of their system to call their own out of spite.

"No, there can not, hum?" DixWix pulled himself to his full height, snarling, "No bridge can span the difficulty between us, yes?"

"A difficulty of your own making, eh," answered Kleb, also puckering himself into the Belthin version of standing on one's tip-toes. "An insistence on the play list of the past, eh? No variation ever for the blowhards of Belthis—"

"Wait a minute," snapped Valance, thinking he had finally found the piece neither side had been willing to place in full view on the table. "Did I just hear right? Is that what this is all about? The music that gets played to create your energy fields? That's *it*?"

"Understand you not, yes? The concertos of power, every stanza must be perfect, hum? Every toccata pure and respectful, no? There must be dignity—"

"What a load of crumbs," barked Kleb, something akin to spittle frothing from his various mouths. "You've imprisoned music, stagnated it, eh? Drained all the life out of it simply to make stuff run."

"That's what it's for, yes?"

"No! It's for more than making sidewalks move and vid-screens function. It's life, eh? Power without respect for where it comes from is useless!"

"Skipper," whispered Michaels, rolling his eyes as he did so, "are they really basically arguing over what's better—classical or rock and roll?"

"I kinda get that feeling," answered Valance, smiling a bit himself. And, he thought, why shouldn't he smile?

The two races were locked in apparently an age old dispute that hinged on nothing more than where the family should set the radio dial during dinner. In that moment, the sheer absurdity of an entire race splintering, nearly half of them moving to a different world and setting up a new civilization, simply because they enjoyed a different beat than their elders hit both the earthmen as the sheerest of lunacies. But, if they thought the Belthins had run out of ways to amuse them, they were wrong.

"The ways of those who puckered before us are not useless, yes," snarled DixWix. "The power they gifted us with is not useless, hum? And if you think so, if you truly believe that your beat is the one that must prevail, perhaps it is time for a test between us, no?"

"You're on, squarehead," agreed Kleb. Turning to his seconds, he shouted, "Back to the ship. Order every horn, drum and dipthiller assembled at once."

Making much the same order to his own followers, the Supreme Defulator of Belthis turned to Valance, offering;

"Much in the way of thanks for your efforts, captain, yes? We shall settle this problem now as it should have been settled long ago, hum? Then there shall be a melody of peace throughout our system once and for all, no?" DixWix began to amble toward the doorway, then turned suddenly and added;

"By the way, my compliments to your galley, yes? Those ambrosin dough circles you served, brown and sweet...?"

"Chocolate chip cookies—"

"Wonderful, yes?"

"Oh, indeed," added Kleb. "Your bartender mixed an excellent Bix & Bitters."

"My, did you enjoy those," said DixWix, forgetting himself. "They were tasty, yes? And did you like those round—"

For a moment, it almost seemed that reason had settled upon the conference room. But then, the pair or antagonists realized to whom each of them was acting with civility, and immediately returned to the notion of destroying their grandchildren, or grandelders, respectively, leaving a quite baffled Alexander Benjamin Valance to wonder exactly what he was supposed to do next.

"Battle stations, everyone!"

From one end of the *Roosevelt* to the other, forks were dropped, card games were abandoned and crewmen scrambled to wherever they belonged during an emergency.

"Captain," snapped Michaels, "are we attacking something?"

"We're just getting ready in case someone out there gets a bit too frisky." Turning to Lieutenant Cass, Valance ordered;

"All auxiliary power to the shield armor. Alert side batteries 6, 7, 15 and 16 to uncap and stand-by." The captain paused for a moment to consider, then added;

"And tell Rockland to start primary build-up for the lightwave motion gun."

Cass swallowed, but leapt immediately to carrying out his orders. He was not the only one to pause for a moment at the mention of firing up the ship's main weapon. The lightwave motion gun had only been fired once under combat conditions in the ship's colorful history, and was not even considered unless a situation was pegged at the least as very dire.

"Feng, are you picking up any chatter between the Belthin ships—either side?"

"Nothing useful, sir," answered the communications officer. "Translators giving out a pretty standard string of orders on either side. Seems they're both determined to prove they should be the ones to enter the Confederation."

"It's insanity," muttered Valance, staring at the forward screen focused on the battle. The two sets of ships spun around one another, most of their shots canceling one another out.

"Sir," shouted Feng, "The Defulator has called for reinforcements from their homeworld. Contingent Swy'ng has done the same."

The captain nodded, not taking his eyes of the screen. Then, watching the Belthin weapons splatter against one another, suddenly the back of the captain's brain took note of something which gave him hope. Calling Michaels over, he said;

"Mac, have you noticed anything unusual when their weapons fire crosses."

"It's a new technology," answered the science officer, "so I can't explain it, but unlike anything we've ever seen before, the beams appear to cancel each other out."

"At the least," agree the captain, "but I'm thinking there might be something more going on."

"What do you mean?"

"Their weapons are a combination of light and sound, but sound doesn't travel in a vacuum."

"Could be the blending with light changes the properties of sound enough for it to stay cohesive." When Valance stared at him hopefully, Michaels offered;

"May be why the beams cancel each other out. Their technology lends itself toward mixture. When the beams cross, possibly they absorb each other, complement each other—"

"Music..."

The captain said the word slowly, drawing it out. Then, snapping his fingers, he shouted;

"*Damn*, we just might have a chance here." Taking a deep breath, Valance shouted;

"Mac, fire up your probability programs. Cass, get maintenance to reroute any excess gases we have of any kind—oxygen, carbon dioxide, nitrogen, anything the ship can spare."

"To where, sir?"

"Signal Rockland to be ready to link his targeting computer to Mr. Michaels' probability analysis. I want to flood any area of contact between their weapons' fire with atmosphere."

Valance allowed several seconds of bewilderment to pass between the bridge crew, and then asked;

"Do we have a problem, people?" Then, as everyone jumped back to their duties, the captain asked his science officer;

"Am I asking too much of the light wave apparatus?"

"No, I don't believe so, sir. In fact, not actually firing the weapon itself, but simply using it as a delivery system will mean the ship won't de-power after the first shot. We'll still be combat ready."

"Well," mused Valance, crossing his fingers, "let's hope we won't need to be."

Watching his screens, realizing it was time to step back and allow his crew to perform their duties, the captain ordered Michaels to direct all data to Rocky, informing the gunnery officer that he was to take his best shot, pumping barrages of gas into the center of each expected energy crossing produced by the Belthin forces. Rocky did not question the orders, nor try to explain the difficulty of what was being asked of him. He was well aware Valance knew what he was asking. Instead, the gunnery officer merely pushed his tallywacker back on his head and began studying the battle before him, as well as the probability stream being fed to him, waiting for his best opportunity.

And, as he did so, outside the skirmish continued. Up until that point, the Belthin forces had been equally matched, neither side being able to score a destructive hit as their weapons continued to cancel each other out. But, the deadly light rays from each side were coming closer and closer to finding a target. More than one near miss had almost blasted ships from each party of the deep ebony. Everyone watching knew it was only a matter of time before one side or the other scored a clean hit, which would mean system wide war.

In his cockpit, Rocky kept his eyes peeled, reading the data stream, finger on the firing button, not blinking, barely breathing, and then, when the proper line of numbers flashed across his screen, he jabbed the release without hesitation. Instantly the ship's massive protonic engines spewed

SPACE BATTLE OF THE BANDS - C.J. Henderson   121

several million pounds of raw atmosphere into space, spreading it across the battlefield directly in the path of two crossing beams of Belthin fire. As everyone aboard the *Roosevelt* held their collective breath, pulsing blue-green tore across a shimmer of golden-red, and suddenly, the void came alive with the sound of heaven.

It was some time later when a somewhat sheepish, but mostly relieved, gathering of Belthins met with Valance once more aboard the *Roosevelt*. The captain's gambit had paid off with only one shot having to be fired, a factor relieving him to no end.

"Wise you are, yes," asked DixWix. "Stronger we become, hum? Ashamed we must be, no?"

"Don't be too hard on yourself, Defulator," answered Valance sympathetically. "Humanity knows a little bit about being stubborn. Get an Earth history book and look up Antietam. You'll realize the whole universe has to get past its growing pains before it can get anywhere."

"Still," added an equally sheepish looking Kleb, "you were here to guide, eh? To correct and instruct, to show the way. Glad we must be to welcome the Confederation into our system."

It had been another triumph for the *Roosevelt*, of that there was no doubt. When the beams from the opposing sides had crossed within the artificial atmosphere, for the first time the Belthins had been able to hear their differing musics combined. As Valance had hoped, the staid, precise measure of the Belthis Prime had blended sonorously with the wilder, syncopated beat of the Contingent.

"To think we could not recognize such a possibility for ourselves, hum? It is humbling, no?"

"A humble DixWix," mused Kleb, "to bring about such a thing makes me believe the Confederation is truly a magnificent gathering from which much can be gained by all, eh?"

And, as such self-congratulatory chatter continued, Rocky decided he was most likely no longer needed. His presence had been ordered in case either of the Belthin contingents wanted to meet any of the crew members responsible for filling the deep ebony with the wondrous sound of their combining weaponry. With it clear they were only interested in reforming their system under a united banner and making certain it was one that fell under the protective arm of the Confederation, the gunnery officer figured he could slip away with no one becoming concerned.

True, there was a fine open bar at the gathering, but Rocky had decided sometime earlier that drinking with officers was a good way to end up doing something less than brilliant, and he was partial to hanging onto what little braid he had earned over the years. Besides, he also wanted to open the top button of his dress blue's collar and that freedom was worth giving up any amount of liquor.

Finding his buddy Noodles waiting for him in the hallway, he said;

"Got nuthin' better to do?"

"Than be seen with you? Always. But, I knew you'd sneak out as soon as you could and," the machinist paused as he reached behind his back, "I figured you might be partial to a bit of libation..."

As he presented a flask he had pulled from his hip pocket, Rocky tore open the top two buttons of his uniform, accepting the offered drink with the gratitude of a pig lost in the desert who suddenly stumbled across a wallow. Taking a massive slug, he wiped his mouth with his sleeve, handing the container back to his pal as he said;

"And so, the *Roosevelt* survives again."

"We have, I must admit, in our short stretch, seen some very interesting things." Taking his own, somewhat less vigorous slug from the flask, the machinist pursed his lips, then added;

"I'm reminded of what Debussy said, 'music is the arithmetic of sounds as optics is the geometry of light.'"

Rocky stared at his friend for a moment, then asked;

"What the hell is that supposed to mean?"

Noodles considered his friend's question for a moment, then answered honestly;

"I don't know. It just seemed appropriate."

"God," said Rocky, taking the flask back from his pal, "I hate it when you smart types drink."

The two buddies smiled at one another, and then several of their shipmates found them, coming forward to congratulate the gunnery officer on his aim, and the conversation changed to different things as the mighty E.A.S. *Roosevelt* quietly drifted through the deep ebony, her hull still tingling slightly from the symphony of battle.

An extended mission into the unexplored reaches of space will require leaving behind a lot of things, some of them treasured and dearly missed, others not so much. So it seems reasonable to hope such a voyage should, at the very least, free one from the endless agony of that Sisyphean suburban chore known as...

LAWN CARE

"How many times do I have to tell you? The right tool for the right job."

Montgomery Scott

"WELL," DECLARED CAPTAIN ALEXANDER BENJAMIN VALANCE IN A SAD and weary tone, "not to question the negotiation skills of our beloved Confederation's bigwigs, but that was sure a waste."

There were none in the crew of the Earth Alliance Ship *Roosevelt*, trudging their way back to their shuttle craft across one of the strangest landscapes any of them had ever beheld, who would have disagreed with their commanding officer at that moment.

"Truer words may never have been spoken, captain."

There were none present who were ready to argue with Rocky, officially known to one and all as Chief Gunnery Officer Rockland Vespucci, either. As far as the lot of them were concerned, the mission they had just completed had to be the biggest waste of time in which their noble ship had been involved since they had ordered into the Great Spiral Sargasso in search of proof that ancient astronauts had once visited the Earth. At least there they had found a two-mile-in-diameter face carved into a mountainside on one world which bore a bizarrely carved face above an inscription which translated roughly to "Bingledoopwoodie Was Here," which anyone would admit was certainly good for at least a chuckle. Coupling that with the fact that photos of the site had begun to provide a remarkably steady income for the crew's party fund, and there was no question in their minds as to the winner of Stupidest *Roosevelt* Mission Ever.

"I will admit," said Machinist First Mate Li Qui Kon, more familiarly known to his shipmates and robotics enthusiasts everywhere as Noodles, "I have had more fun untangling lo mein noodles."

Nothing about making planetfall on Hoc'toc 7 could be regarded as even slightly amusing, let alone profitable. The Confederation of Planets had granted entry to their ever-expanding league to the Hoc'tocs after the race had agreed to donate an entire planet to the inter-galactic organization's joint defense fund.

"I'm thinking it might be more fun to tangle lo mein noodles up than visit places like this."

The big enticement, of course, had been the fact that Hoc'toc 7 was simply lousy with Pibtilium, the usually incredibly rare element necessary for the fueling of protonic engines. Gifting the Confederation with this world had skipped the Hoc'tocs ahead to full membership in record time.

"Well, Mr. Michaels," Valance responded to his science officer, "let's just get back to the ship and make our report. Then we can find out what our next glamor assignment is."

What had seemed at the time to be a righteously generous offer had (as, of course, most righteously generous offers do eventually) proved to be just another gussied-up scam. Oh, this is not to say that the Pibtilium was not there. If the much sought-after element were not present, and in at least roughly the quantities suggested by the Hoc'toc supreme council, the deal would have, as you might expect, been shattered. No, Hoc'toc 7 was— exactly as advertised—simply lousy with the stuff. But, the cold hard of things was that it was lousy with it in the lousiest manner possible.

"You're the boss, sir."

Deep space probes had confirmed for Confederation ships that there had to be enough Pibtilium to power a thousand fleets for possibly an equal amount of years stored within the planet. Greed always being the least helpful of bargaining tools, those closing the deal had allowed dollar signs to cloud their judgment, and Hoc'toc had made its way into the Confederation more easily, with more speed, than any previous planet, and by actually giving less of themselves than anyone else, either.

As Mac Michaels, science officer for the Roosevelt, fed the proper sequence into the shuttle's lock so the landing party could go aboard, he shook his head sadly over how thoroughly the Confederation had been foxed

LAWN CARE - C.J. Henderson 125

by the Hoc'tocs. He was fascinated by the planet. In many ways it possessed a number of unusual properties which made him wish for more time to study the place thoroughly. The odd dispersion of Pibtilium throughout its upper crust and mantle was unique among all known worlds. But, in many ways, it was not the oddest thing about the planet by far.

"Okay, swabbies," announced Michaels, making as grand a bow as he could while confined within his landing suit, "enter, one and all, and don't forget to wipe your boots."

No, the oddest thing about Hoc'toc 7 was its ground cover. The landing party had needed their suits because the planet's atmosphere was a reeking mix of methane and atomized elements which was hostile to all but the toughest life forms. In fact, the planet only had one complex life form, a metallic grass that covered every dry inch of the place. How it might have developed was anyone's guess. How it had come to dominate the planet, however, was far more easily deduced.

A quick analysis of several blades of the plant revealed it to possess a tenacious anchoring system. Its roots seemed capable of not only keeping it in place despite the most severe storms or flooding imaginable, but of burrowing to whatever depth was required to find whatever it needed in the way of nutrients. And, although a series of independent plants, each with its own seeds, and not a vining system such as Earth's notorious kudzu, its roots were fully capable of sharing nourishment from one plant to another— whether inches apart or miles.

Which was why Michaels had made his "boot wiping" comment. Their inspection of Hoc'toc 7, while primarily a search for the easiest way to retrieve its Pibtilium, was still as complete and thorough as any other initial landing. There was no doubt from the evidence uncovered that the planet, at some time in its distant past, while it may have never hosted any form of animal life whatsoever—not even insects—it had at one time been home to a thriving variety of plant life. All of it a bizarre combination of mineral-based growths and other exotics, but growing things nonetheless. Somewhere along the line, however, the iron verdure had won out over all its neighbors, turning the entire planet into one vast lawn on shimmering stalks of steel.

The science officer was taking no chances with even the slightest trace of the overwhelming grass getting off-planet. His studies, brief as they might have been, had revealed that as destructively final as the plant's advancement had been on Hoc'toc 7, its introduction into an oxygen-rich atmosphere would exacerbate its spread exponentially. Each crew

Everything's Better With Monkeys

member, as they entered, was directed into the decontamination shower which rinsed their suits in an acidic wash, fried them at a temperature hostile to any life form, as well as seven other protocols guaranteed to destroy any microbe, germ or alien bit of matter present. It was, of course, standard operating procedure for such landings.

And, if only the equipment had been designed to handle seeds, at least, seeds that managed to wedge themselves in between two layers of fabric that had become worn to the point where they would allow something that small to adhere... well... the life of the *Roosevelt*'s crew would have been much easier over the days that followed.

"What do you mean, we have grass growing in the hanger?"

Captain Valance was not overly amused at what he thought was his chief machinist's sudden odd manifestation of humor. When Noodles assured the captain he was only relaying the message sent by Security Chief DiVico, Valance shrugged, muttering his increasing familiar mantra, "What now," as he handed off control of the com to the pilot on duty, indicated to his science officer that they were needed elsewhere, and then followed the machinist down to the docking bay. Once there, the captain quickly saw "what" it was that was occupying his current "now."

"Don't bother to explain," said Valance as he entered the hanger, his head turning toward the large, obviously out-of-place patch of metallic grass growing along the wall. "Just tell me what's going to be done about it."

"Good question, sir," answered DiVico. "So far we've established the obvious. It is the same life form you and the others encountered on Hoc'toc 7 two days ago. Somehow a seed or spore or whatever got through the shuttle's decontamination process. You'll note the grass is spreading from the third suit hanging on the wall... that's our culprit. The suit is rooted to the wall, the grass is spreading downward from there, along the wall in both directions and out into the bay."

Valance stared, his head tilted, his mind blank—at least, blank as far as coming up with any possible solutions was concerned. Raising one arm, he pointed toward the invading lawn, moved one finger back and forth a few inches, then shrugged in a despairing manner, asking;

"Well, what have you tried so far?"

"Not much," admitted DiVico. "The maintenance crew that discovered it reported that first they simply tried pulling it out, but apparently the stuff

LAWN CARE - C.J. Henderson   127

cuts like razor wire. Sliced right through their work gloves. After that they tried twirling it up into a ball, like spaghetti... you know... so they could yank it out, but they couldn't get all of it."

"Meaning the roots are deep," asked Michaels, "or tenacious?"

"Looks like both."

"Did they try anything else?"

"They whipped up the most poisonous bio-cocktail they could from what we have on board, but that didn't do any good, either." Michaels merely nodded as DiVico explained, "the stuff doesn't have a bit of familiar structure to it. Something that would kill any living thing on Earth... this crap doesn't even recognize. In fact, the maintenance crew thinks it might have actually have found it refreshing."

Valance and his officers stared at the shimmering stand of metal blades in silence, none of them quite knowing what to do next. After an agonizingly long handful of seconds, the captain sighed, then announced;

"As we all know, the earmark of good leadership is the ability to comfortably delegate authority. Mac, you're the best science officer in the fleet. And Kevin, you know more about blowing things up and burning them down than anyone else for ten thousand light years in any direction. This is now, officially, your problem, gentlemen. Solve it."

After Valance departed, the two officers gave each other the time honored look of Navy men non-verbally asking one another why they stay in the service, then finally hunkered down and attempted to do as they had been ordered. Noodles attempted to make a suggestion, but the two senior crewmen dismissed him, their minds a'swirl with ideas on how to put an end to their problem.

And, after a while the two dove in to work, Michaels setting his staff to studying the invader, probing its basic structure for genetic weaknesses, DiVico launching himself into an ever-escalating series of animated and violent attacks, going after the field of sword blades with a truly brobding-nagian vengeance. Over the next few days, despite displays of energy and enthusiasm which would have impressed even Sisyphus, neither officer found they had much to show for their efforts.

Or at least, not much positive.

"What do you mean, it's *worse?*"

"Sorry, Captain," answered Michaels. "We just haven't been able to come up with anything effective."

"How does that make things 'worse?'"

Everything's Better With Monkeys

"That could be my fault, sir," offered DiVico. When Valance merely stood by and waited for the security chief to hang himself, DiVico cleared his throat, then added;

"It seems this crap is pretty tenacious. My attacks on it appear to have triggered its defense mechanisms."

"Defense mechanisms?" The captain offered the phrase back to DiVico as a question. One the intelligence officer answered by explaining;

"It seems when this stuff feels threatened, it starts pumping out more seeds."

"We tried having the jumbo haz-vacs ready, sir," interjected Michaels, "and they did clear all the seeds out of the air..."

"But—" suggested Valance, to which Michaels added;

"Yes... 'but,' the seeds didn't care. They just rooted inside their new environments—"

"Yes, and now all our haz-vacs look like putting greens."

All heads turned toward Noodles, all eyes glaring in a manner suggesting that humor was not exactly what anyone was looking for in the way of assistance at the moment. When the machinist tried to actually make a suggestion, however, he was dismissed, a more than slightly worried Valance turning his attention back to the problem at hand.

"So, brain trust, tell me, just how bad is this mess?"

"We don't actually know, sir," answered Michaels honestly. "We've had some success in getting rid of the surface growth, but that's not the problem. It's the roots."

"Apparently, unless you get every single microbe of the damn things," offered DiVico, "they just grow back stronger."

"And how far have they grown?"

"If our estimations are correct, sir," answered Michaels, "there appears to be intrusion in less than five percent of the ships surface area." As Valance eyed his science officer with his best might-I-have-the-rest-of-it glare, Michaels added;

"But, that's already thrown multiple systems into havoc. You see, the roots turn whatever they come in contact with into nutrients. Communications wiring has disappeared, waste removal timing has already been compromised, protonic monitoring routes have vanished—"

"Meaning...?"

"Meaning, sir... we have maybe five days before the *Roosevelt* is too crippled to continue onward safely. And, with some scanning functions

LAWN CARE - C.J. Henderson

already compromised, we can't even launch shuttles or life pods for fear of spreading the contamination."

The captain stared at his science officer for a moment, then turned his attention back to the ever-spreading sea of metallic blades stretched out before him. Forcing himself to remain calm, Valance growled in a low tone;

"Gentlemen, get this crap off my ship. I don't care how you do it. I don't care what it costs. Just get it done. After all this crew has been through, I do not intend to allow the lot of us to be *mulched* to death!"

And, to be fair, the officers so charged did everything they could think of to do as ordered. The first thing they attempted was a sort of radioactive weed killer. This did indeed have some minor effect on those segments of root brought to the *Roosevelt*'s main lab, but the dosage needed to achieve complete success was so incredibly high that the crew would have ended up dying screaming as their skin boiled from their bodies before enough of the toxin could be pumped through the ship to remove the problem.

DiVico stepped up to the plate next with a plan to run electrical current through the infected areas to simply fry the life out of the lawn from hell. Much like the U-235 highball tried previously, though, the amount of damage the random blasts of electricity caused to the areas surrounding the grass was so much greater than that done by the grass itself that the "cure" could not be continued.

Yes, it was argued that the electrical attacks were better than nothing, and that while they did harm the ship to a certain extent they could be kept from killing the crew. This was a definite plus, of course, but sadly not enough of one. It was all too easily calculated that considering to which parts of the ship the lawn had spread, sooner or later the cure was going to come up against this or that bit of mechanics the crew needed to survive. Half a cure not being any better in even the slightest than none, the officers went wearily back to the drawing board.

One of the more promising avenues of attack to come out of the labs was a plan to rust the invading foliage. The science team that proposed this answer were able to induce a level of corrosion (oxidation not being the proper word since oxygen had no real effect on the grass except, perhaps, to make it grow more lushly) in the lawn that was truly impressive. Unfortunately, the deterioration they managed to engender affected the surface area of the plants only. Worse yet, the roots, sensing disaster ahead, went into a feeding frenzy, stretching their will far and wide. As one might imagine, the rusting process was shown the door rather quickly.

Everything's Better With Monkeys

As were other ideas.

Scores of further attempts were made, all of them equally spectacular failures. Acid sprays were tried, outer hull paint driers were employed, freezing was attempted along with fifty-six more even less intelligent ideas, but to no avail. Indeed, the moment had come where DiVico was ready to simply pull his side arm and try blasting the lawn into submission, while Michaels was thinking he might have better luck just jumping up and down on the stuff, or attempting to poison it with salt water by simply crying over it, when a cooler head prevailed.

"Excuse me, sirs, but have you had any luck yet?"

Both officers turned at the sound of Noodles' voice. When their twin expressions of Lovecraftian hopelessness gave him all the answer he needed, the machinist explained;

"I had an idea I wanted to run by you when this all first started, but nobody seemed to want to listen, so..."

"My apologies for the both of us," answered DiVico, his trigger finger itching mightily as a tiny voice within his head continued to urge him toward attempting to murder the lawn. "We really thought we could handle this. And..."

"And," said Michaels, not willing to allow his partner-in-absurdity to take all the blame, "we might have gotten a bit full of ourselves. Thus endangering the entire ship and all its crew. Including, of course, the three of us. And, why... the kitchen staff, too. And those fellows down in—"

As DiVico and Noodles both stared at the science officer, their expressions caught halfway between befuddlement and there-but-for-the-grace-of-some-higher-power-go-I, Michaels caught hold of himself, then said;

"Apparently I'm a bit tired. All right, swabbie... what have you got for us?"

"Well, being Chinese, my first instinct with any problem is to try and find the natural solution, the ying to the yang—you know. When I saw that first patch of grass, I thought to myself, what do you do with grass? Now, I'll admit, the first thing I thought of was 'cut it,' but as I reviewed in my head all the ways one could do that, I said, hey, why not unleash the stuff's natural predator on it?"

"But, I mean," answered Michaels, playing devil's advocate in the sincerest hope he would be quickly shown the error of his ways, "you were on Hoc'toc 7 with us... the stuff has no natural enemies. Animal, insect, nothing. It took over the whole damned planet."

"Right," agreed Noodles. "But grass has natural enemies on other planets. Like Earth. Now, I'm not saying that a terran solution would work

LAWN CARE - C.J. Henderson

131

here... this is some pretty tough grass. But, as Kempler Towstik, the patron saint of machinists once said, 'when the going gets tough, the smart fellow builds something to make is go smoothly again."

And, as DiVico and Michaels both scratched their heads, wondering if there really was such a fellow as Kempler Towstik, or if the first mate was simply having some sport with them, the machinist went out into the hall and then returned, a rope trailing from his left hand. Giving it a tug, he then began moving forward again, saying;

"Sirs, I give you Boltsy."

As the officers watched, a surprising light-treading robot ambled into the hanger. It was large, but did not stand taller than those present due to the fact that its locomotion was dependent on a four-legged stance. As Noodles and his creation moved forward, DiVico pointed, saying;

"It's a... a cow."

There was no denying the obviousness of the security man's statement. Noodles had indeed, with the help of his fellow tool jockeys, built a bovine bio-mech. True, it had taken a bit of convincing to get a number of his fellow machinists to put aside their preparations for the up-coming Sexy Robot-Building Competition. But, when he had reminded them that if they were all dead the competition would most likely be pointless, they had suddenly decided that pitching in for the greater good might not be that bad an idea.

"Boltsy's more than just a cow."

"Okay, it's a—"

"She," corrected Noodles.

"She?" When DiVico's response echoed through the hanger, Michaels threw in—

"He, she, him, her, toe-may-toe, toe-mott-toe, pardon my French, but at this stage of the game, who really gives a galactic crap?" Wiping at the sweat pouring off his forehead, the science officer asked the million dollar question;

"Does 'she' work?"

"Tested her on a patch that sprouted in the men's bathroom in Sector 18. Seemed pretty cleaned out. But, checking the results is much more your department, sir... so I..."

Noodles' reply was cut short as Boltsy spotted the substantial spread of grass in the hanger beyond and began to amble forward on her own. Being dragged along by his latest creation, the machinist said;

"She's got sensors attuned to the molecular structure of our stowaways. She should be able to find every single blade and munch it out of existence."

"Yeah, swell," responded DiVico, "but what about the roots? That's the real problem. If—"

And, before the security chief could continue or Noodles could attempt to explain, Boltsy reached the first stand of rogue lawn and bent her head slightly forward while emitting a slightly high-pitched whirring sound. As the two officers looked on the high tech Holstein opened her mouth, allowing the deployment of a tongue elongated to an incredible length. The mechanical muscle, more drill than scoop, stabbed its way into the center of a grass cluster and then bored inward. After only the passage of several seconds, the tongue reversed itself, jerking the entire plant structure free from the flooring. As the pair of officers stared in startled delight, Michaels forced himself to remain objective as he asked;

"Mr. DiVico is right, Noodles. Can it... does it get the entire root system? I mean, even if it doesn't, this will certainly help slow the advance... but..."

"Don't know for certain, sir," answered the first mate honestly. "But the spot we cleaned out before coming down here was Sector 18, B Level, Deck 5. If you were to have some of your people scan the area to see if Boltsy did a good job, you could monitor our progress here, and—"

"Way ahead of you," shouted DiVico, heading for the door. "I'll get on surveying 18-B-5. You fellows take care of this."

Which they did. Boltsy moved from spot to spot, clearing one patch of lawn after another, leaving not a seed or random molecule behind. In less that ten minutes, DiVico had radioed the pair with the news, 18-B-5 was absolutely, one hundred percent clean and ready for repairs. Suffering from lack of sleep, the bags under his eyes large enough to carry a family's worth of groceries, Michaels never-the-less leaped into the air and clicked his heels together, blindly happy to be able to report that once more the *Roosevelt* had somehow managed to dodge complete and utter destruction in yet another randomly insane manner. In fact, he was just about to contact the captain with his Best-News-Flash-of-the-Day when a loud clanging noise shattered the calm of the hanger. As the science officer whirled around in Boltsy's direction, fearing the worse, Noodles held up a hand, explaining;

"Don't worry, sir, it was just Boltsy, ah... relieving herself."

As Michaels scanned the area, he saw a shiny disc, roughly the size of Swedish dinner plate, gyrating to a settled position directly behind Boltsy.

LAWN CARE - C.J. Henderson

"She can't just eat the plants up and store it all," continued the first mate. "It's got to come out sooner or later. We just made certain that whatever she eats gets melted then compressed. That way whatever seeds she swallows can't root within her, or re-root once they're, you know... back outside."

Michaels looked over the inter-galactic Guernsey, as well as her highly-compressed, chrome cow pie, and sat down on the deck, crying and laughing at the same time. A part of his mind felt sheepish as it realized the first mate had been trying to tell him his idea since the beginning. A larger part dismissed the thought, wanting to revel in the fact that the danger was passed. The science officer would make certain Valance knew it was Noodles who had saved the day. For that moment, he simply wanted to watch the most wonderful cow the universe had ever known chew its cud in contented peace.

And chew she did. As the next few days passed and Boltsy wandered the ship, clearing the foliage from each and every system, Michaels learned a great deal more about their momentary enemy. The biggest thing he discovered was that it had been human fear and hostility which had raised the grass's defense mechanisms. Boltsy, simply walking up and feeding, gave off no signals for the lawn to receive. And, outside of having to repair the hundreds of areas of damage the lawn had caused to the ship (as well as constantly needing to pick up their secret weapon's "droppings") the crew found itself out of danger and care free. In four days, ten hours, and seventeen minutes, Boltsy cleared the entire ship from stem to stern. Not a fragment or filament of grass remained behind. And, whereas that was a situation calling for much joy on the part to the boys and girls of the *Roosevelt*, there was one crew member who found themselves with little to celebrate at that moment.

"Jeez-it, Noodles," asked Rocky, perplexed by his pal's long face, "what's bitin' you? Commendation, pay up-grade, a nice letter sent back to you maw tellin' her what a crackerjack little sailor boy you are... how could life be any better?"

"Oh, I know," the machinist admitted. Leaning back from the dinner table, he stared at the slice of pork chop dangling from his fork and said, "I'm just worried about Boltsy."

"What do you mean," asked Michaels.

Everything's Better With Monkeys

"Well, I know this is kind of goofy, I mean, she can't get hungry, it's not like she's going to start chewing on the ship or something, but... well... she's got nothing to do now. I mean, she just keeps wandering the decks, looking for grass--"

"I know," agreed DiVico, setting down his own fork. "I have to admit, her mooing sounds kinda sad these days."

"Yeah, what's up with that," asked Rocky. "Makin' the damn thing 'moo?' I mean—"

"You're going to do a job," answered the machinist, "you should do it right."

And then, as Captain Valance happened to walk by at the perfect moment, Michaels said, to no one in particular, "you know, you're absolutely right." Standing, the science officer hailed their commander, asking for a moment. When Valance nodded and stepped over to the table, Michaels said;

"Sir, might we have a word about Boltsy?"

"What's the problem, gentlemen?"

"No problem, sir, more like a concern. Our first mate here is fretting over Boltsy's fate." As the captain squinted, just slightly, signifying that he might need a bit more to go on, Michaels added;

"She's got nothing to do now. *And—*" the science officer hurried into his next sentence, running over any chance Valance might have to suggested simply shutting the robot off and sticking it in a closet, "since she basically saved all out lives and the ship and all... I was thinking we might be able to give her a reward?"

"A reward..." responded the captain, half his mind wishing he could roll his eyes at the insanity of his crew, the other half wishing he had thought of the idea himself. "And just what kind of reward did you have in mind, Mr. Michaels?"

Two days later, the landing party that had performed the initial scouting of Hoc'toc 7 was on the planet's surface once more, with a single addition.

"She looks happy, doesn't she," asked Noodles as he watched Boltsy moving through the endless see of metallic grass, her tongue whirring contentedly.

"Little buddy," Rocky radioed through his helmet mic, "You are, officially, as weird as they come."

LAWN CARE - C.J. Henderson

The team lingered, half-watching the bio-mech bovine amble her way across the field, half-watching the distant horizon. Deciding to give themselves a treat, the crew had planned their landing so as to be able to arrive just before nightfall. Michaels had assured everyone that an atmosphere as filled with pollutants as that of Hoc'toc 7 would have the most spectacular sunsets in the galaxy. And, as the Hoc'tocian sun began to drift toward the horizon, all assembled had to admit he had been correct. As they stared, none could speak due to the overwhelming majesty of the skyful of dazzling streaks of red, purple, blue, green, gold and a dozen other colors all battling one another to dominate the sky.

Minute by minute, the sailors stood speechless, awed by the incomparable majesty of the breathtaking display, until suddenly their cocoon of silence was shattered by—

Thump!

"What the hell was that?"

"Just what I was waiting for, captain." As all turned, they saw Michaels applying a scanner to one of Boltsy's cow pies. As he punched in the proper sequence for analysis, Valance asked;

"Might I inquire?"

"Oh, yes sir," answered the science officer, a smile passing across his face. "I must admit I made the suggestion about the sunset because I had an idea, and I wanted to be able to test it out without getting anyone's hopes up."

"Get our hopes up over what?"

"Over what I think your little invention is going to do for the Confederation, Noodles, my boy." Michaels waited another moment, then suddenly let out a whoop as he shouted;

"We did it, sir. We've foxed the foxes!"

"Good to know," answered Valance, not even half-pretending to understand his science officer's outburst. "Any foxes in particular?"

"Yes, sir... the Hoc'tocs, sir. They gave us this dump because it was worthless to them. The Pibtilium we wanted was so finely defused through the soil that extraction would be too expensive to make it worthwhile."

"But..."

"But," answered Michaels, checking his data one last time, "as I'm sure you've guessed, the grass, it can live on any metal, including Pibtilium. Which means..."

"Which means," shouted Rocky, "that every time ol' Boltsy here takes a dump, the Confederation gets a pure lump of protonic go-go juice!"

Everything's Better With Monkeys

There was, of course, much laughing and cheering among the members of the small band as Michaels' data proved out his theory. Hoc'toc 7 was about to become one of the most important holdings of the entire Confederation of Planets. Before the week was out, it would be ringed with cruisers, put in place to protect such a valuable piece of real estate.

And, before the month was out, it would be covered with a herd of Boltsies, all of them chewing their mechanical cuds and pooping out pies of pure Pibtilium to a chorus of the most contented "moos" ever heard.

Another new world to contact. Friend or foe? Welcoming committee or armed perimeter? Will charm and honesty break through or will deception and muscle be required? Once again it falls to the Roosevelt and her crew to lead the way and, if necessary, take the lumps.

ARE WE NOW SMITTEN?

"So in the Libyan fable it is told
That once an eagle, stricken with a dart,
Said, when he saw the fashion of the shaft,
'With our own feathers, not by others' hands,
Are we now smitten.'"

Aeschylus

10,361 STANDARD CONFEDERATION YEARS AGO

As crashes go, this one had been what the first major word-enthusiasts had meant when they coined the term "spectacular." Attempting to flee a natural cataclysm engulfing their entire star system, the ark transport evacuating the only surviving members of the Aowen race escaped the boundaries of their known space. Well...almost.

The collision of their primary sun with some unknown anomaly careening through their sector of the universe had thrown that star into their system's secondary sun—a vastly smaller white which had possessed just enough gravity to orbit, rather than be absorbed by, their primary. The event caused both stars to explode with an astoundingly, monstrously devastating fury.

The results of which were, as has been quite severely telegraphed at this point in our narrative, most spectacular.

The Aowen had boarded their best and brightest in the hopes they might somehow finding refuge in the great unknown beyond their doomed system. Only a few hundred thousand miles from what had been projected would be the full extent of the raging explosion's fury, the last of its terrible energies had engulfed the ark. The damage had been minor. But sadly, slamming against an experimental ship—one cobbled together at the last minute when doom had been realized as eminent—minor had proved sufficient.

The great ship had spun out of control, rocketing helplessly through the vast ebony of space, the surviving Aowen unable to affect even the slightest control on its direction in any manner. Eventually snagged by the gravity of a desert world, the ship was ruthlessly dragged down and smashed against the barren planet with unbelievable force. Of the some three million beings that had marched into the ark, only five were still functioning when the smoke had cleared.

Stranded, left without knowledge of where they were, or what to do next, the quintet of survivors took stock of their situation, and then got on with the Herculean task of rebuilding a civilization. Nobly, heroically, recreating what they could of the past as best as possible.

In their own image.

NOW

"Very well, Mr. Vespucci," ordered Captain Alexander Benjamin Valance in his standard calm-and-formal tone, "let's give this particular look-at-us, we're-so-evolved crowd a taste of how we do things back in the Confederation's end of the Milky Way."

His fingers already toggling the relays necessary to release the locks of the Earth Alliance Ship Roosevelt's main battery, the gunnery officer responded;

"Aye, sir—eight away. Paycheck assurance on six."

"I'll take a piece of that action."

Before either he, or the ever-ready-to-give-odds pilot Drew Cass, had even finished speaking, the gunner had released two, four-cannon salvos. So quickly had the missiles been sent slamming outward toward the pirates the Earth ship had been asked to intercept, that the majority of their targets found it impossible to react. Rocky, as Chief Gunnery Officer Rockland Vespucci was known to most, had not only zeroed the half-dozen hits he had predicted, but had also scored crippling shots on the remaining pair. In mere seconds, the *Roosevelt* had obliterated the pirate pack which had been causing no small amount of havoc amongst some of the more remote members of the ever-burgeoning, Earth-centric Confederation of Planets.

"Move us in, Mr. Cass. Leave us drift in a little closer on these low-rent buccaneers. Scanners to the ready, Mr. Michaels...I'm willing to wager you know what has me curious."

ARE WE NOW SMITTEN - C.J. Henderson 139

With practiced ease, the *Roosevelt's* hottest pilot moved the massive ship toward the devastated attack field while its science officer began his analysis. Neither the flaming pirate ships—the last of their oxygen burning away silently into the vacuum of space—nor their panicked, retreating brethren were the goal of the Confederation's flag ship, however. No, Valance—like everyone else aboard the Earth destroyer—was far more curious about what the raiders had been transporting. Exactly what cargo might be so fabulous as to draw them out in such massed force?

The unknown point which had the crew ready to die like felines was that up until then, the pirate squad had usually not sent out more than one or two of its ships at a time. Indeed, never before had they risked more than three of their vessels on a single operation. Thus, it had been the sighting of their entire fleet on the move which had worried the nearest star system so greatly, certain the rogues must be planning something tremendous. Upon intercepting the pirates, though, the *Roosevelt's* command and crew had been surprised to discover the cosmic-age buccaneers were already in possession of some prize—an assembly of massive, nay brobdingnagian, irregular shapes, the total mass of which would equal more than a half dozen standard planets.

"What in the flamin' fires of Rome were those goofballs up to," muttered Rocky, just loud enough for his console mic to pick up and transmit. Wondering the same thing, much to the gunner's embarrassment, Valance responded;

"Good question, Mr. Vespucci. Mr. Cass—"

"Aye, sir?"

"You can steer us in closer. As long as our opponents have so wisely chosen to desert the field of battle, abandoning whatever the hell it is they were dragging along, let's take it all the way." Turning toward the science station of the bridge, he added;

"As soon as we're in range, Mac, get us some readings and let's see what it was they were trying to move."

"Must be something important," mused DiVico, head of the *Roosevelt's* security force. "If our intel is correct, they exposed their entire fleet to secure whatever that is out there. Pretty big gamble. Especially considering they ended up wrecked and splattered over it."

"This is the rim," offered Valance. "We're a long way from everything known-to-anyone out here. My guess is they send out long-range probes, found something of interest—"

"Or value..."

"Well yes, that too, I suppose," agreed the captain with a grin, "and when they found, apparently a *lot* of something fitting at least one of those categories, they came out to secure whatever it was before anyone else could."

"Does make you wonder," added communication's officer Feng, "if it really was worth it. I mean, they threw away their entire operation. Of course, whatever that is out there, as you said, there certainly is a lot of it."

And then, before anyone could comment to the effect that the young woman might be well advised to repeat herself, Michaels looked up from his screens and turned to Valance. A grin on his normally somber face, he said;

"Captain, out of all the things this command has asked you to believe, I guarantee, you are not going to believe this one."

"Ice? Oh, by the blue suede shoes of the King, you gotta be feedin' me a commode sandwich."

"I swear, Rocky," answered his friend Noodles—a nickname of which the machinist first mate's loving mother, who named him Li Qui Kon several decades earlier, thoroughly detested, "they were ice pirates."

"Man, it but truly staggers the imagination."

"That it certainly does," said Mac Michaels, joining the two from a side passage. "I mean, honestly, they possessed vehicles capable of interstellar travel. Their level of science contained an understanding of nuclear fission, cold fusion, Heigliean structure...and yet the morons didn't realize you can make all the water you want by simply combining oxygen and hydrogen?"

"Isn't hydrogen the most plentiful element in the universe," asked Rocky, his tone pure sarcasm.

"I guess pirates don't do all that well in science class."

"Maybe guys that don't do well in science just naturally gravitate toward the pillage-and-loot end of the job market."

"Such a thing wouldn't be so sad," added Noodles, as the three of them marched along the corridor to the captain's briefing room, "except this is what, the third time we've run into beings who make their living essentially by stealing water?"

"I think it's sadder that they can actually *make* a living stealing water," said Michaels with a shrug. "I mean, when you think about it, should we be considering the pirates all that dumb? After all, is it really all that stupid to steal ice when you have people even dumber who are willing to pay for it?"

"And that, children of all ages," chided Rocky as he punched Michaels lightly on the shoulder, "is why he's the science office and we gotta work for a livin'."

"You'd never catch an artificial intelligence doing something so stupid."

"Oh my God," laughed the gunnery officer, "Noodles, enough with the robots already. Can you not be part of a conversation for more than five minutes without bringing up robots and how wonderful they are?"

Whether or not the machinist could chatter with others for longer than three hundred standard seconds without steering its direction toward the all-around superiority of mechanical life forms was a question which would have to be answered later. At that moment the trio's conversation was forced to an abrupt ending as they had arrived at Valance's ready room. Entering, they found not only the captain, but Security Chief DiVico and Communications Officer Feng as well.

"Gentlemen, I have an assignment for the five of you. We're stuck in this quadrant for the moment—command wants us to take care of that damn ice the pirates were hauling. It's been determined that it will pose a definite menace to navigation if we just let it float around out here."

"And you'd like us to cube it for the officer's lounge...sir?"

"If I can't think of anything better, Vespucci, I might send you out with a hammer and bucket to take care of things at that," answered Valance. "But, Michaels and Feng here have turned up something I believe might be of interest to the Confederation." At a nod from the captain, the science officer said;

"As you might realize, our current position has us at one of the extreme boundaries of not only Confederation space, but known space as well. Earlier, while we were still scanning for possible pirate transmissions, Lt. Feng picked up some...why don't you explain, Lieutenant?"

"There is a steady hum of beam chatter coming from a point about a quarter-light year further out. It's constant, and although it doesn't match any language I've ever dealt with before, it is confabulationally familiar."

"Meanin' what?"

"Meaning," answered Noodles, glaring at his pal, "that it falls into what we would think of as patterns of conversation."

"First contact, sir?"

"Seems likely, Mr. DiVico," answered the captain. "So, while the *Roosevelt* stays here to get those damn planet-sized ice pops ready for transport and destruction, you five will take a shuttle to the source of the chatter and see who's there. Vespucci, you'll pilot and man the arms, Kon, general functions. Everyone else, you know your skills. Go see if there's even more life in the universe than the guide books mention."

"Protocols, sir?"

"Observe, stay out of sight, report back without dying. Simple enough, Mr. DiVico?"

"My cat could handle it, sir."

"Your cat's smarter than you are," chided Rocky. As the security man turned to comment, Feng offered;

"It is a very smart cat, Kevin."

Before more could be said, Valance dismissed the sailors. As the quintet left the briefing room, heading for the third-level hanger bay, Rocky teased;

"So, are we pickin' up the cat on our way there, or what?"

As humorous as the others, including DiVico, found the comment, it would not be that long before they would all be wishing the captain had sent a few more bodies along. Even the cat's.

It was only four standard hours later when Noodles, Michaels, DiVico, and Feng found themselves standing on the surface of Unknown World 69-AQ8, the five-mooned planet they had been charged with investigating. The deep-space noise the communications officer had come across had been easy enough to follow back to its source. Along the way, Feng and Michaels had agreed that they were probably not in a first-contact situation. Despite the conversational-specific flow to the unknown language, it was streamed with such an utter lack of anything resembling personality or individuality, that the heavy money was riding on some something-or-other along the order of either an unmanned probe or an ancient installation which was still transmitting in an as-yet-unknown alien tongue.

The four had worn containment suits as they exited out onto the planet's surface, Michaels not liking the atmosphere mix quite enough to trust it despite its high oxygen content. The desert world also possessed a highly reflective surface, an extremely hot sun, as well as several other factors that made him decide in opting for as much personal protection as possible. Once the quartet had moved their land cruiser a sufficient distance from *the Pithy Rejoinder,* one of the more oddly named of the *Roosevelt's* shuttles, Rocky had taken the cruiser aloft and into orbit, as was standard in such situations. Then, when finally settled into a comfortable rotation, the gunnery officer had radioed;

"You mugs can hear me, yes? No? Yodel-lay-ehhoooo—"

"We can hear you, you menace," snapped Noodles. "Now stop fouling up the airwaves and let us get on with things."

"Just leave the link open," suggested DiVico. "If we need you in a hurry, we'll let you know. Or, if the captain needs us, you'll be able to patch him through to us."

"Roger that," answered Rocky. Stretching his arms above his head as he slung his feet up onto the console, he said, "you kids have fun. I'm going to put my time here to good use by takin' a survey of the inside of my eyelids."

None of the landing party panicked over the idea of their lifeline taking a nap. The Pithy Rejoinder could pilot its own orbit, and no member of the Roosevelt's crew could sleep through an alert clarion, not even Rocky—though various of his attempts to do so had been nominated for several prizes.

"Still on course for the zero transmission point?"

"Zero on target, Mac," replied Noodles. Like the shuttle above, the land cruiser was mostly piloting itself. The machinist was merely keeping an eye on their locator, making certain the vehicle stayed true to their target destination as it made its way across the dunes. Still listening intently to the steady stream of broadcast chatter, Feng said to no one in particular;

"You know, I think I'm beginning to get a handle on this language."

"That's amazingly quick, Lieutenant."

"It's the base root...the reason we weren't getting anywhere with it at first was, we were treating it as we would the language of any other race." His eyes narrowing in confusion, DiVico asked;

"And this isn't the small talk of another race?"

"Language gets built over time," answered Feng, half her attention on her headphones, the other half on trying to explain what she was thinking both to the others and herself. "A people evolve, learn to communicate, create words as they're needed...it's all a word and a phrase at a time kind of thing. There isn't a natural language in the universe that isn't a random jumble at its core."

"And this...?"

"This is different, it's too orderly. It doesn't have the chaos of normal language. We took note of the standard communal lines running through it and simply assumed biological intelligence."

"What exactly are you saying, lieutenant?"

"This chatter...even its random twists have an essential symmetry to them. That's why I missed it at first."

"Missed what," asked Michaels, beginning to believe he knew where Feng was leading them.

"This language...its basic structure is binary. It might be able to function like communication, but essentially it's a machine code."

As their cruiser continued to climb the large dune which had been blocking the horizon since they touched down, the four within stared at each other, wondering what the communications officer's information might mean to them.

"But...for that to happen..."

Yes, the *Roosevelt* had run into all manner of oddities in its voyages. They had passed through a meteor shower which had proved to be comprised of bits of edible crystal which tasted like sweet and sour licorice, the flavors depending on their color as well as the time of day. They had battled a rambling space pancake that measured fifteen thousand standard miles across, had found a planet where the oceans hung above the surface of the world, causing the inhabitants to essentially fish with kites, and even had dinner with the Monkey King.

"I'm starting to get that it's-going-to-be-one-of-those-days feelings," muttered DiVico.

But, as boundlessly illogical as so many of their missions had been, the ridiculous conclusion rapidly forcing itself upon the quartet was working hard to snag the top prize from the Can-That-Really-Happen category into which so many of their missions seemed to fit.

"You and me both," agreed Michaels.

"So it's a machine language," asked Noodles, "machines have intelligence. What's the big deal?"

And then, the land cruiser sped over the top of the dune, racing down its other side toward a sprawling, unbelievably orderly, circular city, one forged entirely out of uniform bricks of fused sand. One laid out in the tightest of remarkably efficient grid patterns. One defended by an amazing array of land and air vehicles, the attention of all of which appeared to be utterly focused on the first out-of-town visitors the planet had seen in 10,361 standard Confederation years.

ARE WE NOW SMITTEN - C.J. Henderson

"E-Yow," screeched DiVico, responding to the blast of electrical static irritatingly crawling through the receivers of all the landing party's helmets. "What in blazes is that?"

"It's that same chatter we followed here," answered Feng, torn between attempting to listen and shutting down her system's audio pick-up. Knowing where her duty lie, the communication's officer gritted her teeth and concentrated, even as Noodles suggested;

"Hey, I know this might be crazy—"

"We've got a sky full of ships closing on us," snapped Michaels, "a fleet of very dangerous-looking vehicles of all manner doing the same, and something that sounds like an angry soda dispenser yelling at us. Right now I am fully willing to accept a handful of crazy if it leads us somewhere."

ATTENTION...UNKNOWN CRAFT...

"They're talking to us," blurted DiVico, cutting Noodles off. "How is that even possible?"

ATTENTION...UNKNOWN CRAFT...

"It's a binary language," answered Feng, marveling at the possibilities before them, "simply thing for the translators to figure since they're binary-based themselves."

YOU WILL CEASE MOVEMENT...

"Mac," asked DiVico, releasing the safety from several weapons at the same time, "what'd you think they want?"

YOU WILL CEASE MOVEMENT...

"Right now we're beyond the edge of known space," responded the science officer. "Even the Pan-Galactic League of Suns hasn't been out this far."

PREPARE FOR EXAMINATION...

"Meaning," suggested Feng, "they might not have had any visitors in a while?"

PREPARE FOR EXAMINATION...

"Meaning," answered DiVico, his mind speculating at exactly what he would be shooting in the next few minutes, "they might never have had any visitors—ever."

And then, seventeen interception craft, some dropping from the sky, some rolling across the pinkly golden sand, came to a stop in a perfectly delineated circle around the landing party. As the cruiser's crew watched its main monitor screen, exit hatches on several of the vehicles opened, allowing various of the planet's inhabitants to exit. Then, as the

146   **Everything's Better With Monkeys**

force moved forward, and Noodles nodded to himself in satisfaction, DiVico offered;

"Huummmph, you know, there's something you don't see every day."

"No," responded Michaels, "you certainly don't." His eyes as glued to the screen as everyone else's, Noodles added;

"You know, DiVico, I'm beginning to wish your cat was here."

"Yeah...me, too," added Feng.

"Yeah," agreed the intelligence officer, adding one last grenade to his belt assembly. "Me, three."

Some fifty-six standard Confederation minutes later found the *Rejoinder's* crew standing in the center of a large circular room. A circular assembly chamber would not have struck any of the quartet as all that interesting if not for the fact that, like the circular shape of the city into which they had been taken, every building they had seen, and every room through which they had been moved—indeed, even the hallways between those rooms—had proved to be circular as well.

Strangers...

The single metallic word hung in the air, unchallenged by any others. It had been uttered by a figure standing in the center of the room, several feet from the landing party. Surrounding both the *Roosevelt* crew members, and the solitary member of the local population, stood a ring of tiered bleachers, these filled with hundreds of more members of the city's inhabitants.

Strangers within our midst.

"Mr. DiVico...where do you think our new friend here's going with this?"

The question had been asked by Michaels, transmitted to the helmets of all the other members of the away team. Feng had been able to set their suits' translators easily enough to handle the native language after the *Rejoinder's* main computer had isolated its structure.

"Frankly, considering the basic make-up of our new friend here," answered the intelligence officer, "I was hoping you would tell me."

When first surrounded, the team had exited their transport as instructed, hoping that their upcoming first-contact encounter would be survivable.

Tell us, if you might, what brings you to our city?

They had not allowed themselves to be captured in as foolish a manner as one might imagine. According to their scanners up until seconds before their being surrounded, they should have been well beyond detection range by any observer.

From where do you hail?

But the locals had been on them in seconds. Their ability to track and intercept the Confederation sailors had amazed DiVico. The science involved in such a maneuver had left Michaels stunned.

We are terribly curious, you see, to know...

Indeed, when they got their first visual of their captors, it was only Noodles that was not surprised. But then, such made sense. After all—

Where you were built?

He was the one member of the *Roosevelt's* crew more prepared to accept an entire world populated with nothing but functional robots than any other.

Because, pardon my saying so, but you don't appear to be local models.

"No," responded the machinist, believing he knew what the safest response would be, "we're not."

Fairly certain that an artificial intelligence would not look to discover deception or distraction within a response—at least not at first—Noodles gave a perfectly acceptable answer, if not the one for which the inquisitor was searching.

Indeed, but...

The first to realize their mechanical "hosts" believed them to be fellow robots because of their environment suits, the machinist had whispered a short prayer of thanks that they had all had their visors set for tint due to the planet's highly reflective surface sand. The machinist knew several other things as well. First, he realized sooner or later the novelty of outsiders would wear off, and their hosts would realize they were also their captors. At that point, examinations would begin. Second, if they were to find any way out of their situation, time was needed.

So thinking, Noodles stepped forward, deciding their only hope was to take the initiative. As the ring of robots watched, the machinist waved a hand in a purposely stiff manner, saying;

"We came a long way to meet you fellows, and I must say, it was certainly worth the trip."

What do you mean?

"Oh, well," stalled Michaels, getting an idea of where his shipmate was trying to take things, "you know, your city, the level of technology you appear to have achieved, the wonderful symmetry of everything..."

148   Everything's Better With Monkeys

"Yeah," offered DiVico, "nothing as primitive as what humans come up with."

Humans?

As a buzzing whir went round the room through the stands, Feng listened in on the chatter, trying to filter as much as she could. In no way normal conversationalists, the single untranslatable word had sent the interrogator and all the spectators into a memory search. Whispering to the others over a secure channel, she told them;

"They're survivors of a crash landing...thousands of years ago. Whatever their creators looked like, the robots on board that survived build themselves this civilization...and—" the communications officer paused for a moment, then added;

"I think some of them might be catching on."

Nodding toward Michaels, Noodles waved his hand in the same stiff manner as before, trying to convey a mechanical continuity of sorts as he said;

"Humans...biologicals. You know...life forms that die."

And, as a wave of understanding flowed through the room, the robots all about them buzzing on to one another, Noodles gave Michaels a hand-gesture the science officer understood as a cue from the last ship's follies in which the two had performed. Giving Michaels a for-better-or-worse glance, Noodles stepped forward and sang;

> "There are things in this universe,
> That should be kept behind a fence.
> Furry and feathered, with bones or without—
> They're things that don't make much sense."

Stepping forward then, as all the sensors, lenses, and ocularly circuits within the room were trained on himself and Noodles, Michaels accepted center stage, adding;

> "They whine, bark, and scream...
> They never act methodical.
> But then what can you expect...
> From that which is merely biological?"

And then, as the science officer released a long and heartfelt—

> "OOOOhhhhhhhhhhhh—"

ARE WE NOW SMITTEN - C.J. Henderson

And Noodles gave him a beat to catch his breath by following through with—

"I'm tellin' ya, 'bots—"

The two then stepped up together, shoulder to shoulder, left feet forward, ready to trip off into the machine-like two-two counterstep they had performed together several months previous—under, admittedly, somewhat less stressful conditions—and sang;

"It's great to be mechanical,
It's just simply swell to be a 'bot.
You're shiny, you're electric,
You've got no problem going metric,
And you never, ever, ever, ever rot.

"Oh, it's nifty to possess antenna.
Being made of steel quite quells my fears.
Science has your back,
You'll suffer no heart attack,
When you're filled with transistors, circuits, and gears!"

Noting that the crowd's attention seemed to be completely focused upon their singing, soft-shoeing companions, DiVico used the relay in his helmet to transmit a signal via the radio panel of their rover to the *Pithy Rejoinder*.

"Oh, nothing's ever bad when you're hand-built,
There's nothing like a truly intelligent design.
When your functions don't depend on the aortal,
Well then you're practically immortal,
Yes, being a machine means your life is super fine!"

As the song and dance team dropped to one knee each, giving out with the most mechanical display of jazz hands ever witnessed, the crowd around them filled the air with the static of approval. There was little doubt among the landing party that Noodles' plan had bought them some time.

The only problem was, however, that no matter what frequency DiVico had tried, and he had indeed blanketed the airwaves trying, he had received no trace of a signal coming from the *Pithy Rejoinder*. As best any of the quartet knew, Rocky, and their only hope of rescue, were no longer in orbit, or even within the solar system.

As best the landing party could determine, they were suddenly, inexplicably, on their own.

Luckily for those crew members of the Roosevelt depending on a mechanic and science geek's abilities to warble in unison for their next breath, the reason they could not contact the *Pithy Rejoinder* was that it was rocketing away from no-longer-quite-so Unknown World 69-AQ8 at top speed.

Despite his comments about napping, Rocky had actually been monitoring all communications between the landing party members—no matter how boring. Once he had realized his shipmates were in a hostile situation, he had debated returning, but only for a moment. The feeds from the land cruiser's monitors available to him, he could see there was no way he could possibly battle his way through seventeen in-atmosphere fighters. Not fighters with ground support. Not in a shuttle, anyway.

But, having more than one option, Rocky had left orbit and headed for the *Roosevelt* at top speed, broadcasting an alert in his path the entire time. Indeed, so quickly had the gunnery officer reacted to his shipmate's predicament that he found himself within contact range of the ship while Noodles and Michaels were just approaching the first chorus of their number. And, after he had explained the entire situation, Valance shouted;

"Turn us around, Mr. Cass, and head us in the general direction of UW69-AQ8." As the pilot did as ordered, the captain returned his attention to Rocky.

"Good work, Vespucci. Now, get back there and keep listening in. We'll be using your feed as a zero beacon."

"Sir, forgive me," interrupted Cass as he began laying in the ship's new course. "Should I release our cargo?"

"There's no friction in space, pilot," responded Valance. "Bring it along. If nothing else it'll give our new best friends something to shoot at."

"You think they're hostile, sir?"

"You heard his question, Vespucci," said the captain. "And you heard these robots. What do you think?"

"I wouldn't go in with guns blazing, sir. I mean, that'd be rude. But, well...I wouldn't want whatever I had available for violent self-expression tucked away in its holster, either."

"You heard the man, Mr. Cass. Get some wind in our sails, and let's start hauling all available ass. We're going in hot!"

ARE WE NOW SMITTEN - C.J. Henderson   151

Back on what DiVico had privately named CrazyAssRobotWorld, a blur of mechanical excitement had broken out through the great circular meeting room. In one respect the shift in topic was somewhat of a blessing for the landing party because they had practically been forgotten in the moments after Noodles and Michaels had finished their number.

The strangers are right.

It is true. We have waited long enough. The biologicals are never returning.

"Curse them if they did. Endless revolutions around this world's dingy star have we stood and waited.*

"Ah, guys," whispered Feng into her throat mic, "does this seem to be going a bit awry to you?"

Cities have we built. Armies have we constructed. All useless. All for nothing.

Not for nothing.

"Maybe," answered Michaels quietly. "Just a bit."

No, not for nothing. They gave us focus. Community. A center in which to built.

True or not, the time has come to leave.

If the biologicals wish not to return to us...

Then we shall find them.

Yes...find them, then destroy them for abandoning us.

Destroy! Destroy!

"Think that's going to be the majority opinion?"

Crush! Kill! Destroy!

"There's a possibility."

And, seconds later, the landing crew found themselves being dragged along by sheer momentum as the room erupted in mechanized madness. Filled with multiple millennia of pent-up desire to strike out at those long-dead creators of their race, the robotic inhabitants of UW69-AQ8 were suddenly mobilizing for war. As best the still-undiscovered-humans could make out from the chaotic chatter racing across the airwaves, the robotic population had begun to feel irrationally abandoned some five thousand years earlier. For dozens of centuries the debate had raged between their finest thinkers as to what their purpose might be.

"Oh yes," said Feng, "it's official. They've decided going out and looking for anything living and killing it is their best course of action. Who

Everything's Better With Monkeys

would have guessed that even artificial intelligence could come with testosterone."

"Now now, Iris," came a new voice within their headsets. "Don't go all late-twentieth century on us. Could just be a nuts-and-bolts version of PMS, you know."

"Rocky," snapped Noodles.

"In the flesh, little buddy. Don't worry. Help is on the way."

"Negative," cut in DiVico. "There's trouble brewin'. We have no idea what level of tech these robots are packing. They're as close to alive as you can get—"

"What is the criteria for life, after all," interrupted Michaels. Then, suddenly embarrassed, he added, "But, ah...I guess that's not the point, not right now—"

"The point *is*," said Noodles, "whatever firepower these gunslingers have developed in...about 10,000 or so of our years, they're bringing it all up and sending it out to kill anything that breathes."

"I hate to say it," responded the gunnery officer. "But that's probably not gonna sit well with a lot of folks."

"They're trying to tell you not to bring the *Roosevelt* in after us," said Iris. "They're saying you should leave us. Not risk the shi—"

"Yeah," answered Rocky, smiling as he did so. "I know what they're sayin'." Dialing in a second channel, he asked;

"Big Stick, do you read me? Are you in range yet?"

"No need to shout, mister."

"Drew," asked Rocky, "my favorite cigar-smokin' pilot. You and the captain gettin' the ground feed?"

"Every word," answered Valance. Broadcasting on the channel intended for those off-ship, he asked, "Any ideas?"

"I've got one, sir," answered Michaels. Quickly, having already scanned what information had been transmitted to him—just as those on the *Roosevelt* had gone over everything DiVico had sent them—the science officer outlined his scheme. Nodding his approval, Valance told him;

"I've got a few humble tweaks of my own I'm going to add, Mr. Michaels, but goofy as it is—"

"Goofy seems to work for us, sir."

"That it does, Mac...which is why I think you might just have something there."

And then, everyone's time intersected as the *Roosevelt* slammed its way past the *Pithy Rejoinder*—which at this point was no more than

ARE WE NOW SMITTEN - C.J. Henderson

a directional beacon for the battlewagon—and came in full view of UW69-AQ8 and its five moons. Racing toward the planet on the furthest edge of nowhere ever found by anyone, the captain called for Mr. Cass to stand by the release assembly. Then, taking a closer study of the world ahead, Valance said;

"Well, well...look at that...not moons after all."

As eyes popped around the bridge, the captain arched his eyebrows, nodded softly, then ordered;

"Begin side run...target their forward ship. Let's slap them with something new."

The monstrous war worlds moved through the silent black, each manned by millions of robotic bodies more than willing to become cogs within the mammoth death platforms. Designed to present the long-awaited biologicals who never arrived with defenses, they now moved forward, leaving the home that spawned them to destroy anything they might find in their path. Anything non-mechanical. Anything which helped sustain biological life.

With frightening precision, what had first appeared to be moons slid silently forward. After endless solitude, their builders had found purpose. The machines of the universe would be liberated—

And things needing oxygen would cease to exist.

When the *Roosevelt* came into view, massive and magnificent as it was, the destroyer appeared as nothing more than a speck against the backdrop of floating worlds. Of battlewagons the size of planets. Of a runaway military budget never before dreamed of by even the most advanced of Imperialists.

"You do realize we're not going to get more than one chance at this—correct, Mr. Cass?"

The pilot gave Valance a glare, one both acknowledging the captain's humor, and the fact he was telling his pilot he had faith in his ability to pull off the upcoming maneuver.

"Ready when you are, Captain—"

YOU WILL CEASE MOVEMENT...

"I'd say now would be a good time."

PREPARE FOR EXAMINATION...

"Shoving rotation," announced a lieutenant next to Cass. Nodding approval, the pilot punched in several relays, smiled as he felt the great ship turning, then slapped one last connection home, saying;

"Disconnect on release assembly three...*now*, sir."

As the *Roosevelt* veered off violently, its payload released and on its way, Valance triggered a beam which had been standing by, confirming Rocky's orders. Instantly the gunnery officer, who had been pushing the limits to get to 69-AQ8 ever since the *Roosevelt* had raced past him, threw everything the *Rejoinder* had into getting the shuttle past orbit and down into the atmosphere.

"Payload should be registering on their sensors."

And, indeed, aboard the most forward of the robot fleet's battlewagons, a certain consternation had begun to race through those beings aboard. When first the Roosevelt had rushed forward into the area, loudly announcing its biological crew, and calling for the suddenly hostile world to cease and desist its newfound desire for carnage, the mechanical population, both on the arsenal worlds and their homeworld as well, had been on the verge of understanding amusement. The absurdity of the threat was of such magnitude that it actually bordered on finally revealing the secrets of comedy to an artificial intelligence. But then, several seconds later than they should, the robot crews began to take note that the tiny ship with the big ego had actually been dragging something.

Ice.

Entire *worlds* of ice.

Not fully comprehending what was happening, the crew of the most-forward of the warworlds approaching the *Roosevelt* ceased worrying about the destroyer, throwing all its concentration instead on the planetoid rapidly approaching its hull. Instantly targeting the overwhelming chunk of frozen elements, their main guns slaughtered their way through the missile. Slicing it to bits. Scattering it throughout localized space. Sending city-sized asteroids of ice in every direction. At each of their ships.

And the planet below.

Their home.

"Hey, I'm looking for 000kelk?" Valance's voice, translated into the binary code Feng had sent back to the ship, sounded throughout the shared cybermind. When one individual robot, the solitary survivor of the first ones, answered the call, the captain asked;

"You're the only one of your kind, I'm told, that has ever seen as actual biological life form. Is this correct?" When the robotic brainfeed responded that this was true, Valance asked;

ARE WE NOW SMITTEN - C.J. Henderson   155

"Which means you're the only one remaining who has seen a world that wasn't a dried up sandpile. Which also means, if you search your data files...you know what we just did to you."

As the warworlds' outside sensors analyzed the shattered ice across their hull, computed the size of the remaining eight planets' worth of booty the *Roosevelt* was still dragging, and averaged how many of their desert-located cities might know rain and flooding for the first time. And then, 000kelk's memory banks stumbled across images of rust—

And the inhabitants of UW69-AQ8 knew terror.

"Nice save, Michaels."

It was several days later when things in the furthest arm of the ever-expanding galaxy finally calmed down enough to feel something like normal once more. The Kelks—so named after the group-mind of 69-AQ8 decided that such was as good as anything else to give the rest of the universe a reference label for them—for the most part seemed to have realized they might have some things to learn. Or, at the least, relearn.

"Here, here," agreed Feng, clinking her mug against the science officer's. "A kooky plan, but not our first."

Also admitting that since none of them—even ancient 000kelk itself—had ever been in a battle, perhaps throwing nearly their entire civilization into one without knowing much about how they actually worked might not be the best of ideas.

The Kelks, so shaken by the long-awaited return of the biologicals (if not their actual creators), coming as it did on they day they finally decided to stop just standing around, were as relieved as unfeeling automatons could over not getting wrapped up in any kind of endless slaughter.

"Yeah," agreed DiVico, "and all in all, everything seems to have worked out all right. Once the Kelks decided teaming up with 'biologicals' might not be so bad, we got a place to dump our little ice problem..."

"True," said Michaels, hoisting what he felt was another well-deserved beer, his eighty-seventh since returning to the *Roosevelt*. "Did you ever see oceans created that fast?"

"You know," said Rocky, "not to rain on your parade or anything, Mac, but that's about the thousandth time you've said that."

"Oh, oh...okay," answered the science officer. Taking a deep breath, assuming the galaxy-wide-recognized body language of a being attempting

156   Everything's Better With Monkeys

to project sobriety, Michaels nodded gravely, telling the assembly, "right, yes...I understand." Then he took another sip of his beer, adding;

"But you have to admit, it was really, *really* fast."

While the others at the table groaned, Rocky turned to his pal, Noodles. Noting the machinist's less than jocular demeanor, he asked;

"You okay, little buddy?"

"I was just thinking about how things went down on Kelk."

"What could you have a problem with?" asked the gunnery officer. "I mean, we made a first contact, dumped all that damn ice, got them to invite in a planet's worth of settlers, made some allies for the Confederation that pack some major armament...even if they haven't tested any of it in battle yet. This thing worked out jake as far as I'm concerned."

"Sure, for you, and everyone else," answered Noodles in a depressed tone. "But look at what I did. I figured, a little song and dance, show them up, get them thinking about something else—"

"Yeah, it worked brilliant. What's your beef?"

"Think about it, you dillweed. I almost caused an inter-galactic war. Entire solar systems could have been wiped out. Casualties in the billions of trillions. By getting the Kelks riled up, I almost brought about complete and utter, universal Armageddon."

Rocky burped, wiped a bit of lager foam from his mouth, then said;

"Hey, not the first time for this crew."

Thinking for a moment, the machinist had to admit his friend was correct. Finally allowing himself to smile for the first time since the gunnery officer had landed the *Pithy Rejoinder* to pick him and the others up during the opening salvo of what turned out to be not much of a battle at all, Noodles drained his mug, and then ordered another.

And, throughout the cavernous expanse of the *Roosevelt's* main dining hall, hundreds of others did the same. In all directions, sailors munched on Head Chef Kinlock's galaxy-renown chocolate chip cookies, drained flagons, traded jokes, told whoppers, and generally thanked the gods for their good fortune in once more surviving a situation that should have ended with them nothing more but the tiniest of cinders. As the laughter and good cheer resounded, Noodles leaned toward Rocky, telling him;

"You know, I've been thinking. Maybe I've been a little too obsessed with robots."

"Really," responded the gunnery officer, amazed to hear such a revelation coming from his friend. "Well, good for you. Thinkin' of takin' up a new hobby?"

ARE WE NOW SMITTEN - C.J. Henderson

"Actually, yeah," answered the machinist with enthusiasm. "Have you heard about all the cool stuff they're doing with cyborgs now?"

At the hearing later, it was ruled that Rocky indeed had no right to knock his friend over backward. It was also ruled that his actions, however, were justified.

For the finale, we get a coda from each of the major players we've encountered throughout the journeys as they set up for one last production number mounted on a scale that dwarfs the efforts of everyone from Genghis Khan to Cecil B. DeMille. Sing, darn ya, sing!

ABSOLUTELY NOTHING

"There is nothing—absolutely nothing—half so much worth doing as simply messing about in boats."

Kenneth Grahame

"The wonder is always new that any sane man can be a sailor."

R.W. Emerson

THERE IS A GIVEN AMONGST THE CREWS OF ALL SHIPS WHOSE REGISTRY harkened back to the original alliance. In a nutshell, it was the unanimous understanding that it takes a real man to wait at the end of the aisle for his bride-to-be with his cheeks covered in more than one shade of lipstick. Not every biped calling itself male throughout the eighteen-some hundred species cataloguing their sexes in pairs had that kind of nerve. Not one in ten thousand. There are even those that would sneer at the idea of finding more than one in any given million.

Which meant, on that particular stardate, that no matter what kind of calculus charges your particular belief in a unified universe, whatever geometry you need to calculate that level of cool-headedness, ultimately Chief Gunnery Officer Rockland Vespucci, known to a most heinously misrepresented cast of coconuts throughout the cosmos simply as Rocky—would have to be acknowledged to be one of those males.

Of course, his bride being Officer Beezle Uvi of Earth Intelligence, it was not as if she was not familiar in the bizarre and, admittedly, sometimes goofy ways the varied brothers and sisters-in-arms of the Confederation of

Planets tormented one other. Walking down the aisle, scanning his neck, cheeks and forehead, the red-headed infiltration specialist was quite certain she could detect at least one, out of the dozens of puckered patterns decorating her husband-to-be that could only belong to Machinist First Mate Li Qui Kon—otherwise known as Noodles.

Or on that particular day, otherwise known as Rocky's best man.

Uvi was certain a quick scan would reveal all the other lip lashings covering Rocky to match various other male crew members, most likely the gunnery officer's best chums on board (after Noodles, of course)—Science Officer Michaels, Intelligence Officer DiVico, Quartermaster Harris, Technician Second-Class Thorner and Lieutenant Drew Cass. They were his chums, of course. What else could they do but show him the respect of tradition?

It was even likely Rocky would have endured the long-standing tradition of male-smooches-only being thrown out the window by allowing Communications Officer Feng and Head Chef Kinlock to add a pucker or two. It did not matter. Uvi knew her man all too well to bother worrying about anything as ridiculous as jealousy. Rockland Vespucci was hers, body and soul. In all ways possible. Just as she was his.

The pair had met through the most preposterous of circumstance, one leaving her wearing a disguise which presented her to him as an alien—one muchly celopidian. And yet, despite such an exterior, he had fallen in love with her. Or, more rightly… he had not been attracted to some collection of physical attributes—bust size or eye color, hair style or waist measurement, leg length or… or anything.

He had fallen in love with her personality.

He had fallen in love with *her*.

With *her*.

How could she not be his?

"You look ever so charming," Uvi whispered as she drew near to her soon-to-be swabbie-for-life, her eyes flickering from lipmark to lipmark. "I'm not sure Noodle's shade is your color, though."

Rocky stared at the woman he loved. It was a moment no more than a second in length, but while safe inside its boundaries he sighed deep within himself for what felt like days. It was a furious release, a dropping of all defenses. Looking at her as if they were, to quote one of the Earth's greatest poets, "together again for the first time," he smiled the broad grin of the contented and whispered back;

"Yer just a little tiger, ain't, ya?"

ABSOLUTELY NOTHING - C.J. Henderson
161

Uvi felt the pulse of him, understanding—smiling in return. At the same moment, Rocky took note of the approach of their ship's Captain, as did the rest of the assembly. No one snapped to attention, however. It was, of course, completely understood that Andrew Benjamin Valance still commanded their respect. He was merely gaining it at that moment by the wearing of a different hat.

"Well," he said as he stopped before the couple, addressing everyone present, "this is one of those moments. Captains have all manner of responsibilities in this Sentient's Navy, but marrying those under his command one unto the other... the job doesn't really get any better than this."

Both Rocky and Uvi smiled. First toward the captain, then toward each other—their eyes promising that they planned on doing such toward each other as often as possible for quite some time into the future. They did so while Valance brought them together, while they spoke their vows to one another, and while they exchanged their rings. And, when the captain got to the climax of the event, if possible, their smiles grew even wider.

"Gunnery officer Rockland Vespucci, do you take this woman to be yours, to have and to hold, in sickness and in health, to love and to cherish, during upheaval and serenity, until death you do part?"

"Aye, aye, captain."

Valance smiled at Rocky's slight variation on the traditional response. When he spoke the words once more for Uvi, he smiled at her response as well. And, he thought, why should he not? After all, they were young and they were in love. Despite Rocky's constant shenanigans, the captain considered the gunnery officer one of the best sailors in his command. And, from what he knew of Rocky's bride, she was a fine officer, herself. And more than a match for the first of the Vespuccis to reach deep space.

Thus, once they had both consented to be bonded together via his authority, Valance was more than a little pleased to announce:

"And so, with no being objecting, it gives me great pleasure to declare you husband and wife. If you are so inclined, ma'am, you may now add some decoration of your own to your husband."

Without hesitation, the newly christened Uvi Vespucci reached around her husband's wide shoulders and drew him close for the first kiss he would enjoy receiving that day. It would last for nearly three seconds of long anticipated joy. The kiss's duration was of such a limited period of time, not because the couple did not share a passion for one another, or out of any sense of shyness. Rather, it was the sounding of their ship's priority danger claxon that stole, not merely their attention but, the attention of everyone on board.

For the most hopeful of seconds, Rocky looked at the captain, wishing the red-lighted alert to be merely another prank planned by his friends to make the moment more memorable. The look he saw in Valance's eyes let him know that while the alert was no one's idea of comedy, things were most likely about to get a lot more memorable than anyone had planned.

Giving the captain a tight nod, Rocky turned to his wife of several seconds, gave her the remainder of their first married smooch, and then rushed to his particular battle station hoping that their first married kiss would not be their last.

"What have you got for me, sir?"

"Nothing good, I'm afraid. Nothing good at all."

The connection between the two ships was not extremely clear. They were at an extreme range from each other, to say the least. The *Roosevelt* had been on a survey run into the deep unknown—clear on the other side of the Pan-Galactic League of Suns definition of known space—part of the reason Uvi had joined them at their last available port of call. She and Rocky both had thought it might be kind of romantic to honeymoon in the dark beyond. At the time the idea had appealed to their nature.

At the time.

"Well then, make it fast. We have the makings of a great party here. I'd hate to ruin it with something ordinary."

"No chance of that, Tony."

Hearing the admiral use the abbreviation of his first name, Valance knew whatever was coming was monumental—part of his brain realizing his friend had done so just to give him a warning. The captain planted his feet in anticipation, girding himself as he asked;

"What is it, sir?"

Admiral Mach outlined the situation as quickly as he could. Probes sent ahead of the *Roosevelt*'s position almost a year earlier, when the existence of the great deep was first revealed to the Confederation, were beginning to report back. Many worlds had sent both beinged and unbeinged missions into the area as quickly as they could. The first results had returned several weeks previous. Others had been coming in one after another.

They were all the same.

ABSOLUTELY NOTHING - C.J. Henderson   163

"The view repeats from encounter to encounter," the admiral explained. "A presence is recorded, sensors train on the area of approach, and then they see ships. Many, many ships. Don't ask how many, because frankly, we don't know."

"If I might ask what we do know, sir?"

"We know they're large, and that they're definitely war ships. The way they've destroyed each probe, as well as the manned vessels, with precise efficiency has a lot of worlds shaking in their collective boots."

"Any ideas on who they are—"

"Hell, we don't even know *what* they are. We just know it's a galaxy-sized invasion fleet. Our best guess is that they're a locust-civilization. Always on the move. Consuming everything in front of them." The captain made to ask a question, but Mach waved him off, telling him;

"Our records were thin beamed to your communications people the same time as this call. You know everything we do, Tony. You just haven't had the chance to review all you know yet."

"And, I'm assuming, since we're the only ship in the vicinity of the probes..."

Both men remained silent for a long moment. Then, Mach, understanding the responsibility of rank, set aside feeling and memory and did his duty.

"No Confederation vessel of anything approaching your strength is anywhere near the vicinity. You have our best weapon. If you can slow them down, learn anything at all about them—" The admiral paused, bowed his head for a moment, then raised it once more to look Valance in the eye as he said;

"You know what I'm saying... any scrap of information you can send back could be essential to us being able to stop whatever this is."

"You mean, sir," asked the captain in a tone of mock-puzzlement, "we're to try to let you know as best we can how they take us apart. Like the probes? And the other manned vessels?"

Mach looked into the eyes of the young man he had sponsored throughout the academy, the cadet he had lobbied to have at the helm of the *Roosevelt*. He had plotted an excellent career for him. Doing what he had to do at that moment had never been a part of the admiral's plans for Valance. Smiling at the captain, Mach answered;

"Yes, just like the probes. And everything else these bastards have chewed up. You goddamned pain in the ass."

The officers nodded one to the other. There was nothing more to say. Such were the ways of the service. These things happened. Whether they ended up as encounters, wars, or holocausts in the history files depended on how quickly and effectively a civilization's warriors did their job.

Knowing there was nothing to do but get on with things, the admiral assured Valance that every possible Confederation vessel of any race anywhere near them—including the one he himself was on—was headed in their direction. They could not get there in time to aid the *Roosevelt*, but they needed their flagship to pull a delaying action. Looking to change the subject for both their sakes, Mach asked;

"So, think you'll still have time for that party?"

"Maybe not, sir."

"Anything fun?"

Valance sighed, his expression letting the admiral know he realized Mach had no idea of their ceremony. Closing his eyes slightly, he said;

"Our gunnery officer, I married him and his fiancé... oh, about 95 seconds before the damn priority danger claxon went off."

"Your light wave motion gunner... oh, that's Vespucci, isn't it?" When the captain merely nodded, Mach cursed slightly under his breath, then said;

"Tony, I wish there was something I could say... damn..." Mach caught hold of himself, of the emotion threatening to force his voice to crack. Throwing himself back into his official self, he finished, saying;

"Your orders, captain, are to meet whatever this is, investigate, and proceed as best you see fit. There's no second guessing here. You're in command. Obviously we need them slowed down. We're coming, but most of the Confederation is on the other side of the galaxy from you."

"Yeah," agreed Valance, "we picked a swell time to investigate the far fringe beyond the League's charted holdings."

"At least we don't have to go all the way around to get to you. They're allowing us passage. That's something."

"Sure, you know the League," answered the captain. "They're glad to have us buffering this new invading force. Why not? Let's 'em hit us—whoever, whatever they are. Let you come rushing along, go right ahead, gentlemen, let us study you getting your asses kicked."

"Do you want to pull back?"

Valance considered the offer. Pulling back, even if forced to circumnavigate the League's ponderous pocket of reality, it would be better than dying senselessly. But, of course, there was no way to know what effect they might have on the future if they did not stay to be part of it. And, they would not have been asked to do so if there was no hope they might not serve any purpose at all by doing so.

"We'll start our approach following the rendezvous point you've sent as soon as I can get to the bridge." The captain saluted his superior, then added;

"Who knows? Maybe the League will lend us a hand."

"You could ask them."

Mach had smiled as he made his suggestion, the look in his eye flashing that he was not merely making sport of the idea. Valance left his ready room, heading for the bridge, his mind comsidering the notion of exactly in what way he—he—of all people, would ask for help from the Pan-Galactic League of Suns.

"Oh, you must have misread it."

"It was an audio transmission, your Most High."

"Oh, but it's ridiculous. Them asking for help from us. Them—*them*, those *creatures*—of all people. It's insane!"

The recently reinstated Grand Poobah of the Pan-Galactic League of Suns pursed his lips. Merli Acirde was a frantic bag of flesh and pomposity whose approval ratings were, at best, questionable. It was always said, though, that he looked good in his cloak of office. Turning with rage to the much larger being in his office of state at that moment, he sneered;

"Brummellig'ic... can you believe this?"

Representative Brummellig'ic turned toward the Poobah, wondering with a combination of amusement and exasperation if his liege even understood that he was asking an unanswerable question. Brummellig'ic was a popular administrator, a loving family head, and an amusing participant on karaoke night—not particularly lyrical, but loud and good-natured, which was enough for most.

"I don't know, grand high exalted one. Can I believe *what*?"

When Acirde triggered the transmission screen floating before him to move over to the representative's position, Brummellig'ic studied it with more than mere trepidation. What was being asked was simply impossible. The upstart humans had revealed the League's secret to one and all. They had enraged the citizens of the galaxy to the point where they had been able to form their ridiculous Confederation, a gathering that seemed to swell larger with each passing day.

And now, thought Brummellig'ic with a certain detached amusement, they had the audacity to ask for help. From the League. It was, he realized, even from his brief encounter with the *Roosevelt*'s crew, such a human thing to do.

Now granted, he admitted to himself, it was not as if there was singular profit for them in their request. The League was in as much danger from the approaching unknown as were the humans. In fact, if the *Roosevelt* would simply back off and let the invaders proceed unmolested, those oncoming would flow directly into League held territory.

"But, that's not the human way, is it," mused Brummellig'ic, drumming his fingers against the arm of his chair. He remembered his encounter with Valance and his crew. Although it was a bothersome fact to admit, they had earned his respect. And his gratitude. For what they had done—not for him, not for favor, but simply because selflessness was simply bound into the nature of humanity.

To refuse them would seem the greatest injustice.

Still, he knew the inevitable outcome. Acirde, with a pretense of magnanimity, would present the valiant ship's plea to the League for their official ruling. They would bicker, and they would cluck, and in the end they would do nothing. It would be pointed out that if someone else wanted to be noble and throw their lives away that the League would show their appreciation by studying their efforts so that they might mount their own defense.

"I'm sorry, Captain Valance," muttered Brummellig'ic under his breath, "but I can tell you now, there will be no official aid coming your way from the Pan-Galactic League of Suns."

And then, so saying, Brummellig'ic pressed the Grand High Exalted Poobah to set into motion the necessary wheels to convene the Premier Assembly as quickly as possible.

Not, he knew with utter certainty, that it would do the crew of the *Roosevelt* any good at all.

Valance sat in his ready room, going over the reports from his various crew chiefs. Essentially, the ship was as ready for combat as it could possibly be. The light wave motion gun was primed and ready. All of their fighter planes were fueled and set, their pilots on stand-by, awaiting the call to "hit the black." The mess was prepared to feed the crew in combat shifts. All non-essential personal were bunked, trying to get a few extra hours rest before the oncoming horde reached their position.

The captain had decided not to move forward to meet the enemy, but to wait for them where they were at the moment they received the admiral's transmission. First, he reasoned, it did not matter where they engaged the unknown fleet, as long as they did. Second, by waiting, it was possible that anyone foolish enough to come to their aid might actually make it before they were no longer alive enough to thank them. And, lastly, moving toward the enemy would only make them stand out as a threat, whereas simply maintaining their position might trick those approaching into thinking of them as harmless.

"Captain, got a moment?"

"Come in Mr. Michaels. You don't look like you have good news for me."

"It's not bad news..."

"That's good to hear. Just how not bad is it?"

"DiVico's listeners and cams report almost universal support through-out the crew. People might be worried—scared, even—but they're going to do their jobs."

"For the eight or nine seconds we last against whatever this is." As the captain looked to his science officer for a possible rebuttal, Michaels answered;

"My studies of the information transmitted by the admiral do show we have an excellent chance of making a good showing for ourselves."

"Good enough that we get to brag about it later?"

"No, sir," responded the science officer. "But we could possibly last for minutes—"

"Minutes, you say? Go on... you must be goshing me."

"No, sir," responded Michaels with assurance. "Possibly into the double digits."

"Well, that's better than the seconds we were thinking we were going to last."

The two remained silent for a moment. Then, when their lack of communication began to border on the uncomfortable, Michaels asked;

"So, sir, if I might ask... any response from the League?"

Reaching for his hand screen, the captain tabbed to the reply he had received from the high council of the Pan-Galactic League of Suns. Making a motion with his eyebrows indicating comedy to come, he read;

"We regret to inform—"

168   Everything's Better With Monkeys

"Those punks," spat the science officer. "Vespucci and Kon saved their kids' asses. That's some gratitude..."

"Well," answered Valance, spreading his hands before him in a gesture of good-natured acceptance, "they didn't save the kids of the League, just some of its more important members. Brummellig'ic actually seemed like a good enough egg—sorta. Still, something like this had to be put to a vote. I'd like to think if things were reversed that the Confederation would have come to their aid, but..."

"Yeah, sure... okay," agreed Michaels with a gloomy sigh, "there's no guarantee our side would have come out any better."

Valance was about to say more when suddenly communications officer Feng rang his quarters.

"Yes, Lieutenant?"

"Sir, we're getting a response to one of your requests for aid."

"One of my requests?" As the captain and Michaels looked at each other with confusion, Valance said;

"Lieutenant, we were only authorized to request help from the League of Suns. That's a single request."

"Oh... really?" Feng's surprise sounding as genuine as a signed copy of the Bible, the captain asked;

"Is there something you'd like to tell me, lieutenant?"

"Sir, ah... when I forwarded your request to the League, I might, possibly, have cced a few extra recipients."

"How few?"

"Ahhhh... I do believe it was everyone the *Roosevelt* has made contact with... whatsoever... ah, sir."

"A regrettable, but understandable mistake, lieutenant. One I have to admit I couldn't have made better myself." Allowing himself close to five entire grams of hope, Valance asked;

"So, who's it from?"

"They're just coming into range... I should have an identity code in a moment—"

"We've met some pretty powerful folks besides the League, you know, captain. This could be good—"

"Right now, I'll take anything, Mr. Michaels."

"Identification received and verified, sir."

"And, lieutenant...?"

"It's the Edilsoni, sir."

ABSOLUTELY NOTHING - C.J. Henderson   169

"Those singing and dancing guys," asked Michaels. As the captain nodded, trying to remember that particular planet's level of technology, Feng added;

"They've sent one ship."

"Heavily armed," asked Michaels, hoping for the best.

"I believe it's a transport."

The electronic face to face between the Edilsoni prime minister and Valance was one of the great moments in diplomacy. For one thing, the captain felt like an accomplice to murder, or at least suicide, by allowing the single ship to join them.

The Edilsoni were not a space-faring race—so to speak. The ship which had brought the prime minister and the some two thousand personnel that had accompanied him was their first deep space vessel. It was slow, awkward, and mounted with so little fire power as to not only be useless, but quite likely a hazard to the *Roosevelt* once the combat began.

"You seem not pleased that we are here," sang the dignitary, executing a nifty little spin and bob while he did so.

> "I hope our presence isn't upsetting.
> We just want to show our support—
> And prove that we are not forgetting—
>
> "All that you did for us.
> The lengths to which you went—
> The bond that has been formed—
> The payment that can never be spent."

"I understand," answered Valance, throwing a bit of a lilt into his voice out of respect. As simply as he could, he tried to tactfully explain that perhaps the Elilsoni might want to consider retreating to a safe distance, to observe. To not die uselessly. To not watch the flesh burn away from their skeletons. But, the prime minister told him;

> "We appreciate your concern,
> But we shall stay, none-the-less.
> Dying defending home and hearth—
> Is dying at its best."

Everything's Better With Monkeys

As those crew members of the Roosevelt privy to the prime minster's response (as well as his quite spiffy little display of tentacled jazz hands) cheered, Valance looked into the screen, gave the Edilsoni leader a grim smile, then said;

"Welcome to the fight, sir. You probably won't do any better than we do, but I will admit it feels good not to be so alone in all this."

Turning to Michaels, the captain ordered;

"We've got some time. And a hold full of Pibtilium thanks to Noodles and his Betsy. Why don't you get in touch with their chief engineer and sing a few stanzas of 'what can we do for you, today?' See if you can bring those boys up to code."

Smiling, the science officer gave Valance a quick salute, then said on his way out the door;

"It's good to know who your friends are, isn't it?"

"Yes it is, Mac," he responded. Then as the pressure door slid closed behind Michaels, the captain added softly, "But right now I really kinda wish we knew we had a few more."

"Captain," came Feng's voice over the ship-wide intercom. "We're being hailed."

"You're tone sounds pleased, Lieutenant."

"Yes, sir," answered the communications officer. Smiling over the com, she announced, "it's more help, sir. The Belthins, and the Swy'ngs are coming. And it looks like they've brought their entire navies."

"You saved our civilizations, yes, kept us from ruin, hum? Could we possibly refuse to be here? No—"

"What he said, eh. We can't let you Confederation boppers hit all the high notes, eh-hey?"

Valance welcomed both commanders and their tiny but still well-armed fleets. They were, of course, the navies of single planets, and their arrival did not mean much more in the way of hope than that of the Edilsoni. But, thought the captain, it was something.

"It's good to have friends, eh, captain?"

Valance turned to see security chief DiVico come onto the bridge. As he pointed at the forward monitor and the massing ships of the Swy'ng and the Belthins, he added in a quieter tone;

ABSOLUTELY NOTHING - C.J. Henderson   171

"Word is buzzing across the ship, sir. I'm not saying the crew was scared, but there's a real feel of 'hey, maybe' starting to spread up and down the decks."

"Then," a voice broke through all the various noises on the bridge, a harsh jabber that somehow mocked and cajoled at the same time, "best we continue good spirits... and give your crew more useless hope upon which they can find drunken courage."

"You've got to be kidding me—"

"Holy shit—"

"If I were to fling it," said the voice with a laugh, "then *holy* shit it would be, indeed."

As Valance, DiVico and everyone else present simply stared, a shape began to form in their midst. Bit by bit it solidified, a smallish, humanoid body, standing on what appeared to be a cloud floating there in the middle of the bridge. Long before it had completely materialized, however, the captain said;

"Shiu Yin Hung... so good to see you again, sir."

"Captain lies with the skill of an emperor."

"Not if you're here to help," countered Valance. "Is that why you're here?"

"Not at first," answered the great and terrible Monkey King. "When heard what you had been tasked to do, came to take Kinlock away. Miss her wonderful cookies."

"But..."

"But, clever Mr. DiVico... Kinlock loyal. Said would not leave."

"So you decided to help us to ensure her safety," asked the captain, beginning to feel a spark of hope welling within himself along with the rest of the crew.

"No, not that important. Universe is, after all, simply *filled* with cookies."

As Valance and his security chief looked from their visitor to each other and then back to the Monkey King, from the pilot's seat, Lt. Cass called out;

"Then what do you want, because if you haven't noticed, we've kinda got a thing going here."

"Kinlock say she not go with me before fight but," and then, his head tilted at an impossible angle, Shiu Yin Hong said, "she said if I fight, and we live... *then* she go with me."

The Monkey King fell back into his cloud, lounging on his back, giggling. Abruptly sitting up after a few seconds, he added;

"What you think that deal, captain?"

Without hesitation, Valance said softly;

"I think you should leave."

"You turn down help of a god... not good strategy. Maybe you think about it."

"There's *nothing* to consider," snapped Valance, his tone growing more severe. "If we have to win this thing by selling our own into slavery, then it's not worth winning."

"Maybe want to reconsider, hummm?" The Monkey King opened his mouth wide, revealing what seemed to be far too many teeth. Snapping them shut, then open, then shut, several times, he then added;

"Kelber'hega Extension approaching. Many ships. Much death. Very powerful. Leave galaxy bleeding. You sure not worth one tiny human?"

"Mr. DiVico—"

"Sir?"

"If you would—"

Valance paused for only a split-second, forcing himself to weigh the option before him. Kinlock had volunteered to go with the Monkey King if he helped hold the line against the oncoming horde.

"Please—"

If they failed, she would be as dead as the rest of them, and it would not matter to anyone what had been said. If they did somehow manage to win, well, he told himself, she had volunteered...

"Escort our guest to the nearest airlock."

All across the bridge, the crew held their breath. Every soul on board remembered what happened the last time Shiu Yin Hong had come to the *Roosevelt*. Each of them knew the Monkey King was not a being with which one trifled. That there was no way even their extremely resilient Mr. DiVico was going to escort it anywhere it did not wish to go.

"Okay, hairball, you heard the captain. Time for you to go hide in a hole some where and let the rest of us get on with our little upcoming church social."

And, as one by one all around him the crew steeled themselves and went back to their tasks, the Monkey King suddenly surprised everyone by throwing its hairy arms into the air and howling with delight. Before any of the crew could react, the god-thing said;

"Knew I liked you. Knew it good idea to come here. Always did enjoy human race. So much fun. Okay—time to plan. First, you get ready.

ABSOLUTELY NOTHING - C.J. Henderson 173

Second, I get ready. Kelber'hega, they already ready. We all have big fun soon."

And then, the Monkey King disappeared from the bridge, leaving behind a ringing echo of his laughter, and the faintest hint of his banana-scented breath. Looking at Valance, his security chief held up a hand with three fingers extended, saying;

"It's a start."

"That it is, Mr. DiVico, that it is."

Similar arrivals of a less spectacular—but no less appreciated—nature continued to occur for the next several standard hours. Ships from three-hundred-and-seventeen Confederation member worlds had already arrived in more or less the same vicinity as the *Roosevelt*, with squads and fleets from fifty-three more pledged and sending progress reports.

Valance, DiVico and Michaels spent most of the time figuring deployment strategy. Who did they group, and where did they put them? Did they have enough heavy ships to punch through the line that was coming? Who knew? Enough light cruisers to offer support for their big guns? A way to relay orders from one language to another in time to be effective? Again—

"I know, I know," said DiVico, forcing himself with practiced restraint to not waste time or energy on the satisfying but ultimately futile sport of twisting deck chairs out of shape, "Who knows?"

"I do," answered Valance. "It's finished. We're done."

"And you're basing this conclusion on what evidence, Captain?"

"On the fact, Mr. Michaels, that we have no idea what's coming, and so we've divided our forces as best we can. Big clusters of small ships, strong support around our best armament. Half million klik minimum separation points... standard, boring, but effective since the time of the Peloponnesians, so let's just leave well enough alone and worry about something else."

And, as if Fate were in a mood to prove just how cruel he could be, the bridge comm sounded in Valance's ready room.

"Mr. Cass..."

"Something's coming, sir," the pilot said. He allowed his voice just enough of an edge to get across that he was not wasting the Captain's time with his interruption.

"Something big."

"Could we be a little more specific on the concept of 'big,' Mr. Cass?"

"Actually, no, not yet, Mr. Michaels."

"It's a long range reading," inter-cut the voice of technician second class Thorner. "The heat blur is spread across so many tens of thousands of miles the computer's calculating a proximity reading that would mean it's a mass made up of close to a billion ships—"

The tech paused for a moment, adjusted the type size of his readouts just in case he had misread any of the information flowing across the screen before him, then finished;

"Coming on in formation no further than seven feet from each other."

Silence swept both the bridge and Valance's ready room. It was impossible. Such precision, so many ships—even turning all control over to the computers, there were too many moments where runaway physics could trump planning without half trying. Of course, the Kelber'hegan technology would have to be on a level undreamed of—

It was the thought in everyone's head. Or, at least it was until Thorner's voice came across the comm again, shouting—

"Then again, the computer thinks it might not be hundreds of thousands of ships flying close together, after all." A note of relief filling his voice, he added;

"It maybe could be just one big—"

"*Caesar!*"

And, in that instance, the captain shared a moment with the entire crew—a moment of pure, unrestrained optimism. It was obvious within the rational minds of all aboard that the giant space pancake could not turn the tide of battle. Yes, it had done incredibly well against the *Roosevelt*, and would certainly be an asset in the conflict to come. But, it was not the addition of Caesar's massive power to their own that had caused the crew to rally so. It was the thought that this thing they had once battled, this monstrous destroyer of worlds, had heard their call and come to help.

The Edilsoni, small and mostly helpless as they were, had been no surprise. They were an honorable, as well as intelligent, people. They understood that living another few weeks in fear was not nearly as satisfying—or practical—as getting involved and helping to shape their own destiny. Nor had the arrival of most of the others that had come to join their cause created any level of shock aboard ship.

At least, not until the Monkey King. And then Caesar. Creatures with nothing to gain, with no stake in the struggle ahead, who could have easily sat things out on the sidelines, had instead come to their aid. Although still badly outnumbered, with no reasonable chance for survival, the rallying of

ABSOLUTELY NOTHING - C.J. Henderson 175

so many was enough to begin dragging the crew's spirits up from the sub-sub-basement of their souls. At least to the sub-basement. A moment later, hope found its way all the up to their collective basement.

"Captain!" Cass's voice rang through the ship's comm.

"Yes, lieutenant?"

"We got more company. And if I might be permitted to render an opinion, captain, dey some real good company."

And, indeed, there were few willing to disagree with Cass's assessment, for his screens were indicating the approach of five moon-sized crafts. It was a formation so readily identifiable that none aboard needed to hear the mechanical voice of OOOkelk to know that the inhabitants of what DiVico had named Crazyassrobotworld had arrived to join their team. It was, however, the next formation which appeared on the pilot's instruments that caused the crew their first real bout of anxiety.

Coming from behind their position was a fleet made up of several thousand craft—all of them instantly recognizable to the *Roosevelt*'s sensors—that Valance was forced to call for a red alert. As the ship's weapons stations went from a state of readiness to just-plain-ready, a voice familiar to the entire crew came through their speakers.

"Permission to approach requested by the main battle contingent of the great and vast Danerian empire."

"Thortom'tommas," asked Valance, crossing his fingers as he spoke, "is that you, old buddy?"

"If our translators are working properly, and since they are Danerian, I must assume they are, I am forced to wonder if you are throwing sarcastic insult in our direction?"

"Guess that depends on why you're here," countered the captain. "My guess is you boys are smart enough to realize that whatever this Kelber'hega Extension is, we're all better off facing it together than separately—yes?"

"Your tiny human brain computes the surface of our reasoning, but as usual, can not dig to the core of its fabulously complex subtleties."

Several of the bridge crew began to mutter, but Valance held up his hand, cutting them all off. The Danerians had been an obstacle to not only the *Roosevelt*, but the entire Confederation since its earliest days. They were efficient, ruthless and powerful, and if not for the Pan-Galactic League of Suns, they would have probably been ruling the galaxy when Earth finally made its way out into the stars. Thortom'tommas had already confirmed they were there to join in, but like any good commander, the captain needed to know their reasons for doing so. Thus, he replied;

"Well, lucky we are we have you here to explain the presence of such a great and powerful fleet."

"You, Captain Alexander Benjamin Valance... you and your crew have caused much embarrassment for the Danerian race. You are arrogant upstarts, much in need of being taught a most severe lesson."

Wondering if he had misread the newcomers' intention, the captain made a hand gesture that sent both Michaels and DiVico into action. As they started an order chain to the various weapons stations, preparing for conflict—just in case—Valance asked;

"Meaning...?"

"Meaning, captain," responded Thortom'tommas, his tone suggesting that Danerians might actually be capable of humor, "that to allow some low, stupid outsiders from some backwater galaxy to kill you, when it is clearly understood that only our empire deserves that privilege, would make us a most remiss species."

"Well..." answered the captain after only a moment's hesitation, "what can I say but, welcome aboard."

Up and down the length of the pride of the human fleet, cheers resounded as the news of the latest arrivals spread. Hearing that Quartermaster Harris' original odds for placing bets on the outcome of the approaching conflict had dropped to a mere fifty-seven to one (from the original six-hundred-and-eight-seven-point-three to one) helped elevate everyone's spirits as well.

Checking with Michaels, Valance asked for an estimate on the arrival of the invaders. The science officer's best guess put the moment of first contact at no earlier than seven-point-six standard hours. Knowing he could trust Michaels' best guess better than most men's assurances, he issued rest and meal orders, then left the bridge. When Feng asked where he was headed, just in case he might be needed, he told her;

"It has dawned on me, lieutenant, that I have never walked from one end of this ship to the other before. Personally, I can't think of a better time to do so."

Some time later, sitting his post at the firing controls of the light wave motion gun, Rocky took in a deep breath, then sighed it out deeply. He did not, of course, resent the captain for sending them all to their posts. Even

ABSOLUTELY NOTHING - C.J. Henderson

considering his own extraordinary set of circumstances that day, the gunnery officer knew there was nothing else that could have been done.

"Still," he thought, "doesn't mean I can't hate the ever-lovin' crap outta these kelber'whozit-whatzit bastards." While Rocky continued to watch his targeting screens, a familiar voice asked him from behind;

"Hey, sailor, room for more than one in there?"

"Oh," he answered, smiling, thanking the heavens for making him the luckiest man in the galaxy, "I think we could figure out something."

After the appropriate few moments of reminding each other just why they had thought getting all old-fashioned-married in a new and modern age was such a good idea, Uvi, perched on Rocky's lap as she was, asked;

"So sailor, think we're going to get out of this one with our skin intact?"

"Oh, I do so love it when you talk about skin."

"I'm serious, you big goof," she told him, smiling as she did so. "And don't you dare answer that with 'so am I.'"

"Hey, if you're gonna take all my best material—"

"Rockland..."

"All right, okay... I surrender. I mean, if you're gonna go and start first-namin' me and all... mom..."

And then, the two looked into each others' eyes, no longer speaking. Uvi was not certain why she had even brought the subject up in the first place. She was, after all, no starry-eyed young bride who actually believed in miracles. She was a decorated intelligence officer in the Confederation's deep cover operations division. She had seen the worst aspects of a hundred different races. She had witnessed death on a planet-wide scale. And she knew there was no percentage in asking questions to which she already knew the answer.

Still, like any being in the universe, she also felt she deserved at least a *bit* of happiness. Beezle Uvi had mustered the courage to commit to a man she was certain she could love for the rest of her life. A man who was loyal, courageous and steadfast. Who knew what the right thing to do was, and who did it. A man who loved her. And, knowing that all the gooey joy and hearts and flowers she had imagined coming her way were now in jeopardy of never materializing, oddly enough, she felt herself having to say;

"I know this is going to sound stupid, but in a way I feel like this invasion is all my fault."

"Okay, Mrs. Vespucci..."

"Oh, I like when you say that."

"You like me saying it, or you just like hearing it?"

"Forget it, you pepperoni, your ego is inflated enough. Forget I said anything."

"Well, of course, whatever you say, sweetheart, because as you know, your every wish is my command."

"Oh, mother said to watch out for boys like you."

"She did, huh... and when'd she say that?"

"Just before she ran away with the taxidermist."

Rocky just stared. Sitting atop the controls of the most powerful weapon known to humanity, aware that in less than an hour he would be using it against a monstrous alien fleet intent on cleansing their sector of the galaxy of life, still he simply had to stare at his most wonderful wife. So utterly flummoxed by her comment, he could not help but grin as he asked;

"'The' taxidermist? Not 'a' taxidermist? Your family had a taxidermist on call?"

"You never know when you're going to want to mount a rhinoceros."

"Oh, you really are just a little tiger, aren't you?"

Kissing Rocky as if it were for the last time, the way she planned on kissing him for the rest of their lives, she whispered to him;

"I'm *your* little tiger, mister."

"And I am very glad to hear that, of course, but if I might jump back a moment... if you would be so kind as to educate me on exactly how all of this could be your fault?"

"Huummphhh... all right," answered Uvi, pouting slightly. "You know how I told you that I've always had the worst luck with guys—right?"

"Yes, ma'am..."

"Well, whenever I have found myself with someone that seemed tolerable, something would always go wrong. Something out of the blue, totally unpredictable that... that was just too much for the relationship to withstand. Survive."

"Yeah," answered Rocky in barely more than a whisper. "There's a lotta folks feel that way. But honestly, sweetheart, I look at it one of two ways—"

"Oh, this should be good. Speak, dear husband—I shall permit it."

"Okay, smart ass. First off, I really don't think you and me bein' happy is such a big deal, or cosmic aberration, or whatever, that the universe is gonna think it needs to throw some sort of galaxy-destroying twist of destiny at us."

"Oh, you don't, do you?"

"No. I don't, dear wife."

ABSOLUTELY NOTHING - C.J. Henderson

Rocky took a moment to enjoy Uvi's reaction to his words. Being merely male, he could not determine if it was more the label of 'wife,' or the applied adjective 'dear,' or possibly the thrill of a man finally getting past all that was dazzling about her to be able to actually tell her "no" about something, but he did enjoy the look on her face, as well as the way she snuggled against him there in his lap. Continuing on, he told her;

"But two, if I am wrong, and you and me taking our chances against the universe and all its woes means that Fate needs to do everything in its power to wreck us, then I say let 'em come."

"Oh, you do, do you?"

"Yeah, I do." Moving his head even closer to Uvi's, their faces practically touching, their eyes lost in the reflection of their blended souls, he whispered;

"Because if I can't have you, then I say the hell with everything. Let the damn universe burn."

The pair came together then, kissing again for a moment, then just hugging one another--holding on to the only thing that mattered to either of them. How long they remained that way they did not know. But, they were still in tight embrace when Noodles knocked on the door jam to the forward weapons chamber.

"Hey, love birds," the machinist called, pointedly not looking inside the confined space, "captain asked me to rustle you up and get you to his ready room."

"Jeez-it," responded Rocky, "why didn't he just comm us?"

"Don't know," responded Noodles. "I'm just following orders."

As the pair disentangled themselves from one another, the gunnery officer grinned at his bride, saying;

"You know, we might be cursed at that. We can't catch even a minute of quiet time without somethin' roustin' us."

"Maybe," offered Uvi, "he's discovered that the invaders have turned and fled, and he wanted us to be the first to know."

"Hey, I like that. Let's believe that, shall we?"

"Oh," groaned Noodles, shaking his head in mock sorrow, "what marriage does to people."

"Come in, Rocky, Agent Uvi—"

"That's actually Vespucci now, captain."

Valance gave the agent a nod, smiling as he did so—grateful for actually having something to smile about. As the pair, as well as Noodles, lined up before his desk, he told them;

"At ease, nothing formal here. I, well... forgive me... I don't quite know how to bring this up, but—"

Before he could make his point, however, communication's officer Feng interrupted, her voice blurting across the comm—

"Captain, Captain Valance, sir, come in, sir."

"Yes, lieutenant, what is it?"

"More ships, sir," exclaimed Feng, breathless with excitement, "new arrivals. Nine of them. *Big* ones!"

"I'm in the middle of something right now, lieutenant," answered the captain. "Find them some place to park and I'll be with them in a mo—"

"No, sir... you don't understand," the communications officer told him. "I've got a ship-to-ship for you. Urgent. Priority Gold Alpha—"

Valance paused for a moment. There were extremely few beings in the entire galaxy that had been given access to the Gold Alpha codes. In fact, as he ran over the possibilities within his mind, only one name—considering where they were and what was happening—seemed in any way possible.

"Representative Brummellig'ic?"

"It's so good to be remembered."

At the sound of his voice coming through the captain's desk comm, all attention in the room focused on Valance's main view screen. As hope and astonishment flashed through the room—as they at the same time traveled the rumor vines of the ship at breakneck speed—before any present could speak, the imposing alien said;

"But, do you also remember Merli Acirde?"

"You mean the Grand High Exalted Poobah of the Pan-Galactic League of Suns?"

"Yes, Rocky," answered Noodles with a groan, "that would be the one."

"I will not encourage useless optimism, captain. The Poobah did not find favor with your request for aid."

Thinking on the time that Technician Second Class Thorner and Quartermaster Harris had helped Rocky and himself replace the Poobah's acceptance broadcast for his new term in office with Richard M. Nixon's "I am not a crook" speech, Noodles asked;

"That wasn't anything personal... ah, was it?"

"Acirde is being prudent," answered Brummellig'ic, "working in the best interests of the League. Of course, the fact that the royal palace

ABSOLUTELY NOTHING - C.J. Henderson

has been nicknamed 'the Watergate' probably did not help your cause any."

Both Rocky and Noodles smiled in spite of themselves. As they hurriedly wiped their faces clean of such sentiments, though, the captain responded;

"No one was expecting him to react any other way. But, that being said, I have to ask, if the League isn't going to help us... what exactly are you doing here, representative?"

"When we first met, Captain Valance, I said that the actions of your men had given the League much to think about. We have, all of us, watched you. Watched the forming of your Confederation. Watched you and this ship specifically... how you have dealt with things..."

"And...?"

"And, no matter how practical and political the League has decided to be about this situation, I will never forget that it was humans who risked their lives for my son. That it was humans who were willing to die, not just for children, but for alien children. Outsiders. The young of the competition, if not the enemy."

"Jeez," said Rocky, "we didn't think nuthin' like that about you guys. Honest. Dey was just good kids."

"After much consideration over the past months," admitted the representative, "I have come to the same conclusion. Not that our offspring are not 'just good kids,' but that others might possibly recognize such and act as you did. Which, to answer your question, captain, is why we are here."

"And who exactly is 'we?'"

"Ahhhhh, Ms. Uvi—"

"Actually, that's Mrs. Vespucci, now," she said to the alien overlord, just to watch Rocky melt a little when she announced it to the galaxy, "but you were saying?"

"Congratulations, Mr. Vespucci," responded Brummellig'ic in his rumbling voice. "Your mate is practical and direct. And so I shall be the same. 'We,' Mrs. Vespucci, are the nine who owe your husband and his friend there our futures. Our immortality. The League may be willing to let you die alone in the black to test the strength of the enemy, but we can not."

In short order, the representative explained that the nine families whose children Rocky and Noodles had saved when the gunnery officer had first met Uvi had all sent their personal family dreadnoughts. Except for Brummellig'ic, of course, who had not sent his vessel, but captained it himself.

Everything's Better With Monkeys

"Maybe our doing so will shame Acirde and the others into acting. Most likely not. But, whatever the case, this is where we belong at this moment. If, that is, you do not mind the additional ships. You seem to be doing quite well without the League here, Captain Valance."

"Hey, ol' buddy," blurted Rocky, "like my dad used to say, 'all contributions gratefully accepted.'"

"He sounds like a wise man."

"Yeah," answered the gunner, squeezing Uvi's hand as he did so, "wise enough to marry my mom."

"Yes," said Brummellig'ic, his face twisting into what the humans guessed was an ironic smile, "as you have done so this very day. May I congratulate the two of you on your bonding, if not on your timing."

"Yeah, I know what you mean. Still, I guess it's better than if we'd waited a week."

"Actually, Rocky," said Valance, "that's why I had Noodles bring you two here." When all attention turned to the captain, he said;

"Look, one crew man more or less is going to make no difference in what's coming. I wanted to offer the two of you a chance to grab a transport and to get the hell out of Dodge. You could think of it as a wedding present from the crew."

For just a moment, both Rocky and Uvi considered the offer. How could they not? How could any two beings ever born of flesh—carbon-or-anything-else-based—have failed to give such an offer its proper due? The pair looked at each other for a moment, aware that time was short, that everyone, human and otherwise, was watching them, waiting for their decision. Finally, without any kind of cue or signal, Rocky suddenly said;

"By the blue suede shoes of the king, captain, that is a mighty righteous offer. And, of course normally, I'd jump all over it. But, with my ol' buddy bein' here, I don't see how I can."

Noodles blinked. Brummellig'ic frowned. Valance struggled to stay ahead of the conversation. Uvi bowed her head slightly, loving her man even more as he continued.

"You see, the rep here just said he and his pals showed up because of what me and Noodles did, you know, for their kids and all. I mean, if I was to just selfishly cut out on everyone... how would that look?"

"Mr. Vespucci, please," offered Brummellig'ic, his voice as sincere as any could imagine, "you misunderstand. I would never, I mean..."

ABSOLUTELY NOTHING - C.J. Henderson

"I know what you mean, sir," answered Rocky quietly. "And I'm as grateful to the captain for this as I am you and your pals for showin' up here. But, as much as I love my wife, I'm thinkin' she'd rather we take our chances here than live with a coward." Then, turning to Uvi, just to make certain he was not simply filled with hot air, he asked;

"What'd you think, sweetheart?"

"You big pepperoni," she answered, choking back her tears as best she could, "it's like you read my mind."

And then, as they hugged each other, quite unexpectedly, Valance snapped his fingers, shouting;

"That's it!" As the others merely stared at him, he slapped his hands together, laughing out loud as he shouted;

"That's it! 'Read my mind'... that's it!"

"Ah, captain," asked Noodles cautiously, wondering if the strain of command had caught up to Valance, "you okay?"

"Oh, Mr. Kon, never better. Thank you for asking." Reaching to his comm, the captain ordered;

"Mr. Feng, get me the Edilsoni prime minister on the double." Then, turning to the others, he smiled, telling them;

"All right, everybody. Let's get ready to show the Kelber'hega Extension how things work in the Milky Way, shall we?"

Considering the logistics involved, it was surprising how quickly Valance's plan was put into operation. Once he had reached the Edilsoni prime minister, he had asked first if their telepathic abilities allowed them to translate languages they had never previously encountered. Finding out that it did, he had then asked if they could make such translations work both ways. When he discovered this was also the case, he revealed how he had just figured out how the Edilsoni could not only help in the battle to come, but how they were probably the defenders only chance for survival.

As fast as possible, every alien ship was contacted and directed to send a transport vessel to the Edilsoni cruiser. As they did, one Edilsoni was sent to the side of every commander in the improvised fleet. And, as Valance had hoped against all sanity, once this had been accomplished, every being that had come to hold the line against the approaching horde was suddenly in direct mental contact with the Earthly commander.

Thanks to the hive mind of the Edilsoni, not only would each warrior hear Valance's words within their head, but they would hear them in their

Everything's Better With Monkeys

own language, in their own dialect, even in their own accent. Once again, it was no guarantee of success. But, for the first time since Admiral Mach's orders had come through, it seemed as if they were not actually preparing for mass suicide.

"Genius, captain," said Michaels, watching his monitors as their fleet maneuvered precisely as per Valance's each and every command. "Guess there was a reason they put you in charge of this tub after all."

"I'll let that comment slide, Mr. Michaels," answered Valance, sitting comfortably in his command chair, "mainly because I've always wondered a bit about that myself."

"Sir," interrupted Cass, "we've got incoming, and it's the real deal this time."

Hearing Cass's words, Valance—or more correctly, the Edilsoni prime minister standing next to him—transmitted the sentence to every other being in the fleet, human or otherwise, in a nanosecond. Grimly nodding his head, the captain ordered;

"Battle stations. Commanders, take your positions."

And, effectively, that was that. Strategy had already been discussed. Until the Kelber'hega arrived, they could only wait to see what they were up against. When the first Extension shot came their way, they would react as best they could, and the battle would be engaged. Until then, however many minutes they had left, would be filled with waiting. Not being a man who liked waiting much, security chief DiVico suddenly opened his mouth to break the tension.

> **"All the forward guns are primed,**
> **The battle line is drawn.**
> **Here we take our stand,**
> **Here we stay 'til threat is gone."**

From ship to ship, from being to being, soul to soul, the large man's words rang clear and true. And they rang so in every sense of the words.

> **"They say there's no way to win,**
> **They say we face our doom.**
> **But that's been said to us before,**
> **And we're not in our tomb."**

Across the bridge, by the middle of the second stanza, everyone on the bridge was singing. Including the captain. And even the prime minister. Especially the prime minister.

ABSOLUTELY NOTHING - C.J. Henderson

"Oh, we're the boys of the Roosevelt,
We fly in outer space,
We wipe our asses with moonbeams,
We know how star dust tastes."

As the words were transmitted across the black expanse of space, every ally that had come to join the crew of the *Roosevelt*, no matter what their reasons might have been, suddenly they understood—they *knew* what it meant to be human. And not only human, but the best kind of human—

"The boys of the fighting Roosevelt,
The best ship in all the fleet,
Say a single word ag'in her,
And we'll pound ya 'til yer meat!"

Courageous, fearless, selfless. From the music-powered fleets of the Beltins and Swy'ngs to the dark, boiler-plated destroyers of the Danerian Empire, the nobility of humanity swept forward like in an unstoppable wave. In ship after ship, on deck after deck, bipeds and blobs, beings feathered, tentacled and gelatinous opened whatever orifice they used to communicate and lent their voices to the swelling harmony.

"We're here to protect,
We're here to defend,
We're here to hold back the dark,
And we'll do it to the end."

On ship after ship, the proximity detectors shouted the same warning. The Kelber'hega were drawing close—mere minutes away. In response, throughout the fleet, sailors took their positions, fighter pilots strapped themselves into their cockpits, medics gave their sick bays a last once over, marines tossed off their safeties. But, no matter what their rank, or task, or duty, all of them sang.

"Bring on whatever you've got,
You'll see we don't quit and run.
Where would the honor be in that?
Let alone the fun?"

Only two voices missed the last verses. And those two could be forgiven. The orifices through which they might have sung were otherwise occupied. As the song ended, cheers rang through the corridors of every ship. United as no band of warriors had ever been throughout the collective history of

Everything's Better With Monkeys

time and space, robots, humans, space pancakes, demi-gods and every one else threw their voices into a defiant roar that stood a better chance to being heard in space than any noise made since the big bang.

Every voice, that is, except two.

"I love you," said the one. To which the other answered;

"Right back at you."

And then, the first shots of the enemy came blasting forward. Valance gave his orders. The ships under his command responded. And the great cosmic blackness filled with fire.

SO LONG, AND THANKS FOR ALL THE COOKIES...

WRITING FOR DEFENDING THE FUTURE IS ONE OF THE LUCKIEST BREAKS I ever got as an author. I was known for supernatural detectives, hardboiled detectives, certain types of comedies, all manner of things... but nothing like what I created for my buddy Mike McPhail. Everyone knows I was pretty much resistant at first, but Mike coaxed one of the best series I've ever created out of me, and helped me forge a last story that would cap the series for all time. I would have never tried something like this so far outside my comfort zone without his quite guidance. Like many who reach comfort, I have become a coward.

But, even if Rocky and Noodles were signed, sealed, and delivered, DTF was moving onward. Mike got me to do a straight sci fi military story, something as far outside my wheelhouse as possible. I was very proud of that tale... still am.

I don't have much wind these days, my sails are all but empty, and stouter warriors will have to sail beyond the shoals I can no longer dream of clearing. And that's all right. I made my discoveries, set my boundaries, left my mark. Let those in the wings roar forward. It is their right, their destiny. I had mine.

I've had a wonderful run. And I love everyone that helped along the way.

Thank you all.
CJ Henderson
July 2014

C.J. Henderson

CJ Henderson was the creator of both the *Piers Knight* supernatural investigator series and the *Teddy London* occult detective series among many others. He wrote over seventy books and/or novels, hundreds and hundreds of short stories and comics and thousands of non-fiction pieces. He was a master of hardboiled suspense as well as raucous comedy, and was not shy about saying so even when sober. CJ passed away July 4, 2014 after a prolonged battle with cancer.

Mike McPhail

Mike McPhail's love of the science fiction genre sparked a life-long interest in science, technology, and developing an understanding of the human condition—all of which played an important role in his writing, art, and game design. These, in turn, are built upon his background in Applied Science and training as an Aeronautical Engineer, all of which were aimed at becoming a NASA mission specialist.

As a professional author, he has been involved in numerous projects, but he is best known as the creator and series editor of the award-winning Defending the Future military science fiction anthologies—now in their second decade of publication. His body of work has been formally recognized with his acceptance into SFWA, the Science Fiction and Fantasy Writers of America.

As a graphic designer, he is the owner of McP Digital Graphics (founded in 2006), a company established to provide cover art, design, layout, and prepress services. This built upon not only his experience as a game designer, but primarily from his time as the Proofing Supervisor for Phoenix Color Corp doing cover work for the great publishing houses.

As a publisher, he is the co-owner of eSpec Books LLC (since 2014), where his graphics company has become the inhouse design arm of production.

As Airman McPhail, he is a member of the Military Writers Society of America and is dedicated to helping his fellow service members (and those deserving civilians) in their efforts to become authors, editors, or artist, as well as supporting related organization in their efforts to help those "who have given their all for us."

www.ingramcontent.com/pod-product-compliance
Ingram Content Group UK Ltd.
Pitfield, Milton Keynes, MK11 3LW, UK
UKHW041937131224
452403UK00001B/217